Tourist Trap

I turned on my flashlight for a better view.

Head pointing away from me, facedown on the beach, was a body with sprawled arms and legs. Oh, God. There was a thin shaft rising skyward from its back. The body was clothed in a black crinkle cotton caftan.

Sand flew in the air as Angie ran to my side.

"Don't touch anything!" she cautioned.

We stood shoulder to shoulder, looking at the body at our feet.

"Holy Mary Mother of God," Angie exclaimed, "it looks like Zena!"

It was Zena. But now she was the late Dr. Sheffield. The woman was dead. Very dead indeed.

MORE MYSTERIES FROM THE
BERKLEY PUBLISHING GROUP . . .

Death Dances
to a
Reggae Beat

Kate Grilley

BERKLEY PRIME CRIME, NEW YORK

This is a work of fiction. Names, characters, places, and incidents are either the product of the author's imagination or are used fictitiously, and any resemblance to actual persons, living or dead, business establishments, events, or locales is entirely coincidental.

DEATH DANCES TO A REGGAE BEAT

A Berkley Prime Crime Book / published by arrangement with the author

PRINTING HISTORY
Berkley Prime Crime edition / June 2000

Chapter

1

PROMOTIONS ARE NOT what they're cracked up to be.

I thought when I accepted the job as general manager of WBZE, the top rated radio station on St. Chris if not the entire Caribbean, I'd landed in a bed of frangipani.

I would still host my regular weekday radio show from six A.M. 'til noon, then shuffle a few papers, sign paychecks, morale boost the troops, and saunter out the door at one P.M. for a real lunch instead of a carton of pineapple yogurt inhaled during a sixty-second commercial break, my workday done.

Talk about self-delusion. Before you could say Johann Sebastian Bach I was up to my toffee-colored eyes in trouble.

That's Trouble with a capital *T*, which rhymes with *P*, which stands for political infighting.

If I'd known there was also a very dead body in my future, I would have jumped the good ship WBZE faster than my cat Minx can pounce on a mousie and joined Mrs. H on her six-month 'round the world cruise.

Mrs. H is the owner of WBZE and, prior to my ascension, also the general manager. She offered the promotion with a generous raise and bonus attached, like a diamond-studded carrot, the previous Christmas when my life was in twenty-four-hour-a-day holiday bedlam. I decided to accept the offer on Old Year's Day, it was official February first. Even rated page one in the *Coconut Telegraph*, the St. Chris daily newspaper, "Kelly Ryan to Run WBZE." Heady stuff.

There was one fat zircon among the diamonds.

Chairmanship of the annual Navidad de Isabeya parade committee. Mrs. H casually added it to my job description during one of our last precruise meetings in late February.

"By the way, Kelly, would you do something for me while I'm gone?"

"Sure, name it." I thought she meant a simple favor, like watering plants.

"Take over the birthday celebration parade committee." Mrs. H, noticing the are-you-out-of-your-bloody-mind? look on my face, quickly added, "Piece of cake, the committee practically runs itself."

I knew she was lying through her capped teeth when she said, "You're the boss, take off any extra time you need. I don't expect you to abandon your personal life for the station. Or the parade."

She handed me a slim file folder labelled "Parade." "Our second committee meeting's tonight."

Without missing a beat, she segued into, "How's Jeff? Will he be back in time for my bon voyage party?"

"Smooth, Mrs. H. Very smooth."

Notice how deftly she switched the topic to my love life? Jeff—Jeff Payne, son of the old island family who founded the local rum distillery, he's the chief detective on the St. Chris police force—and I had been seeing each other since early December and were quite cozy. When we had time. Between his job and mine there weren't enough hours in the day, especially when I went to sleep by nine every work night in order to get up at four-thirty to be on the air by six.

"I'd love to help you out, Mrs. H, but this isn't going to work. I hate group poop. I'm allergic to Robert's Rules of Order." I placed the file back on her desk.

Mrs. H looked at me over the top of her rose-tinted horn-rimmed reading glasses. "Nice try, Kelly. You'll be perfect. Can't stand that camel building committee stuff myself. See you at the library at seven."

I recognized an exit line when I heard one.

My parting shot was to stroll out of Mrs. H's office with the file tucked under my arm, whistling "Nearer My God To Thee."

A throaty chuckle was her only reply.

Chapter
2

I WAS RUNNING late for the parade committee meeting.

Driving east on Kongens Gade—Danish for King Street and Isabeya's one-way version of a main street—I was all the way to Government House at the town square and still keeping my eyes peeled for a parking spot close to the library.

After a nasty encounter with the Carib Indians on his second voyage in 1493, Columbus beat a fast retreat along the northern coastline of the newly named St. Cristofero—modesty was not *numero uno* on his list of virtues—to the main harbor area of our little island.

Grateful for the hospitality shown by the peaceful Arawaks residing there, he christened the Arawak Indian settlement "Isabella" to honor his patroness Queen Isabella the First of Spain, planted a wooden cross as a mark of Christian dominance, then skipped town.

Through a spelling error, or bad handwriting, the original Isabella became Isabeya; but here everyone calls it "town"; there's only one on our crescent-shaped thirty-five-square-mile island. The original cluster of palm frond-roofed Indian huts was expanded haphazardly by the Spanish, English, French, and Knights of Malta; then rebuilt from scratch by the Danes in 1764 in a six-by-six grid pattern fanning out from Government House after a catastrophic town fire that some called "Danish lightning."

Isabeya is long on charm but short on parking.

The narrow left-side drive streets were originally designed for horses, foot traffic, and the carriage trade. In the maze of one-way streets crisscrossing Isabeya we still see stray horses, also chickens, dogs, cats, an occasional mongoose and the normal trucks, cars and taxi vans.

I nabbed a semilegal space in the Fort Frederick parking lot and hoofed it across the grass to the library.

The library is quartered in the former Customs House, a square two-story building close to the fort. Built by the Danes over two hundred years ago, the library's coral and molasses walls—the tropical equivalent of Elizabethan wattle and daub—were two feet thick. In accordance with the guidelines established by the Historic Preservation Act, the library had recently been repainted from faded peach to the original mustard yellow. I hoped the Caribbean sun would soon bleach the color to something less eye-jolting.

The ground floor housed the library administrative offices and the children's collection. The parade committee was meeting in the general library on the second floor.

As I sprinted up the broad fan-shaped welcoming arms staircase, I heard voices coming through the open doors and windows. Behind me resonated the strains of "Yellow Bird" from the steel band at Dockside, a hotel and restaurant complex fronting the seaside boardwalk, converted from an old ballast brick warehouse dating back to the days of the pirate Blackbeard and his cronies.

The meeting began decorously, then veered toward disaster.

The bright spot was seeing Angelita Sanchez, Jeff's associate on the police force and my ex-husband's latest love. Angie was on the parade committee as a police liaison to handle crowd control and street closure. She was wearing her standard jeans, sandals, and message T-shirt. The scarlet "don't rain on my parade" shirt contrasted nicely with her glossy shoulder-length black hair.

Mrs. H introduced me to the other three members: Reverend Calvin Stowe, Mr. Elijah Daniel and Dr. Zena Sheffield.

I knew everyone by sight but Dr. Sheffield.

"Hi Kelly, call me Cal." Reverend Stowe, looking like one of Santa's roly-poly elves in clerical garb, was a familiar fixture around town.

"Good evening, Miss Ryan." Mr. Daniel's smile flashed on and off like a caution light, his eyes never warmed above freezing. After the last election he'd been appointed the assistant commissioner of education by a grateful governor who happened to be a distant family member. Suddenly I felt like I was sixteen and had been caught passing notes in study hall.

"My dear, it's so nice to meet you. Please call me Zena. I love what you do with the classics every morning." Zena was zaftig, or Reubenesque, on the order of a Wagnerian heroine. Clothed in a loose crinkle cotton caftan, her flaxen hair styled in a braided coronet, she clutched an enormous tote bearing an Ivy League crest to her breast like a battle shield.

Mrs. H segued into her hostess mode. "Zena's here on sabbatical to finish her biography of Queen Isabella. She teaches Renaissance history. You two must chat. Kelly's an amateur Egyptologist."

"Really?" said Zena. "How amusing for you. The period's a bit early for me. Have you read Herodotus?"

"Sure," I replied, "I keep it on my bookshelf next to Aesop's Fables."

Zena threw her head back in a laugh that began at her

toes. "Very good! You and I may have something to talk about after all."

Mrs. H called the meeting to order. We took our seats at the round reading table in the center of the room.

Zena plumbed the depths of her tote and dug out a box of Island Delights, liquor-filled chocolate-covered island fruit confections sold at Posh Nosh, the upstairs restaurant at Dockside and St. Chris's leading purveyor of gastronomic sin. She removed the pale avocado ribbon from the peach-colored tin box and offered the treat around the table.

Everyone politely declined, Reverend Cal adding that unfortunately he was a diabetic and must pass. "Lead me not into temptation," he said. We all chuckled on cue; Angie and I tried not to smirk. Reverend Cal was famous for boring additions of Scripture to the most mundane conversations. Don't ask him about the weather, he'll get started on Noah. All forty days and nights.

The first order of business was to announce Mrs. H's resignation and my appointment as her successor. That's when the dust flew in the fan.

Mr. Daniel vehemently protested. "I do not want to appear out of order, but I think it proper that the chairmanship of this committee go to a regular member, not a replacement. It is, after all, a government function."

Mrs. H quelled that insurrection in short order. "The actual birthday is a government holiday, but the parade is not a government function. This started in the private sector as a way to boost tourism during the slow season after the Easter holidays, remember? Since we broadcast the parade live every year I think Kelly's the perfect chairman and coordinator. I've already cleared it with Miss Lucinda, the general chairman. However, to be entirely fair, we'll put it to a vote."

I was in by one. Two ayes, one nay, two abstentions and I didn't vote. This was not getting off to a good start.

Round two was a temper-flaring debate over award categories for interpretation of this year's theme, "New Worlds to Conquer."

In addition to the standard float, troupe and floupe categories that comprise a Caribbean parade, we also had individual entries, unaffiliated bands and a half-mile of drum majorettes. On St. Chris every young girl owns a pair of white boots and knows how to twirl a baton.

Mr. Daniel proposed an award program so broad that every schoolchild was guaranteed an award merely for showing up on parade day.

"That rather defeats the purpose of the competition, doesn't it?" asked Mrs. H. "I suggest two categories of school awards. Grade school and high school. With three awards per category. One for best float, one for best troupe, and one for best floupe. Six trophies total. That's it."

"What, pray tell, is a floupe?" asked Zena.

Mrs. H explained. "A float is an entry confined to a single flatbed truck; a troupe is a group of street marchers without a float; and a floupe is a combination float and troupe entry."

"How quaint." Zena began ravishing the last Island Delight.

Mr. Daniel's eyes went from chocolate slush to frozen fudge. "I cannot guarantee participation by the schoolchildren unless there is sufficient motivation. They have worked long and hard on their arrangements and deserve recognition."

"Virtue is its own reward," piped Reverend Cal.

Zena licked the chocolate remnants from her fingertips. "What about historical correctness?"

"Historical what?" asked Reverend Cal. There was an impish tone to his voice I couldn't quite comprehend.

"Navidad de Isabeya is in celebration of the birthday of Queen Isabella the First, born April twenty-second, 1451," lectured Zena. "I think there should be a special award for the entry that most accurately depicts the period."

"That rules out Columbus on a spaceship," quipped Angie.

"Or Izzy astride a moon rocket," I added. We both giggled.

"I fail to see the humor in those remarks," said Mr. Daniel. "The celebrated history of our island is part of our proud heritage and should not be made the brunt of sophomoric jokes."

Mrs. H's mouth twitched, Zena ignored us.

"I will personally sponsor a special historical award and present it from the grandstand at the end of the parade," said Zena in the tone of a monarch bestowing a royal favor.

"Do the historical award qualifications apply to transportation?" asked Mr. Daniel. "I sincerely doubt the diesel engine had been invented then, and most of our floats rely on flatbed trucks for locomotion."

"Don't be an ass," snapped Zena. "I don't expect horse-drawn floats, although it would be more appropriate to the period."

"Oh, my. Are we going to allow live animals this year?" asked Reverend Cal.

We all smiled, even Mr. Daniel, remembering an incident from an earlier parade. Mrs. H retold the story for Zena's benefit.

"There was a woman here, a Continental, who used to dress as Lady Godiva, draped in yards of scanty fishnet, and ride her horse in every parade. One year as she was followed by a troupe of majorettes, her horse relieved himself in front of Government House. The entire parade came to a halt for half an hour until one enterprising soul, armed with a shovel and wastebasket, cleaned up the street." She added, "I think we'll maintain the ban on live animals."

Angie said, "We should also ban imbibing by the truck drivers."

That remark led to a story from another year about a drunken float driver who stopped his truck in the middle of Kongens Gade, dropped the ignition key down a sewer grating, then disappeared in the crowd. I remembered the agony of trying to fill forty-five minutes of live airtime while a backup driver and duplicate key were found.

At nine-thirty Mrs. H adjourned the meeting.

Angie and I retreated to the Lower Deck at Dockside for a quick drink.

We sat outside, waiting for our drinks at a small round table overlooking the harbor. Dockside's steel band had quit for the night so we were serenaded by crickets, the slap of waves against the dock, twanging boat lines and the chug-chug of the ferry shuttling the three hundred feet from town to Harborview, formerly the Danish governor's residence and now converted to a high-priced hotel, located on its own little island in the middle of the harbor.

The meeting demanded a rehash. "Kel, whatever made you take over that committee? Are you nuts?"

"Mrs. H twisted my arm. What's the story with Mr. Daniel? He seems a little scratchy."

"Don't mind him. He's throwing his weight around. I hear he's planning on running for the local Senate next fall. That's why he wanted to be chairman of the committee, so he'd get some free publicity. I'm not surprised he voted against you. Don't take it personally. Zena and I will back you all the way."

"Thanks. Zena's quite a . . . character."

"Character is right. She's almost a majority stockholder of Posh Nosh. She puts away a box of Island Delights at every meeting."

"At twenty-five bucks a box? She must have gotten one hell of an advance on her book."

"If she says 'historically correct' one more time I'm going to poison her bonbons. You weren't there last week. She used that phrase at least fifty times. By the end of the evening everyone was pissed off. What was that crack she made to you before the meeting?"

"A bit of historical—"

Angie threw up her hands in horror. "Don't say the *C* word!"

"Humor, Angie. I was going to say historical humor. Actually she was testing me in a pretty subtle way. Herodotus . . ."

"Yeah, yeah. The father of history, what about him?"

"Many Egyptologists regard him as a b.s. artist. The father of the 'I came, I saw, I exaggerated' school. She was trying to find out where I stood."

"Well, it worked. She obviously agrees with you." Angie paused to sip her drink. "I'm not sure I like her. I think she's one of those women who climbed the ladder then kicked it over once she got to the top. I also think she's an intellectual snob. She may be big trouble."

"Why?"

"She's new here. She doesn't know people and she comes on very strong. She could ruffle a lot of feathers."

"Cheer up, Angie, eight weeks from Saturday it'll be all over for another year."

"We should all live that long."

We clinked our glasses in a toast to our mutual survival.

Chapter
3

I WAS ALMOST late for work the following morning.

Not a good way to begin the day or end a work week. But ever faithful Minx, my calico cat, was persistent. She started by tapping my face with her paw, followed by breathing heavily and licking my ear with her sandpaper tongue, and finally resorting to the ultimate alarm: sitting in the middle of the bed, barely out of reach, shrieking at the top of her little lungs.

That shriek did the trick. I bounded out of bed at four-forty-five, only fifteen minutes behind schedule. Minx sped toward her food dish, a smug smile on her sweet little face, to await breakfast cat crunchies.

Minx has been my anchor since my divorce. Having a job that's essentially sitting alone in a soundproof room talking to myself, I missed having someone to come home to.

I found her one rain-sodden afternoon by the side of the dirt road leading to my house. She'd been abandoned before she was weaned and was scrawny, flea-ridden, almost too weak to move. When I scooped her up in my hand, she nestled her tiny head against my body and purred. We bonded in that instant. Minx quickly became my faithful alarm clock and constant companion.

On the twenty-minute drive from my house to the WBZE studio, I savored the early-morning sea air and drank a second wake-up Tab. I glanced at the ocean to my far right as I drove along the east end road toward town. It was still too dark to see any sign of the out islands forty miles to the north.

From the air St. Chris looks like a fat lima bean floating in the Caribbean Sea. On the northern side, the inverted side of the crescent, is the coral reef-enclosed harbor and town. A range of mountains, topped by Mt. Bellevue, 1,074 feet, runs from east to west. The sparsely populated southern shore lacks the protection of the reef, is prone to occasional sharks and is rather rocky.

Most of our weather comes from the east, not the west. During the June to November hurricane season we're glued to marine weather reports for news of storm clouds bouncing off the western coast of Africa. At times the air is hazy with airborne Sahara sand.

Contrary to the belief that life in the Caribbean is year-long endless summer, we do have seasons.

The changes here are subtle. Winter is dry with cool nights and warm days. The trade winds blow steadily from the east, gusting to rattle the collection of Woodstock wind chimes that line my screened-in gallery.

In March a quiet transformation calms the winds to balmy breezes, and the earth smells green and warm. The hazy air, soft as an old flannel shirt, is delicately scented with frangipani and the elusive fragrance of the filament-blossomed Mother Tongue tree.

At sea the annual spring cross-migration resembles rush hour on the oceanic freeway. Whales leap and frolic as they swim north; beneath the waves, leatherback turtles stroke steadily south to their birth beaches for nocturnal nesting.

Turtle season begins March first and involves nightly patrols of the nesting beaches, protecting the egg-laying turtles and their sand-covered urn-shaped nests from destruction by nature or human poachers. Slogging quietly up and down a deserted beach is my contribution to an endangered species and my own mental health.

I really had to get my work/play/sleep act together. My day job takes top priority. It pays my mortgage.

After my divorce I was feeling rootless. I was living in a rented guest cottage, my life revolved around my radio show and spending time with friends. I acted in a few shows with the community theater and indulged my passion for travel, treating myself to one off-season trip a year at bargain rates. I went to London at Thanksgiving to see new plays and shop for Christmas, Egypt in August to cruise the Nile, and viewed the Acropolis under an October full moon before embarking on a week-long Mediterranean cruise to Turkey and the Greek islands.

At my best friend Margo's insistence I sunk the balance of my life savings, and a hefty chunk of my earnings until hell freezes over, into a real estate investment.

Did I mention that Margo's also a real estate broker?

She sweet-talked me—"Kel, you're over forty, you're divorced, if you buy a place now you'll have the mortgage paid off by the time Social Security kicks in and you'll never be a bag lady"—into buying an old Danish one-room schoolhouse on two acres of north shore land nestled in the east end hills overlooking the ocean.

"It's a fixer-upper, Kelly. Just needs some TLC and a little paint," Margo said with a disarming smile, handing me her cherished Mont Blanc pen to sign the Offer to Purchase.

I bought the property for a song, but spent a fortune on renovations. Beginning with a new corrugated tin roof, I painstakingly converted it from a goat-dung-infested ruin into cozy—real estate lingo for *very* small—but comfortable living quarters. Now I was thinking about adding a hot tub or tiny swimming pool. More expense and upkeep.

It was time to get on the job. I really needed the money.

The WBZE offices and studio are located on the ground floor of a two-story building on the western side of Isabeya. The Gothic multispired Anglican church is three blocks to the east; less than a half-mile away is the former Danish barracks that now houses our prison population. Our transmitting tower is a two-mile drive away through Isabeya to the northeastern edge of the harbor.

On the side wall of the studio is a large safety-glass picture window, covered with an iron security grille, overlooking the parking lot.

As I parked my ten-year-old Japanese hatchback in my reserved spot—another diamond on the promotion carrot—I could see Michael, the ten P.M. to six A.M. deejay, doing a Marcel Marceau drum solo.

He switched to an audible version of "Hail to the Chief," using his fist for a bugle, when I walked from the reception area, past the offices and the broom closet housing the Teletype machine, into the studio.

"Put a sock in it, Michael."

"Hey, Mama, I hear you're into self-abuse!" His hands became a Rudy Vallee megaphone as he belted "I Love a Parade."

I laughed at our resident retro hippie in his garish Magnum P.I. aloha shirt and baggy shorts when he imitated a drum majorette, complete with imaginary baton. Michael knows how to get my attention and also how to get me out of a snarky mood.

"Watch it, sweetie, or I'll put you in charge of the damned parade," I said.

"*Moi?* Are you demented? No way, Jose! I'll coanchor the broadcast, but that's it, Mama. I don't do committees."

"Draft dodger! But you're still in charge of the road march competition."

"No big t'ing, Mama. I'll start scouting the steel bands tonight before work." Michael cued his sign-off, "Thanks for the Memories," my sign-on, "Fanfare for the Common Man," then baton-twirled his way out the door humming "Seventy-six Trombones" as I began the six A.M. news.

I was hoping for quiet until eight-thirty when Emily, our receptionist, arrived to take over phone duty. Emily's nineteen, has the attention span of a sated sand flea and an audible fondness for chewing gum. She's also Mrs. H's granddaughter.

After the news, I settled back with a fresh Tab to enjoy the morning classics. Beginning with Handel's *Concerti Grossi*. Two minutes into the opening, the music was accented by the blinking of all three telephone lines. Sure looked like SOS to me.

I went through "Good morning, WBZE, the breath of fresh music in the Caribbean, please hold," sounding like a crazed parrot, and got back to line one.

"Kelly, dear, it's Zena. Might I have a word with you about the parade?"

"Can you hold? I've got two other calls."

Onto line two. "Miss Ryan, this is Mr. Daniel." The third line had to be . . .

"Hi Kelly, Cal here." Spare me. Could I turn this into a conference call?

Back to Zena on line one.

"I won't take much of your time, Kelly, I know you're working. But I was thinking about the parade after our meeting last night, and I thought it would be so much more authentic . . ."

Authentic? Was this a new way to say "historically correct"? I'd have to warn Angie.

". . . if we started the parade with a reenactment of the actual landing ceremony at Columbus Bay."

If we did that we'd have to reincarnate the Carib Indians. The first time Columbus met the Caribs his crew was greeted with poison-tipped arrows. It was time to nip this in the bud. Take charge before the committee took charge of me.

"Zena, bring it up at the next meeting. We'll discuss it then. Don't forget the post office will be using the site for Stamp Day. Thanks for calling, I've got to get back to work." Over and out.

The gentlemen callers had a few suggestions of their own. Mostly what to do about the lady. Cement overshoes were implied but not articulated. I deflected their self-serving intentions until the next meeting and put the parade out of my head as I segued from Handel to "Summer" from Vivaldi's *The Four Seasons*.

The phone was mute until after the seven o'clock news break. A relief. I hate telephones. It's not a phobia, merely an active dislike. I'd lived for years without a phone at home until this past Christmas, and still resented its presence in my house. And hated paying the monthly bill even more. The only plus was having an unlisted number.

Margo, instigator of my home phone, was my next caller.

"Hi, Kel. I tried calling you last night. Were you out or antisocial?"

"Out."

"Anyone I know? Anyone Jeff should know about?"

"Mrs. H, Angie, Reverend Cal."

"Sounds like a committee."

"You got it. The parade."

Margo laughed until she choked. "Oh, no. How did you get roped into that? Don't tell me. You've got the backbone of an angleworm."

"Thanks, sweetie."

"This won't interfere with turtle season, will it?"

"No way!"

"Good. I wanted to remind you about the beach walk and picnic tomorrow afternoon."

"I didn't forget. We're on for two, right?"

"Right. Gotta run and peddle some real estate. See you tomorrow!"

Chapter
4

SATURDAY AFTERNOON WAS tourist weather. Temperature in the mid-eighties, bright sun, high wispy clouds, the gently rolling sea lapping the beach at Leatherback Bay like the tongue of a tired dog.

The beach walk was in full swing, with Margo as field marshal. The nightly patrols were two-person teams, but everyone joined in the preseason cleanup. We scoured the half-mile length of south shore sand like the Normandy invasion on D-day.

By late afternoon we'd bagged enough trash to sink the *Santa Maria*, found $4.83 in small change, and were ready to collapse with a cold beer while hamburgers cooked on Margo's portable charcoal grill. It would be the last fire on the beach until early fall when all the turtle nests were hatched out.

Margo flopped beside me on the sand. We sat drinking Heineken and watching the undulating sea. After trudging up and down the beach for several hours, she still looked as cool and fresh as if she'd stepped out of the shower five

minutes earlier. Her khaki shorts held a crease, and her
long, sun-streaked blond hair was done in a neat French
braid underneath her sun visor. I felt gritty and knew my
gamin-cut espresso brown hair was popping off my head
in salt-laden spikes. I couldn't wait to get home and bathe.

"When's Jeff coming back?" she asked. "I've got you
two down as a team for Friday nights."

"He's supposed to be home next week. I haven't heard
from him since Tuesday, but I don't think his plans have
changed."

"If he's not here, I'll pair you with someone else. How
about Pete?" Margo smiled in Shirley Temple innocence.

I look over at the group lounging on blankets near the
grill where Pete, my blond drop-dead-gorgeous-with-a-
Robert-Redford-smile former husband, sat with his arm
around Angie. "I don't think so, Margo. Try again."

"She's much too young for him, but they look good
together," Margo said, putting her hand on my arm. "How
do you feel about that? You okay?"

"Yeah. Sure." I smiled and gulped air from my empty
bottle.

"This is me, Kel. 'Fess up."

"Pete and I've been divorced for five years. It's about
time we both found someone else."

"Kel, cut the crap. Remember, I know what that hot
pants son of a bitch did to you after fifteen years of marriage. When you got divorced your self-esteem was lower
than whale doo-doo."

"Thanks for the memories, sweetie."

What I never told Margo was that Pete and I had a one-
night fling before Christmas. It happened after an early
holiday party the weekend following Thanksgiving, before
I started dating Jeff. One of those nights when I was feeling very lonely. Pete was at the party without a date, I
didn't have a date either, we both drank a little too much . . .
and nature took its course.

I remembered how I felt the next morning. It was strange waking up at Pete's condo in a king-sized bed that wasn't my own, and even stranger seeing my ex-husband's tawny hair on the next pillow. What had seemed right the night before—"Auld Lang Syne" and all the sentiment of the approaching holiday season really warped my judgment—suddenly felt very cheap. I quickly dressed and got the hell out of there.

Pete may have thought we were on the road to reconciliation—not very likely, after more than five years apart—but I quashed any hopes he might have been harboring by dating Jeff. Jeff and I costarred in the fall community theater production of Noel Coward's *Private Lives*. After closing night, our onstage romance blossomed into one offstage. On New Year's Eve Pete surprised all of us by showing up at a fancy hotel party with Angie as his date. From that night on they were inseparable.

Margo flashed her hand in front of my eyes. "Hello in there. Kel, I know how it is. St. Chris is a very small island. We're all friends. We all run into each other ten times a day. We all go to the same parties, belong to the same groups. Don't you feel that's a little too cozy at times? If you think Pete's dating Angie sucks, for God's sake say so!"

I surrendered. "Margo, if I didn't have Jeff in my life, I might feel differently. Okay? But I'm glad it's Angie. She's great. Wait until I tell you what she said at the committee meeting."

Margo and I put our heads together for a good gossip. Paul, a retired Navy pilot who flies for a local airline and Margo's long-term live-in lover, joined us with fresh beers. When Pete yelled that our hamburgers were on the grill and if we wanted them rare we'd better haul ass, we joined the rest of the group at the fire.

The sun dropped over the hills behind our backs as we ate. In the tropical latitudes there is no real twilight; once the sun goes down it's only a matter of minutes before it's totally dark. The length of our days varies by only two hours between summer and winter. On the summer solstice the sun rises at six, sets at seven; at Christmas it's light at seven and dark by six.

In that last gasp of light before darkness, the sea lost its peacock colors and became a navy ribbon between the sand and the horizon. Stars popped out like rhinestones on black velvet. Overhead Orion stalked his prey. By eleven we'd be able to see the Southern Cross hanging low in the sky.

Margo handed out folders containing schedules, log sheets, and the list of rules and procedures for tagging and reporting. Most of us had been turtle-watching for several years; we knew the drill cold, having established the routine our first year out, but Margo ran a tight ship. Paul collected five bucks from each of us for the pool.

We had begun the pool seven years earlier when our group adopted Leatherback Bay as our watch site. Each year the first team to find a turtle had their names and the date added to a special plaque we had made, and had custody of the plaque until the next season. The money we put in the pot paid for the engraving and a bottle of very good duty-free French champagne for the winners.

During our marriage, Pete and I had our names on that plaque two years in a row and I secretly hoped I'd be on the first team this year. Screw Pete. I wasn't in line for sainthood; chairing the damned parade committee had depleted my stock of noble gestures.

I pooped out early and went home. Being a single on a Saturday night in a crowd of couples was straining my smile.

I hoped Jeff would call. I really missed that man.

If you ask me, spring skiing is an idiotic sport.

Chapter

5

I DIDN'T HEAR from Jeff until Tuesday morning, and then I wished I hadn't.

When I drove into the WBZE parking lot at five-forty-five A.M. I could see Michael relaxing in the studio. He was leaning back in his chair, feet propped on the console, talking on the phone. I flashed my lights twice, our signal to let him know it was me and not alien visitors. He mouthed the words "It's Jeff, for you," and in case my lip-reading skills were deficient, kept pointing to the phone and then to me.

I raced into the studio. Michael had the call on hold. "You might want to take this one in the office."

Jeff sounded like hell. But, then, it was still the middle of the night in the Rockies.

"Hey, Kel. How ya doin', baby?" He also sounded very drunk.

"Jeff, you sound awful. Are you drunk?"

"It's the pain medication. Makes me woozy."

"What pain medication? Where are you?"

"I'm in the hospital." Jeff laughed, more in irony than
mirth. "What a lousy way to end a vacation."

"What happened?" I wasn't sure I wanted to know.

"It's like this. Oh, shit, Kel . . . look, um . . . well, I
slipped on some ice."

"Jeff, spit it out. What in the hell happened?"

Michael picked that second to come into the office. I
looked at the clock: 5:57. Damn. I had to get on the air.
He handed me a note that read "I'll cover for you," tore
the news copy off the Teletype machine, and ran back into
the studio.

"Kel, are you still there?"

"Yeah, it's airtime, Michael's covering. Tell me what
happened before I break your bloody arm!"

"You're too late for that."

"What do you mean?"

"I broke my arm. Make that arms. Plural. I broke both
of them."

Oh my God. He'd slipped on a patch of ice in front of
the ski lodge, fallen backward, put his hands out to break
the fall, and broken both arms just below the elbows.

He was now in the hospital, looking like Boris Karloff
in a mummy movie, and wouldn't be home for another six
weeks. Six long weeks. Christ. I didn't even have time to
cry or fume; I had to get on the damned air. I was so
rattled I forgot to get the name of the hospital or the number where Jeff could be reached. I didn't even know exactly where he was in Colorado. He'd been traveling from
one resort to another in search of perfect snow.

I ran into the studio as Michael was finishing the
weather.

"Chance of rain twenty percent, pissable showers this
morning, clear skies by noon."

Pissable showers? Michael! But how angry could I be
with someone who covered for me and had already segued

into my show with a new recording of Beethoven's *Fifth*? I owed him, big time.

"Tough break, Mama."

"Michael, any more bad puns and I'll rip out your tongue!"

He smirked and said, "Guess that gentleman won't be resting on his elbows anytime soon. You'll have to dust off your copy of the Kama Sutra." He was out the door before I could retort.

The Andante second movement of the *Fifth* had barely started when Michael was back, bearing a tall takeout cup.

"This'll take your mind off your troubles. Drink up before the ice melts. Doctor's orders."

Bless his elfin heart. A Bloody Mary. Made exactly the way I like them. Lots of ice, regular nonspicy Clamato, fresh key lime, Jane's Crazy Salt, Original Mrs. Dash, cheap vodka and no Tabasco. In our land of duty-free liquor, a quart of Clamato costs more than a fifth of vodka. Drinks are poured with a heavy hand on the booze and light on the mix. What the hell. I sipped the drink. It tasted great.

I picked the wrong morning to start drinking on the job.

In addition to having a walnut-sized bladder—my next chair was going to have a built-in porta-potty—the phone never stopped ringing. The parade committee was making me crazy. Give it a rest, folks.

Emily called in to say she had a flat tire and would be late. What was this? Sunspots?

When I thought I had everything under control, the power went out.

We were temporarily off the air for seven minutes while I got the generator started and left a note for Emily to order more propane. We were down to our last tank. The way the generator slurped LP, if the outage lasted more than an hour we'd be SOL and permanently OTA until power was restored.

The outage was my excuse to ignore the phone.

To conserve gas and keep the generator running as long as possible, I turned off everything not required for broadcasting, including air-conditioning.

The studio was as dark as a molten tar pit and equally hot. At least I'd worn my usual Lands' End shorts, tank top and Dr. Scholl's sandals. Otherwise I'd be doing a quick strip down to my bikini panties. Being a deejay in the tropics is not a dress-for-success occupation.

I grabbed an icy Tab from my cooler and held the can against my sweating face before I popped the top and plopped in a straw. Tab definitely qualified as nectar of the gods.

After a zillion tries I managed to get through to the power plant. The outage was islandwide.

A prerecorded voice said, "We hope to begin restoring partial power within the hour, we'll rotate feeders on an hourly basis until full power is available."

Sure. Rotate on this, power company. But I began announcing the rotation schedule on air and reminded my listeners to check their latest electric bill for their feeder number.

I kept trying to call the gas company. No answer. No Emily to make the call for me. What was she using to change that tire, an electric jack?

I sat in the dark, playing jazz, updating the power rotations, calling the gas company, checking the generator, and drinking Tab.

I was sweating so much that trips to the loo had become unnecessary. Reminded me of Aswan in Upper Egypt on an August afternoon. I felt like a peanut buried to roast in the Egyptian sand.

By noon life was back to normal. Emily was at her desk, cracking her gum like a contented bovine. The gas company was on the way. Just in time. The generator had coughed to a halt seconds before the power was fully restored.

My airtime was over and I was calling it quits for the day, heading to the Watering Hole in town for a lazy lunch with Margo before I went home to get ready for Mrs. H's bon voyage party.

Margo and I were sitting in our usual spot at our permanently reserved round table immediately outside the restaurant and directly across from Margo's Island Palms Real Estate office, under the shade of a faded yellow canvas umbrella, mushroom bacon cheeseburgers and fries on order, when Zena descended upon us like a hawk on a coconut rat.

"Found you! The girl at the station said you'd be here. My dear, you must tell her not to chew while she's talking. Very rude. But at least she answered the phone. I tried calling you all morning."

Without waiting for an invitation, Zena settled herself in the chair to my right.

"Now here are some of my ideas for the parade." As she spoke, she pulled a stapled sheaf of papers from her tote. "Didn't have time to type these properly, power was out this morning . . . does that happen often? I won't be able to make my pub date if that sort of thing continues."

She thrust her papers toward my hand—"Kelly dear, read these now and tell me what you think"—ignoring the glass of iced tea I was holding, resulting in a shower in my lap and on my bare legs. Oblivious to my discomfort, Zena began scribbling a note on a small pad, muttering to herself, "Call power company. Tell hotel to install backup power for my room."

Margo handed me a napkin to mop up the mess as the waitress arrived with our orders.

Zena sniffed audibly and said, "Meat? You eat meat? The smell makes me sick." She stuffed the notepad in her tote, grabbed her papers and quickly rose from the table.

"I'll call you at home. Are you in the book? Never mind, I'll get the number from the operator." Fat chance, I thought, I'm not listed. She departed like a dust devil in a swirl of beige cotton.

Margo tracked Zena's departure with raised eyebrows. "Who in the hell was that?"

"That, my dear, was Dr. Zena Sheffield." I couldn't resist a wry smile.

"A little self-absorbed, isn't she?"

"Only until you get to know her," I replied, "then she's completely one-track."

"If I were you, I'd derail her. Fast."

Chapter
6

MRS. H'S PARTY was in high gear when I arrived at Harborview at six.

I love Harborview, but don't get there very often. It was fun to take the ten-passenger ferry from the wharf at Dockside over to the pier at Papaya Quay, where Harborview's main building was situated on a small rise, nestled amid lush gardens and artificial waterfalls tumbling toward the sea.

The history of Papaya Quay includes a ghost.

When Columbus fled the Caribs in 1493, his fleet traveled east, from what we now call Columbus Bay, along our northern coastline, until he came in sight of Papaya Quay. Known then by the Indian name Cibuguiera, meaning "stony land," Papaya Quay was used by the Arawaks solely as a lookout post. Taking no chances on grounding his ships in the meandering shoals, Columbus anchored outside the reef and sent a launch ashore to explore.

This time the meeting was cordial on both sides. The Arawaks showered the invaders with hospitality. Fearful of a retaliatory visit by the Caribs, the Spaniards did not overstay their welcome. Columbus dispensed a few trinkets, some rosary beads made of glass, planted a wooden cross where Fort Frederick now stands and headed for points north.

Papaya Quay continued to be used as a lookout post by the Spanish and then the English. Until the fire that destroyed Isabeya in 1764, it remained uninhabited but was a popular holiday outing spot for the planters and their families.

After the fire, the Danish government was homeless, with only Fort Frederick left standing to house the soldiers and dispossessed town residents. Temporary Government House quarters were established on Papaya Quay.

The original governor's mansion was later expanded with outbuildings for the customs inspector, harbormaster and the governor's aides and their families.

When the first phase of the new Government House at the foot of Kongens Gade was completed five years later, Papaya Quay became the governor's private retreat.

Island legend tells us the governor had a mistress, an enchanting beauty who claimed descent from the original Arawaks, who he stashed at Papaya Quay until her death during a yellow fever epidemic. She was buried on the quay, but her grave has never been found.

It is said she haunts her former home to this day, walking back and forth along the terrace waiting and watching for her lover to come to her by boat.

Standing on that same wide terrace surrounding the dining room, I could see the lights coming on in town three hundred feet away, the gazebo bandstand in the small park between the fort and the library, and hear the hourly bell from the Anglican church on the western end of Kongens Gade punctuating the faint laughter of diners at Dockside's Lower Deck.

I breathed a sigh of contentment. Moments like this reminded me why I had moved to St. Chris a decade earlier.

"Town looks like a stage set from here, doesn't it, Mama."

I turned to reply and did a double take.

"Michael? Michael!" I couldn't believe my eyes. The party dress code was formal, and Michael looked absolutely magnificent in black tie. Gone were the baggy shorts and luridly flowered shirts he wore to work. If formal clothes made the man, Michael was a ten plus. He'd even had his auburn hair, moustache and beard trimmed. I still couldn't believe my eyes.

"Close your mouth, Mama, you'll draw flies. Let's get some bubbly." We walked arm in arm to the bar, housed in the former Danish kitchen, where the guest of honor was holding court.

"There you are," Mrs. H cried gaily, "and don't you two look nice. Stunning little black dress, Kelly. I know that label. Your pearls are fabulous." She wrapped us in a hug. "Without you two taking care of the station, I wouldn't be able to go on this trip. Thank you."

I thought I detected a teary tremor in her smile.

"I think Mama's grown a foot since you put her in charge. She's almost lifesize now." Leave it to Michael to save the moment with a smart-ass remark.

"Be careful she doesn't cut you down to size," Mrs. H retorted.

"I think she already has," he shot back. "Nah, it's only her three-inch heels."

When I was barefoot Michael topped me by mere inches; in our formal togs we were almost eye to eye.

"Have fun, darlings." Mrs. H whispered to me, "Relax, Kelly, no one on the committee was invited. I'll talk to you again before you leave."

The invitation was for cocktails. As new residents of St. Chris quickly learn, that phrase implies drinks and a lavish buffet, as opposed to a sit-down dinner. Michael and I

filled our plates and found seats at a table on the terrace
overlooking town where we were serenaded by a steel
band softly playing Bach's "Jesu, Joy of Man's Desiring."

I felt slightly off balance. Michael and I had never before socialized away from the station. This dress-up version of Michael was going to take some getting used to. I
generally thought of him as an amusing flake with lousy
taste in clothes and a preference for music that gave me a
headache. But it was obvious there were sides of Michael
I'd never seen. Beneath his raffish exterior there possibly
lay a prince.

Pumpkin time came for Michael at nine; he had to be
on the air at ten. After he left, I went to say good-bye to
Mrs. H.

She hugged me again and said she was sorry to be leaving at a time when she knew I'd be wanting to get on a
plane for Colorado to be with Jeff.

"To do what?" I asked. "Watch him vegetate in a hospital bed? I don't think so." I couldn't tell her I didn't
have the vaguest idea where he was.

"When you call him, charge it to the station," she said.
"Don't let that blasted parade committee get you down,
either." Mrs. H cupped my face with her hands. "Tread
lightly with Zena, but don't let her walk all over you. I
think she'll pull any trick to get her own way, but I know
you can handle it." She kissed my forehead in a farewell
benediction, leaving behind a faint lipstick print as a mark
of her protection.

Chapter
7

MRS. H'S ADVICE echoed in my head two nights later at our regular Thursday parade committee meeting.

It must have been the approaching full moon, because everyone was in a foul mood. Sniping, baring fangs, determined not to agree on anything, and looking upon me as either Glenda the Good Witch if I agreed with them or the Wicked Witch of the West if I didn't. I wanted to sic the winged monkeys on them or crack a whip and toss raw meat into their cages. Angie excepted. She skipped the meeting, using the flimsy excuse of police business. Smart lady.

Zena was by far the worst offender. It was obvious she'd won her black belt in academic infighting. I was beginning to take her continual interruptions and condescending asides personally.

I called a five-minute break, slipping outside to stand at the top of the library steps for a much-needed breath of fresh air. Zena was right there, stuck to my side like flypaper, chomping away on Island Delights.

"My dear, are you aware that—"

"Zena, I'm sure the entire committee will want to benefit from your insight. Please wait and share it when we've reconvened." I was beginning to sound like a stodgy academic myself, in danger of permanent lockjaw from smiling with my teeth clenched.

Her wonderful insight was the latest in a laundry list of inconsequential lore about the life and times of "Our Venerable Queen." What Columbus's 1493 discovery of the pineapple in Guadeloupe had to do with anything except the decimation of Island Delights or the invention of the piña colada escaped us all.

Zena was not one to be deterred by the lack of an enthusiastic response. "On his second voyage," she droned, "Columbus introduced sugarcane to the West Indies, which the Spanish had brought from Asia to the Canary Islands. The first locally produced sugar was transported back to Spain in 1512."

I stifled a yawn and refrained from asking if the sugar had been shipped in bottles labeled "151 proof."

Instead I tapped on the table to bring the meeting back to order and said brightly, "I think we should return to the subject of float decoration."

My innocent request set off another round of Family Feud.

"My schoolchildren do not have the resources to acquire . . ."

"If ye have faith in a grain of mustard seed . . ."

"It would be historically correct if palm fronds and natural vegetation . . ."

Reverend Cal slammed his fist on the table. "The tongue no man can tame, it is an unruly evil."

The room became suddenly and ominously silent.

Zena's icy rage would have rendered the dinosaur extinct. "You false prophet!"

Reverend Cal turned bright red.

Mr. Daniel laughed.

Zena's anger found a new target. "You! What are you laughing at? You're nothing but a political hack."

I rapped on the table for attention. Too late.

Only Mr. Daniel heard me say, "Cal, will you get in touch with the Chamber of Commerce about material donations for the school floats?"

Mr. Daniel paused in the doorway, fury emanating from his body in pulsing waves. "We would not be having these difficulties if I had been appointed chairman of this committee. I will not involve myself further while Dr. Sheffield is still among us."

My final words, "We're adjourned for three weeks," echoed in the empty room.

In the distance I heard two cars speeding out of the fort parking lot. One of the cars badly needed a new muffler.

Chapter
8

ANGIE WAS MY new partner for the weekly turtle walk.

We met on the point in the middle of Leatherback Bay on Friday evening at six, a few minutes before sunset. The air was heavy, like breathing cotton. Reminded me more of late August hurricane season than early spring.

Minx was better than a barometer at predicting storms. When I left for the beach she was curled in a tight ball, calico-striped tail over her pepper-freckled pink nose, snug against the pillows on my king-sized bed. I was glad I'd tucked a plastic rain poncho in my fanny pack.

Leatherback Bay is shaped like two side-by-side smiles. Angie and I walked a figure-eight pattern, using the point as our starting and meeting place. We headed in opposite directions, taking thirty minutes to cover our quarter mile of beachfront, a fifteen-minute rest at the far end of the bay with a brief check-in by walkie-talkie, then thirty minutes back to the starting place. Another fifteen-minute rest when we'd compare notes and fill in our log sheets, then we'd change directions and head off again to the far ends of the beach.

We only used our red gel-covered flashlights when absolutely necessary. Extraneous lights distracted and confused the turtles. At least once during nesting season, Fish and Wildlife would be called to rescue a turtle from a beachfront swimming pool.

The pungent sea air was a heady tonic after the hours I had spent in the confines of the radio station. I tasted salt on my lips, like licking the rim of a margarita glass. I inhaled deeply, the way a leatherback turtle uses its sense of smell to find land.

A quarter-mile offshore a thirty-year-old female leatherback—T–001, nicknamed Eve, the first turtle tagged at Leatherback Bay—raised her head above water. Fueled by a diet of jellyfish, she traveled thousands of miles, from the African coast up to Europe, then across the Atlantic and down to the Caribbean Sea, to reach her St. Chris nesting beach. She swam slowly toward Leatherback Bay until her hind flippers easily touched the sandy bottom, her twelve-hundred-pound body buoyant in the sea. There Eve remained to rest, floating in the shallows, until dark.

By the end of the second round I was dead-ass tired. My calf muscles were throbbing. Angie worked out every morning at the health club while I sat on my butt at the radio station. My main exercise was kayaking in Top Banana, my bright yellow molded plastic sit-on-top Ocean Scrambler. At thirty-nine pounds, it weighs slightly more than two cases of Tab. Kayaking is great for the upper body, but doesn't do much for toning leg muscles. I groused to Angie as I flopped on my back on the beach during our rest break.

"Poke me with a fork, I'm done."

"Kelly, you're such a tenderfoot. You need to get out more. Take up bicycle riding."

"You'd think I'd be in better shape after running away from Zena this past week."

"You said she really put her foot into it last night."

"More like her mouth," I quipped.

"Tell me again what she called Reverend Cal? A false what?"

"Prophet."

Angie shook her head in amusement. "She actually said Mr. Daniel was a political hack? To his face?"

"You got it."

"Kel, I told you that woman was going to be big trouble."

"Let's hope she keeps her mouth shut tomorrow at Columbus Bay. Or stays away."

Angie's reply was masked by the rising wind. Within seconds a squall dumped rain on us in chilling torrents. We hastily abandoned the beach walk, racing to our nearby cars to head for home before the dirt road turned to tire-sucking mud.

After the storm passed, Eve roused herself from the shallows to head for the beach. When her belly touched bottom and she could no longer swim, she used her powerful front flippers to pull herself along the sloping sandy bottom, emerging from the water to scout a secure nesting site above the high tide mark.

She first dug a shallow pit with her front flippers to cradle her underbody. Then, using her hind flippers in alternating cycles, she carefully sculpted her urn-shaped nest in the damp sand.

The outer edges of her back flippers curved into scoops to grasp the sand and fling it far from the nest. Dig, scoop, lift, toss. Right, then left. Dig, scoop, lift, toss. When the nest was eighteen inches deep, with a top opening ten inches in diameter, she folded her hind flippers away from her tail and began filling the nest with Ping-Pong ball-sized soft-shelled eggs. The laying process ended after approximately one hundred eggs had been deposited in the nest.

Eve used her back flippers to cover the nest carefully with sand, patting the top layer into place.

She then made laborious circles in the sand, using a front flipper and opposing rear flipper for locomotion, to obliterate all traces of the nest.

Mustering her last gasp of energy, Eve headed back to the ocean, two hours after she'd left it, for nourishment and rest before repeating the nesting process nine days later.

Chapter
9

THE FIRST TIME Columbus landed at the mouth of the bay that would later bear his name, a small Carib Indian village was located in a cove on the bay's eastern shore.

It was mid-November, 1493, the end of a prolonged hurricane season. The sea was too rough to allow the seventeen-ship fleet—which included the legendary *Niña* from his first voyage—entry through the narrow channel in the coral reef. A small launch with a crew of twenty-five was dispatched to explore.

At the sight of the monstrous ships blocking the bay entrance, the Caribs fled their village to hide in the bush. The children wore small bells tied to their arms to enable their parents to find them later.

The landing party ransacked the abandoned village, taking what they pleased from the lean-tos. As the launch left the cove to return to the fleet, a canoe containing four men, two women and a small boy approached from the mangroves to the south where the Caribs had been hunting game for food.

When they saw the ships, the canoe's occupants were dumbstruck. For an hour they sat still in the water, within bowshot of the invaders in the launch and in plain view of the anchored fleet.

The staring match was broken by the invaders advancing toward the canoe. The natives retaliated by shooting at the invaders with poison-tipped arrows. One arrow pierced through the shield of an invader, inflicting a nasty wound, which resulted in the sailor's death three days later.

The launch then rammed the canoe, spilling the Caribs into the sea from where they were immediately captured and later sent as booty to Spain. One Carib continued firing arrows as he tried to swim to safety. He was caught with a grapple, hauled over the gunwale of the launch and instantly beheaded.

I sat in Top Banana in the middle of Columbus Bay, kayak paddle straddling my lap, the morning sun warm on my swimsuit-clad body, trying to visualize the scene from five hundred years ago.

I looked toward the reef and saw nothing but an empty sea and clear skies stretching to the silhouetted out islands forty miles north. But in my mind I heard the muted tinkle of tiny bells, the raucous cries of the invaders, the swish of the canoe approaching from the mangroves.

The former Carib Indian village was now a footnote in history books, the site later occupied by a long vanished star-shaped French fort, presently home to the small marina where I'd parked my car and launched my craft.

When I docked and secured my kayak to a palm tree for the opening ceremonies of Stamp Day, the western shore of Columbus Bay resembled Brigadoon on the beach.

A huge tent had been erected on the sand, the St. Chris flag flying from the main tent pole. Over the entrance was an official post office sign bearing the special one-day Columbus Bay cancellation—a bare-breasted Carib maiden in a traditional feather headdress holding an arrow in her hand seated in front of a billowing sail embellished with a Spanish cross—that would be used on all outgoing mail.

Members of the St. Chris high school steel band pounded their hearts out in a vigorous rendition of "Yellow Bird," serenading the stamp collectors chatting in a queue that snaked from the parking area to the beach.

St. Chris was selected as the first day post office for the issuance of the commemorative four-stamp panel depicting the voyages of Christopher Columbus. The Italian government was issuing identical designs in Genoa, the first day Italian city. Collectors in St. Chris and Genoa would be able to purchase both sets at either location with first day cancellations.

The excitement was contagious. Children raced up and down the beach with gaily colored helium-filled balloons, imprinted with the first day cancellation, tied to their wrists.

The church ladies had risen early to prepare the johnnycakes, meat pates and fried chicken legs they offered for sale along with home-brewed maubi and ginger beer. Miss Maude waved and called to me from her table.

"Good morning, Kelly."

I smiled and waved back at her, "Good morning, Miss Maude."

I approached the table where St. Chris's favorite retired schoolteacher sat on a folding cane-seated chair. A wide-brimmed straw hat shielded her face from the sun.

"Have you come to taste my ginger beer?" I detected a twinkle in her bright blue eyes. Eyes that could still spot a spitball in the making from twenty paces.

"How can I resist?" I dug a bill from my waterproof fanny pack and received a plastic cup filled with ice and ginger beer. The spicy taste of the grated ginger root tickled my tongue.

"Try a johnnycake. I made them this morning." She

waved away my attempt to pay her. "How have you been keeping? You haven't come to see me to get cuttings for your garden. I've got a special strain of catnip I've been growing for your sweet Minx."

Miss Maude, a lifelong St. Chris resident, lived in a stone cottage near the west end rain forest. In her childhood she'd stood in a new pink dress clutching her mother's hand to watch the red and white Danebrög, the world's oldest national flag, lowered for the last time and the new blue, white, green and yellow St. Chris flag rise triumphantly in the freshening breeze. Seventy-six years after Transfer Day, her speech still bore a faint Danish lilt. Miss Maude spent her retirement days tending her herb garden and fruit trees, selling her produce and herbal bush teas in a stall at Isabeya's marketplace and from a little stand in front of her house.

"Miss Maude, I've been meaning to." A flimsy excuse. "But with my job and the parade and turtle season . . ."

"Melee," she said, smiling and handing me another johnnycake.

"I'll come by to see you soon. Promise."

I left Miss Maude and worked my way through the crowd to where Margo and Angie were standing near the folding chairs set up for the opening speeches. A makeshift podium, flanked by portable speakers, listed on the sand.

Margo was the first to greet me. "Kel! How did you get here? Swim? I didn't see your car."

I pantomimed paddling. Margo looked incredulous. "All the way from your house on the east end?" I shook my head, pointing eastward and mouthing, "Marina."

Angie laughed. "After last night? I thought you'd be carried here on a litter."

"Uh-huh. With all the glamour of Cleo entering Rome," added Margo, eyeing my water-spotted nylon shorts and strapless one-piece bathing suit. "I hear you two bugged out early."

"Rained out," I said, smiling innocently.

"No one's seen a turtle yet, so I won't take away the gold star on your attendance chart."

The steel band paused between songs, the momentary silence broken by voices shouting in Italian and English.

"Basta!"

"I'm telling you, it's wrong. He was never here. It's all wrong!"

"I am asking you to leave quietly."

Three heads whipped around to find the source of the dissension.

Zena stood behind the podium at an easel where the original rendering of the newly minted stamps was on display. She jabbed at the artwork with a stick she had picked up on the beach. The postmaster grabbed her arm, but Zena held fast to the stick.

"Kelly, isn't that your new best friend, Dr. Sheffield?" asked Margo.

"My God, what is Zena up to now?" said Angie, sprinting for the podium.

"Margo, look." I pointed at Zena's hand.

"I can hear the woman, I don't need to look at her."

"No, look. Look at what she's holding in her hand."

"A stick."

"Look again."

"Oh, no," said Margo. "That's manchineel. Doesn't she know any better? Someone should tell her."

Angie apparently conveyed the message, because Zena immediately dropped the stick and began wiping her hand on the voluminous skirt of her dress. She ran to the sea to wash her hands, then quickly left the beach. Angie used a fallen saucer-sized sea grape leaf to dispose of the stick in a nearby trash can.

"Can you believe Zena? She certainly has a talent for trouble." Angie sighed.

"Or being conspicuous," I mused, wondering why she'd

chosen such a public occasion to make a total ass of herself.

"Angelita, I must thank you for diffusing a most unfortunate situation," said Mr. Thomas, the St. Chris postmaster. "We are lucky the artwork was not damaged, otherwise an immediate arrest would have been necessary."

Dressed for Stamp Day in a three-piece wool suit, French cuffed white shirt and a silk tie, Mr. Thomas wiped his perspiring brow while introducing us to his Genoese counterpart.

"What can that woman have been thinking of?" said Mr. Thomas. "Picking up manchineel. Even a schoolchild knows better."

"What is this manchineel you speak of?" asked the Genoese postmaster.

"It is a tree that is indigenous to our lovely island," said Mr. Thomas. "Innocent in appearance, but very deadly. If that vexatious woman had studied her history books she would have known the tree sap was the poison the Caribs used on their arrows. The Spaniards even consumed the small fruit, often with fatal consequences, believing it was related to the apple."

Mr. Thomas smiled ruefully at the foolishness of ignorant outsiders. "Now, if you will excuse us, we must begin this auspicious event. The sun is very hot and our collectors are becoming impatient."

From different parts of the beach, two bystanders watched the scene unfold. On each man's face was a malevolent smile.

Chapter
10

THE WEEK BETWEEN Stamp Day and the next turtle walk was mercifully quiet.

Perhaps too quiet. What felt like a lull before the storm was, in retrospect, the deceptive calm of the eye of Hurricane Zena.

Blissfully unaware, I put the parade committee out of my mind and spent the week getting a life: on the air in the morning, lunch with Margo and assorted friends at the Watering Hole round table, kayaking before dinner in the reef-protected sea near my home, quiet evenings spent re-reading Agatha Christie's *Death On the Nile* on my screened-in gallery with Minx nearby on lizard patrol. To Minx, the small bug-eating chameleons were both a toy and a delicacy.

Phone calls from Jeff were sporadic and beginning to depress me. With omnipresent Nurse Perky—I didn't know her real name, but from her bright chirping voice I pictured her as a fluffy-haired, flea-brained nymphette—always holding the phone to Jeff's ear, we had as much

privacy as talking on a speakerphone. I was also beginning
to wonder why he wouldn't give me the number or tell me
where he could be reached. He always said it was easier
for him to call me.

Minx and I went for nightly walks before bedtime, then
ended the evening with a fast game of hockey. Our version
consisted of batting a plastic mesh cat ball containing a
small jingling bell back and forth across the floor. Her end
zone was under my brass bed; mine was anywhere the ball
wasn't. Minx was especially adept at shooting the ball
from under the bed to the thin wedge of space under a
bookshelf. She usually won.

By Friday night I felt rested and ready to pound my
beach beat.

Angie and I met again at the point at Leatherback Bay
at six. The sun was a half-hour from setting. The waning
moon wouldn't rise until eleven, so we'd spend most of
the evening walking in darkness. Shapes are deceptive in
the dark. It's easy to mistake a rise in the sand or a partially
submerged rock for a nesting turtle.

I set off briskly on my first trek, heading east. The cool
easterly breeze felt good on my face, the setting sun warm
on my back. I shed my flip-flops, securing them to the
strap of my fanny pack, tramping barefoot in military ca-
dence on the hard-packed sand along the water's edge.

The breeze made it difficult to identify the origin of
sounds. The bell of the Anglican church in Isabeya tolling
the half hour sounded closer than the splash of a hungry
pelican fifty feet offshore.

As I walked, I memorized landmarks and scanned the
beachfront for signs of turtle activity. The distinctive trails
of tractorlike tracks leading to and from the sea were as
identifiable to a knowing eye as a poacher's footprints.

I followed one trail leading to nowhere. Probably a false
crawl by a turtle seeking a nesting site and going back to
sea without depositing her eggs. Before the nesting actu-

ally begins, turtles are easily distracted by lights, unfamiliar scents, human presence or an instinct that conditions aren't quite right.

I reached the end of my route, moving to the soft, dry sand above the high water line for a rest break. Time to check in with Angie.

"Mother Hen to Chicken Little."

Angie's voice squawked in my ear. "Chicken Little, my ass. I'm three inches taller than you! *Que pasa*?"

"Nothing. What's happening at your end?"

"Same here. *Nada*. Keep on truckin', Kel. See you in thirty."

It was darker than the inside of my pocket when I made my way back to our starting place. I kept to the water's edge, but my pace slowed as my eyes strained to perceive movement. The clicking palm fronds masked the sounds of digging, so I walked even slower in order not to miss any signs of activity.

Angie was noshing on trail mix when I arrived at our meeting place. She pointed to a Tupperware bowl at her side.

"Have some. My mom made a big batch for us."

"What's in it?"

"Picky, picky, Kel. You want some or not?"

"Allergies. I can't eat citrus."

"Oh, yeah? What happens to you?"

"My tongue breaks out in hives, my stomach turns into a washing machine full of rocks and I get the shakes. Trust me, it's not a pretty sight."

"So how do you drink Bloody Marys?"

"That's different."

"Tell me another one."

"I'm a masochist; I like to suffer."

"This is Mom's special blend: sun-dried papaya and coconut from our yard, mixed with lots of peanuts. I added the M&M's for color. And chocolate."

I reached for a handful. Angie lay back on the sand, looking up at the stars.

"Hey, you can see Mars!"

I craned my neck to look. "Where? I don't see it."

"See Orion? Lie down, Kel, it's easier. Okay. Look at the club in his upraised hand. On the left. See it? Mars is up, about center sky, and left of that."

"Oh, yeah. I see it." The dusky red orb shimmered like a rare Burmese ruby or a Vicks cherry cough drop. "Angie, look. There's Sirius. Star of the Egyptian goddess Isis."

"Where?"

"Straight down from Mars, toward the water. The bright one."

"Got it."

We settled back to stargaze, our hands dipping into the trail mix bowl between us. Laughter and party sounds, complete with a reggae band playing old calypso numbers, trickled down to the beach from a home in the eastern hills.

As the soporific sea air coupled with whooshing waves tickling the beach pebbles lulled me toward sleep, from an unidentifiable point in the west I heard someone trying to start a car with a bad battery or faulty starter. It finally caught on the third try. Apparently the car needed a new muffler as well. The sound seemed to grow louder, then died.

The next thing I knew, Angie was saying, "Kel, are you nodding off? It's after eight. We've overstayed our break time." I shook myself awake and grabbed a Tab from my cooler. A pit stop would have to wait until I was at the western end of the beach.

Half an hour later, after a discreet potty stop in the bush, I squatted on a large piece of driftwood for a break. The hands on my waterproof Indiglo sport watch pointed to 8:47.

"Wonder Woman to Tiny Tim."

"Bag the short jokes, Wonder Woman," I laughingly replied. "What's up?"

"Nothing. Absolutely nothing. This is getting very bor-ring." She gave the final word a singsong lilt.

"I'm with you, Wonder Woman. Tell you what, in another couple of hours the Southern Cross will be up. If we haven't seen a turtle by then, let's call it a night."

"That's a plan. See you in thirty, Tiny Tim. Mom also made meat loaf sandwiches for us."

A meat loaf sandwich sounded really good.

I was close enough to the point to almost smell rather than imagine the sandwich, when I spotted a black lump in the sand ahead of me. I stopped in my tracks to radio Angie.

"Angie! I think I've got a live one! Where are you?"

"Really? Great! I'm at the point, where are you?"

I quickly looked around for a landmark. "The twin palms, before the land curves toward the point. That's where I am. The turtle's ahead of me, about thirty feet due east of where I'm standing. Nesting site about ten feet above the high tide line."

"Gotcha. Be right there."

I carefully approached the nesting turtle. Was it Eve? I'd been part of the team that had tagged her our first year. She hadn't nested the prior season, so she was due to show this year unless something dire had happened to her. In my excitement over finding the first nester of the season, it failed to register that there were no tracks leading to the nesting site from the water.

As I drew closer, I could tell it wasn't a turtle at all. I'd been tricked by a large rock I hadn't noticed earlier. I was ready to radio Angie to stay put at the point, when I looked again. This rock had arms and legs.

I turned on my flashlight for a better view.

Head pointing away from me, facedown on the beach, was a body with sprawled arms and legs. Oh, God. There was a thin shaft rising skyward from its back. The body was clothed in a black crinkle cotton caftan.

When I got within touching distance of the figure, Angie approached at a sprint from the east, a beam of light from her gel-covered flashlight bobbing ahead of her on the sand like a floating red carpet.

"False alarm," I called out. "This isn't a turtle, I think it's—"

Sand flew in the air as Angie ran to my side.

"Don't touch anything!" she cautioned.

We stood shoulder to shoulder, looking down at the body at our feet.

"Holy Mary Mother of God," Angie exclaimed, "it looks like Zena!"

It was Zena. But now she was the late Dr. Sheffield. The woman was dead. Very dead indeed.

Chapter

11

GONE WAS MY friend. In her place stood Detective Angelita Maria Sanchez, all official business.

"Kelly, stay right where you are. Don't. Touch. Anything. I'll be back in a few minutes." She ran down the beach toward the point and the parking area where we'd left our cars four hours earlier.

I looked down at Zena's body, trying to identify the item sticking out of her back. Could it possibly be a spear? Sure looked like one. Visions of Caribs with their poison-tipped arrows going after the Spanish invaders filled my mind.

I leaned down for a better look, being very careful to stay outside touching distance. I'm no forensics expert; but I couldn't see any blood around the entry point of the shaft. But the night was dark, her dress was black and what did I know aside from being an avid reader of mystery fiction?

I looked at Zena's feet clad in coordinating black flats, never before having noticed what tiny shoes she wore. They looked smaller than my size six.

I turned to face the sea and saw Gacrux, the uppermost

star of the Southern Cross, twinkling on the horizon.

Angie returned in a few minutes, as promised. A row of flares now marked the path from the point to Zena's body. Angie's gun was in its holster on her hip, on her belt were a set of handcuffs and a billy club, the walkie-talkie we used for our turtle walks had been replaced by a cellular phone.

"I've called this into the closest substation, the backups should be here anytime now. Did you see anything else?"

I pointed out that the shaft looked like a spear, adding that I didn't see any blood around the entry point.

"Probably postmortem. Good observation. I wonder what really killed her?"

Her flashlight tucked under her arm, Angie continued writing in her police notebook. In the distance we heard sirens approaching the beach road.

Angie had been careful to retrace her steps on the beach as closely as possible. I removed the red gel cover from my flashlight for better visibility, and let the light play over the north side of the beach between Zena's body and the trees. I didn't think for one minute that Zena had died where she now lay. My suspicions were soon confirmed.

"Angie, look!"

She stopped writing. "What am I looking at? Where should I look?" The words flew out of her mouth in a clipped, staccato fashion.

"Over there. In the sand." I remained in place, tracing the path with my flashlight beam. "See that depression in the sand? It looks like the body was dragged here."

"You may be right. Whoever brought it here tried to cover up their tracks after the body was dumped. I wonder what was used?"

"A palm frond?" I asked.

Angie nodded in agreement. "Could be. I'm going to have a closer look." She walked a few feet away and hunkered down, gazing at the sand.

I looked at the body. No sand on the clothing. It must have been wrapped in something before being laid out on the beach. Whatever had been used for a shroud was no longer in evidence.

The sirens came closer. Then, with a final wail, they fell silent. We heard car doors slamming, then running footsteps approaching the beach.

"Sanchez! You there?"

"Over here." Angie waved her flashlight skyward in an arc like a klieg light at an opening night. Police officers soon clustered around the body.

I walked a few steps closer to the water. This was now police business and I was merely a bystander. I stood gazing at the gently moving water.

Orion had taken his exit stage left and Gacrux, Mimosa, Del Cru and Acrux, the four stars that comprise the Southern Cross, were now fully visible. The moon had not yet risen.

A black hump appeared in the shallows, followed by a raised head slowly turning left then right. I heard a whoosh of expelled air. A turtle scouting a landing site?

"Go away. Go farther down the beach," I implored under my breath.

The hump unfolded, stretching skyward, completely black against the sapphire sky like the creature from the black lagoon. In the creature's upraised hand was an object that looked like a bow. Or a club.

I couldn't help it. I screamed until the air was gone from my lungs.

Angie yelled, "Kelly! Have you lost your mind? What's wrong?"

All I could do was point at the water. I was momentarily distracted when I stepped on a small sea urchin, which was like tromping barefoot on a pissed-off baby porcupine. Its black needled spines embedded themselves in my foot.

Two policemen raced to the water's edge.

The creature struggled, then fell back into the water.

The officers pulled him from the sea, hauled him to his feet, cuffed his hands behind his back, then brought him to where Angie and I stood watching.

The masked creature was a scuba diver in a full-body wet suit, complete with hood. One of the officers held a speargun, seawater dripping from the handgrip.

The diving mask and scuba regulator were removed from the diver's face.

Before us stood Mr. Daniel.

One of the officers intoned: "You have the right to remain silent."

Chapter

12

I WAS UNDERWATER, hitching a ride on the back flippers of a leatherback turtle in order to escape from a giant black squid.

In the distance I heard tiny bells tinkling. I relaxed my grip on the turtle to listen to the bells, scraping my foot against fire coral as I sank to the ocean floor. Searing pain from my foot radiated up my leg in nausea-inducing waves. The bells kept ringing. Louder and louder.

I woke with a start and threw back the covers, tossing Minx onto the floor. She reacted with an angry yowl. I looked at my bedside battery-operated clock: 10:30. Damn. I was late for work. My shift was almost over. I'd really blown it. I raced across the room to the ringing phone.

"I'll be right there!" I slammed down the phone and ran to my closet. The phone rang again.

"Kelly! Don't hang up, it's me. Margo."

"Margo, I can't talk. I'm late for work. Really late."

"It's Saturday, you twit. You don't work on Saturday."

I felt like someone had let all the air out of my body. "Are you sure? Is it really Saturday?"

"Cross my heart. Are you okay? What's the matter with your voice? Have you got a cold?"

"I'm in recovery from a goddamned heart attack. I was sound asleep, having the strangest dream."

"Grab a Tab, sweetie. You'll feel better. I'm coming right over with breakfast. I want to hear all about last night. Abby called me this morning. She heard about it from her secretary Barbara, Angie's cousin. What do you want to eat? Sausage McMuffin or biscuit with bacon?"

"One of each. Don't forget the hash browns." I was starving. I never did get to eat the meat loaf sandwich Angie's mother had made.

I collapsed on my couch. Minx sat next to her empty food bowl, glaring at me with narrowed eyes, whining for breakfast.

I put my right foot on the floor, rose halfway from the couch, then promptly sat down again. Ouch. My foot really hurt. Why was I wearing one sock?

Treading lightly on my right heel, I hobbled to the kitchen. Cat crunchies and a quarter can of turkey with bacon for Minx, a cold Tab in foam holder emblazoned with the WBZE logo for me. Perhaps now I could begin thinking clearly. I had half an hour to get my act together before Margo arrived with breakfast.

Margo and Paul live in a two-bedroom unit at Sea Breezes, a seaside condo complex located on the north shore, west of Isabeya. It was a five-minute drive from the condo to the open-air minimall due west of town housing the supermarket, video store, and McDonald's. Another twenty-five minutes from the minimall to my house. If traffic was light.

I spotted a small silver tube lying on my coffee table. The St. Chris hospital label read: "For external use only."

Two small white envelopes also lay on the table. One read: "For pain. One every six hours. Not to exceed four tablets daily." There were seven tablets inside the envelope. The other envelope was empty and bore no label.

Then I remembered. Zena's body clothed in black. That was no dream. But the fire coral? Had I really injured my foot on fire coral? When? I carefully removed the sock I didn't remember ever buying. The sole of my right foot was swollen to twice its normal size and covered with small purple pinpoint marks. It felt like I'd had a ball bearing implanted. I also had an odd tickle deep in my throat.

A vision of the Southern Cross appeared and disappeared in my head. A figure rising from the sea. I heard myself screaming. I remembered stepping on something.

Of course. The damned sea urchin. The sterile sock was put on my foot in the hospital emergency room before I came home at three A.M. I was groggy from the sleeping pill the doctor insisted I take before retiring. Dumb move. I should have known better.

I prayed the feeling in my throat wasn't a harbinger of laryngitis. That's all I needed. A deejay who couldn't talk wasn't part of my job description.

The last time this happened I was working as an actress in a national company of *Hello, Dolly!* playing Minnie Fay and lost my voice during the closing night performance right after I'd screamed my lungs out when I saw a man hiding in the closet. Purely stage business, but for a closing night prank, one of the crew stood in the closet and mooned me. The stage manager saved the show by reading my lines over a backstage mike while I lip-synched on stage. That ended my career as an ingenue. When I got my voice back a week later I sounded more like Julie London than Julie Andrews.

While I showered I mentally reprogrammed my radio shows for the coming week, deciding it was time for a nonstop airing of Wagner's *Ring Cycle* with Anna Russell thrown in for comic relief. I tossed on an ankle-length tropical print sarong we call a Java Wrap, making sure the square knot was securely tied above my breasts.

Minx finished breakfast, then disappeared outside into the bush on safari. I think she was still holding a grudge over having been so rudely ejected from my bed. I'd make amends later with Matanuska Thunder Struck, special Alaskan catnip a friend had sent in a Christmas box.

"What's all this?" I asked when Margo entered from the parking area through my kitchen door with a McDonald's bag in one hand and plastic grocery bags in the other.

"You've got company coming. Jerry and Abby are lagging behind me in separate cars. Pete's stopping for ice and beer. I didn't know if you'd shopped recently, so I brought Bloody Mary makings, cheese and crackers. Sit. I'll put everything away. Eat your breakfast before it gets moldy."

"Where's yours?" I asked.

"I couldn't wait. I ate in the car."

I devoured my hash browns in six bites. "How come Paul isn't with you?"

"He's got a flight to Sint Maarten today. Won't be back until late afternoon. By the way, you really look fabulous in that wrap. It gives you cleavage."

"Coming from a friend who hasn't seen her toes since she bought her first bra, my so-called cleavage may be an understatement. But thanks anyway." I smiled to let her know I was teasing.

I retired to the couch to focus on food while Margo put the groceries onto the tiled island in the middle of my kitchen that also serves as a dining table.

The interior of my house is one room, a northwesterly facing rectangle with kitchen and bath on the west end, sleeping area on the east and living space in the middle. The front opens through sliding glass doors onto a screened-in gallery overlooking the Caribbean Sea. To

form the interior walls that enclose the bathroom and util-
ity area next to the kitchen, I had a carpenter build two
large free-standing closets with outward-facing bifold lou-
vered doors. I use the closet facing the living room for
clothes and linens; the one fronting the kitchen serves as
a pantry and storage area for seldom-used unmentionables
like my vacuum cleaner and ironing board.

The weathered brick and coral walls of the original
structure rise twelve feet to exposed beams supporting the
red corrugated tin roof. Frosted glass jalousie windows on
the east, west and southern walls begin four feet from the
floor, creating the ambience of life in a tree house and
leaving me plenty of floor space for bookshelves.

The decor is early eclectic: easy care tropical rattan and
wicker furniture with overstuffed cushions covered in blue,
green and yellow prints. Handwoven silk rugs from Egypt
and Turkey dot the terrazzo floor.

Ceiling fans in the sleeping area, living room and
kitchen twirled lazily on low, while trade winds tickled the
twelve wind chimes hanging across the front of the gallery.
Margo swears I saw the movie *Body Heat* too many times.

My smart-mouthed friend walked across the room toward my Tennessee Williams brass bed, stopping to finger
the floor-length sheer white curtains bordered in a blue
Greek key design that were hanging on a long rod suspended from roof support beams, currently tied back for
daytime against the front and rear walls.

"Oh, Kel."

I swallowed the last mouthful of biscuit. "What?"

"Your new divider curtains. I love the effect. Very
Gatsby. Where did you find them?"

"I made them with a bolt of fabric I found on sale in
Greece. I got the idea from the movie. Same sort of thing
Redford had next to his swimming pool."

My voice cracked on the word "pool." I was instantly
reduced to the vocal range of a bullfrog.

"Are you sure you're not coming down with a cold?"

"Damned sure. I think it's laryngitis."

Margo handed me a copy of our local paper. "Here's today's *Telegraph*. There's nothing in it about the murder."

"Are we surprised?" I rasped. We both smiled.

Most of us read the *Coconut Telegraph* for a laugh and the do-it-in-five-minutes-in-ink crossword. The paper is famous for typos and transpositions and equally famous for being behind on the news. St. Chris must be the only place where you can buy a paper on Sunday, dated Monday, printed Saturday, full of Friday's news.

I wadded the wrappings from breakfast into a ball and hobbled barefoot to the kitchen to drop them in the trash.

"Now that you've stuffed your face, Kel, I'm ready for one of your famous Bloody Marys. To hell with waiting for everyone else. Let's sit on the gallery and you can spill the beans about last night. I can't believe you actually found a body. Was it gruesome?"

Before I could answer, we heard the crunch of tires spitting gravel on the road leading to my parking area. I filled three more glasses with ice and continued making Bloody Marys assembly-line style.

"Hi Kel, Margo said to bring beer and ice," called Pete, hefting a large cooler from the back of his Jeep. "Hope I brought enough." I opened the kitchen door to let him enter. "On the floor okay? Does one of those Bloodys have my name on it?" He picked up a glass and did a tour of the room with his eyes. "This place really looks great. You haven't lost your touch."

"Thanks."

"What's the matter with your voice? Are you coming down with a cold?" He paused to sip his drink. "Angie's meeting me here later. She's busy at the cop shop this morning. I hear you two had quite a night."

Two more cars came up the drive.

"Who do I have to kill to get a drink around here?"

asked Jerry. "Nice curtains, Kel. Are they new?"

"Where's Heidi?" yelled Margo from her perch on the gallery.

"Home doing the *New York Times* crossword. In ink," replied Jerry.

"Hi, Kelly. Margo said to bring food," said Abby, her trademark two carat diamond studs twinkling in the sunlight in bright contrast to her raven-black blunt-cut hair. "I stopped for a bucket of extra crispy KFC. Where do you keep your plates? I'm famished."

"Kel, get your tush out of the kitchen and let those laggards take care of themselves. I want to hear what happened. Talk fast before your voice goes," said Margo.

"What's the matter with your voice?" asked Jerry, heading for the gallery with a fresh drink in his hand.

"Are you coming down with a cold?" asked Abby, reaching for one of the paper plates I was putting into wicker holders.

"Angie said Kelly screamed her lungs out when she saw the killer coming out of the sea," said Margo. "Shut up, guys. Let Kelly tell it her way."

"You caught the killer? Barbara didn't tell me that part," said Abby, moving to a chair on the gallery. "Who's defending?"

"Ambulance chaser," quipped Jerry.

"Swamp seller," Abby retorted with a broad grin.

Jerry, a former insurance executive, and Margo work with Pete at Island Palms, the real estate office across from the Watering Hole. Abby handles most of their closings in her nearby law office.

"Kel, Jerry needs a coaster. His glass is making nasty wet rings on your mahogany table," said Margo.

"They're in a basket on the shelf under the tab . . . ," I croaked.

"Under the what?" yelled Margo. "Did you say Tab? That's an odd place to store coasters."

I opened my mouth but nothing came out. My voice was history.

Chapter

13

TRYING TO TELL a story without words reduced me to playing charades.

Margo prompted with questions while I pantomimed what actually occurred.

"Wait a minute, let's back up. Where were you in relation to the point?"

I pointed to the west.

"How far west?"

I held up two fingers, pointing to the palm tree outside my gallery.

"Two screens? No? Trees? Two trees? Ohhh. The twin palms. Then what?"

Now came the tricky part. First I pointed to my chest, then my eye.

"I, eye?? Are you saying Ay-Ay, the pre-Columbian name for St. Chris?"

"No, Margo. She means 'I see' or 'I saw,' " said Abby. "Remind me never to be on your team if we ever play this for real. Kel, what did you see?" Abby was always the lawyer after the facts.

I made a semicircular motion with my hand.

"I don't get it," said Jerry. "Try a 'sounds like.' "

First I tugged on my earlobe.

"Sounds like. I get that part. Sounds like what?" said Jerry.

Then I made a rocking motion with my pelvis.

"Got it," said Jerry, beaming. "You saw a truck!"

I gestured "no, no, no" with my hands.

"The word is hump, Jerry. Sounds like hump," said Abby. "Right, Kel?"

I nodded.

"Lump?" asked Pete.

I nodded again.

"Ohhh, I get it," said Margo. "You saw a lump in the sand. You thought it was a turtle."

Now we were getting somewhere. By the time we got to the part where I stepped on the sea urchin, I was exhausted. We called time-out to refresh our drinks and put more food on the table. I was saved from further charades by Angie's arrival.

"Wait until you hear what really killed Zena," Angie said, eyeing the Bloody Mary makings. "Can I have one of those? I'm off duty now. How's your foot, Kel?" When I didn't respond, she looked at me and said, "What's the matter? Cat got your tongue?"

"She lost her voice," said Margo. "It's taken her an hour of charades to tell us what happened last night. I wish we'd taped it for *America's Funniest Home Videos*. Especially the part about the truck." Margo collapsed in giggles, wiping tears of laughter from her face.

"Truck? What truck? There was no truck," said Angie, setting Margo off in another fit of stomach-holding laughter.

"Never mind, honey," said Pete, giving Angie a quick hug and kiss before handing her a drink. "You had to be here."

We settled back on the gallery. I lowered the white vinyl blinds to keep the afternoon sun out of our eyes.

Angie picked up the story where I left off.

"Mr. Daniel was released after questioning. He claims he was poaching lobsters out of season. There's a statute on the books about poaching, so we had to give him a citation. He wasn't happy about it, there's a hefty fine involved. He threatened to fight us in court."

"A poaching ticket beats a murder rap," said Abby.

"He may be facing that, too. There are a lot of holes in his story," replied Angie. "But it wasn't the spear from his gun that killed Zena, even though it fit the gun perfectly. Kelly picked up on that right away."

"Cut to the chase, Angie," said Margo. "What really killed Dr. Sheffield?"

"Manchineel."

Five mouths dropped open. You could have heard a lizard hop. Then a babble of sound.

Margo: "I don't believe it."

Jerry: "Holy shit."

Abby: "Absolutely incredible."

Pete: "Amazing."

I scribbled "historically correct" on a notepad and flashed it at Angie, who chortled and applauded.

"Very good, Kel!" said Angie.

"Let us in on the joke," said Margo. After Angie explained about Zena's mania for H.C., everyone laughed.

"When we first found her, Zena was lying facedown on the sand, her arms and legs spread-eagled. How did you describe it? Like she was making a snow angel, right Kel?"

Angie excluded, the rest of us had grown up in the States and knew all about snow angels. Even Jerry, a transplanted Texan, remembered that frozen white stuff.

Those memories were one of the many reasons we all stayed in St. Chris, especially in winter when our favorite indoor sport was watching the Weather Channel and making rude comments about Stateside conditions in our former hometowns.

Snow tires and skis were two of the first items I sold at my garage sale before Pete and I made the move to St. Chris. I kept a fur coat. Just in case. After ten years, it was still in storage.

Pete and I had discovered St. Chris on vacation. What a paradise, contrasted with a grey, subzero Chicago winter. We went home and toyed with the idea of making a move. It sounded especially attractive during a mid-March blizzard. Two years later we said "good-bye Chicago, hello St. Chris" and came back on one-way tickets.

There are two types of Continentals—transplanted mainlanders, or "expatriates in paradise," as we refer to ourselves—who move to the tropics. Retirees who have come to clip coupons in the sun and others who have abandoned the rat race of the States for a more relaxed lifestyle. My friends are abandoners. We can't afford to sit around sunning ourselves on a daily basis. That's a pleasure reserved for weekends and the twenty-three government holidays. Without our jobs we would have been bored silly, dead broke or slobbering drunks. In a land of duty-free liquor and a *mañana* work ethic, it's easy to procrastinate over one for the road.

Abby had made her move within two months of Margo a year before I arrived. Jerry and Heidi were practically natives, after living on St. Chris for eighteen years. Paul was a newcomer at seven. Angie was born on St. Chris and was related to practically everyone on the island.

Angie continued her saga. "When the paramedics arrived, we turned Zena over. Her lips were horribly swollen and distorted. Her poor swollen tongue was protruding from between her lips. The autopsy report said her gastrointestinal tract looked like she'd consumed a can of lye."

"Lye's wicked stuff. Like drinking drain opener. My aunt Grace swallowed some when she was a kid one summer day when my grandmother was making soap," said Jerry. "I don't know how they pulled her through, but they did. I think my grandmother doused her with castor oil and salt water. Poor Grace ended up with a voice like yours now, Kelly. For the rest of her life she always sounded hoarse."

I clutched my throat. Visions of an aborted broadcasting career flitted through my head.

"Zena wasn't stupid enough to eat manchineel on purpose," said Margo.

"Lord, I hope not," replied Angie. "Not after Stamp Day. Did you know manchineel means 'little apple'? The botanical name means 'horse poison.' Be careful when you eat Kallaloo, some land crabs are known to thrive on the fruit and carry the poison in their systems. My mother always purges her crabs with cornmeal for seven days before she makes her crab and okra Kallaloo."

"If Zena didn't eat the fruit on purpose, how did it get into her system?" asked Abby.

"In a box of Island Delights."

This time I swear I heard a lizard hop.

Chapter

14

I DIDN'T GET my voice back until Wednesday.

Four days in the world of the mute was a curious experience. Not from my inability to communicate vocally, but the reaction of those around me. Once the amusement at my predicament became yesterday's news, it was like I'd been rendered deaf and invisible. I'd be sitting with the lunch group at the Watering Hole, but people would ask Margo about me as if I were on another planet.

"How's Kelly doing? I hear she lost her voice. What does she want for lunch?"

I wanted to pound the table in frustration. "Excuse me? Take a look, people, I'm sitting right here. I can speak for myself." Wrong.

I soon grew tired of scribbling notes. Conversations flew by too fast for me to participate nonvocally. I fumed silently, drinking so much hot tea with lemon and honey to soothe my throat that my citrus allergy kicked into overdrive. I gave up and sucked throat lozenges instead.

Angie gave me a get-well present, a T-shirt from her

collection that read "I'm not deaf, I'm ignoring you." I wore it everywhere.

At home my answering machine became my voice. My previously recorded message, "I can't talk now, please leave your message at the beep," was greeted with hoots of laughter. I had lots of calls, but no more from Jeff. I couldn't call him to explain why I couldn't call, he couldn't call me unless Perky Poo did the dialing. *Catch 22.*

Zena's death, "Tourist Found Dead on Beach," was front-page headline news in the *Telegraph* on the stands Sunday, dated Monday, March 15, and the hot gossip topic. As usual, the *Telegraph* story had a whiff of the truth but not all of the facts.

On Tuesday news of an impending property tax hike moved further developments, "Death Caused by Manchineel," to page three. The details were sketchy. There was no mention of the Island Delights in her stomach.

Zena was no contender for the Miss Congeniality Award, nor was I the president of her fan club. The woman was a pushy, overbearing, know-it-all pain in the ass and I was glad to have her out of my life. But she died an unpleasant, untimely and painful death, possibly not of her own devising. That disturbed me. But I wasn't sure I cared enough to start turning over rocks or go around poking Jack Spaniard nests to find the truth behind her demise.

On Wednesday morning I awoke with a song in my heart and, to Minx's startled surprise, one on my lips as well. I sounded like the Tin Man badly in need of an oil can, but complete recovery was imminent. The swelling in my foot had deflated to a stage where I could comfortably wear sandals.

Michael was playing "When Irish Eyes Are Smiling" as I walked into the studio. He turned on the mike and announced to anyone listening: "The first Irish eyes I've seen this morning belong to our resident colleen, Kelly Ryan.

This next number's especially for her. Put your hands together."

He segued into a boisterous Calypso version of "Happy Birthday," then whirled me around the studio.

"Another year, Mama. Funny, you don't look any older. You've probably got a portrait stashed in your rafters." Michael sported an impish grin. "Is this one of the significant ends-in-zero-type birthdays?"

"Only if I get prezzies and ice cream will it be significant," I retorted. "Other than that, I'm not telling."

"She talks!"

"Watch it, I've got four days of silence to make up for."

I skipped out of the studio to fetch news copy off the Teletype machine and grab the Irish music I'd hidden away in the music library. Part three of the *Ring Cycle* could wait.

Michael was still hanging around when I finished the news and began a cut of Enya's haunting Celtic music. Normally he's out the door and burning rubber to get to McDonald's for his bedtime snack when it opens at six A.M.

"*Que pasa?* Isn't it past your bedtime?" I asked.

He handed me an envelope. "It's from all of us."

Inside was a gushy card, the kind that puts me into a diabetic coma. "Emily picked it out." Tucked in the card was a gift certificate. For parasailing off Papaya Quay in the Isabeya harbor. "That was my idea, we thought you should see the world as the rest of us see it."

"No short jokes on my birthday!" I smiled and hoped it looked genuine. "Thanks for the gift. I'm really touched and surprised."

"Surprised" was not the word. Panicked was more like it. I get the Stan Freberg "Hey there, you with the sweat on your palms" willies merely looking at my stepladder. A complimentary root canal would have been greeted with greater joy than bobbing high over water suspended from a parachute tethered to a speedboat.

"Since Jeff's not here, how about if I take you out for an Irish dinner? We could go to the Lower Deck for Guinness, corned beef and cabbage."

Everyone on St. Chris is Irish on St. Pat's. The bars and restaurants all serve green beer and whatever imaginative concoction they think will pass for authentic Irish pub fare.

"Guinness tastes like the scrapings from a tar pit. Make it a corned beef on soda bread with a bottle of Harp and you're on. What time?"

"I'll pick you up."

I shook my head. "Nah. It's silly for you to drive all the way out to the east end and back when you've got to be on the air at ten. I'll meet you there."

I knew Michael lived somewhere on the west end. The trouble with living at either end of the island was that your friends invariably lived on the other end and didn't want to make a long drive at night on our unlit, unmarked and poorly maintained roads. I find it axiomatic that my enthusiasm for long drives shrinks in proportion to the size of my environment.

"Make it six-thirty sharp. If you're on time you might get Bailey's Irish Cream on the rocks for dessert." He raced out the door.

Later in the morning Emily cautiously opened the studio door. I waved her inside, but she disappeared from view, returning a few seconds later bearing a large arrangement of multihued carnations—my favorite flower, I love spicy scents—topped with helium-filled birthday balloons bouncing off the doorjamb. It had to be from Jeff.

"Happy birthday, Kelly. Dahlia just delivered this from her flower shop for you."

"Thanks, Emily, and thank you for the beautiful card. Michael said you picked it out."

Emily blushed. I'd said the right thing.

"I'm glad you got your voice back." A ringing phone took her out of the studio and back to her reception desk.

Elated that Jeff remembered my birthday, I dug for the card hidden in the flowers.

"Happy birthday, dear Kelly. Wish I could be giving you this in person. Hope Zena's behaving herself. Mrs. H."

If she only knew.

Chapter

15

ON A SIGNIFICANCE scale, so far my birthday was pushing to reach a one.

Nothing from Jeff—no flowers, no card in the mail, no message on my home answering machine. My friends made themselves scarce at lunchtime. There were no familiar faces at the Watering Hole round table, only drunken tourists celebrating the wearing o' the green.

By six-thirty the Lower Deck at Dockside was a madhouse. There wasn't an unoccupied chair in sight. Bottles, cups and discarded plates were piled on every table. A steel band pounded out "Irish Rover" punctuated by the shrill sound emanating from dozens of plastic green whistles, a beer distributor giveaway.

I couldn't find Michael anywhere. A harried waitress paused briefly in mid-flight from bar to table to say, "Hi Kel. Yeah, I think I saw Michael a few minutes ago. Check upstairs at Posh Nosh. The overflow crowd's up there tonight."

In addition to being a cozy hotel, Dockside boasts two

restaurants: the Lower Deck, where Angie and I had drinks after the first parade committee meeting; and Posh Nosh, upstairs along a wide enclosed gallery overlooking the harbor.

The Lower Deck occupies a cobblestone courtyard with lots of umbrella-shaded tables. Food is served on paper plates in wicker holders, drinks come in oversized plastic cups and the menu is scrawled on a chalkboard.

Posh Nosh is linen napkins and tablecloths, fresh flowers in crystal vases, a printed menu, elegant food and service, and matching prices. It's the place we entertain visiting relatives or celebrate special occasions. Both advertise on the station. Posh Nosh on my show, the Lower Deck goes for Michael's younger listeners.

Victoria, Dockside's owner, greeted me at the top of the stairs. Instead of her usual Laura Ashley long skirt dinner crowd attire, she was wearing khaki Bermuda-length shorts and an emerald-green alligator logo polo shirt with one of the green whistles hanging from a beaded chain around her neck. Except for the whistle, we might have dressed out of the same closet.

"Hello, Kelly. I knew we wouldn't have any gourmet diners tonight. Where's your whistle? Here, I've got an extra." She tore open the plastic wrapping and draped the whistle around my neck like a lei. "Michael's here. I've put you at a table at the far end. You asked for Harp? It's on the way with a chilled mug. Enjoy your evening." She tooted merrily on her whistle before greeting the next group of customers.

I wove my way through tables filled with revelers to the end of the gallery where Michael was seated at a table for eight. With him were Margo and Paul, Jerry, Abby, Angie and Pete. In front of the unoccupied fan-backed chair at the head of the table were a pile of gaily wrapped packages.

"Surprise!"

"Happy Birthday, Kel."

"Bet you thought we forgot."

At the end of an Irish-inspired dinner, instead of the customary silver dessert plate bearing an Island Delight in a fluted paper cup for each member of the dining party, the Posh Nosh version of fortune cookies, our waiter appeared holding aloft a multilayered torte blazing with more candles than I cared or dared to count. "With Miss Victoria's compliments and best wishes for many happy returns." Everyone sang while I made a wish and blew out the candles. Got 'em all with one breath.

Our party was the last to leave Posh Nosh. Michael disappeared after dessert to be on the air at ten. The din from the Lower Deck had wound down to a dull roar. I stopped at the office behind the reservation area to thank Victoria for the lovely dessert. A counter-height glass case next to the reservation desk was filled with Dockside souvenirs for sale.

"Must you rush off?" she asked. "Do join me for a spot of Bailey's." She opened a new bottle, filling two cut crystal tumblers to the halfway mark.

"Ice?"

"Please."

Victoria drank hers straight up.

"You've had quite a run on Island Delights," I said, pointing to the glass case. "Your cupboard's bare."

"When Angelita came to see me last Saturday morning I was completely taken aback," she replied, pausing to take a generous swallow of her drink. "Fortunately the media hasn't picked up on the Island Delight aspect yet. Can you imagine the headlines? The odds of my staying in business would be as good as Prince Charles assuming the throne. I won't sell or serve Island Delights again until this matter's settled."

"Vic, no one thinks you had anything to do with Zena's death."

"I'm not so certain, Kelly." She paused for another sip. "May we keep this conversation private? Abby suggested I not discuss it unless she was present. She's warned me that if I'm implicated I could lose my green card or risk being deported back to England."

I nodded.

"You do know Dr. Sheffield was staying here at the hotel."

"How long had she been here? I didn't meet her until the end of February."

Victoria replied, "She checked in January seventh, the day after Three Kings Day."

"Did she have a reservation?" I asked.

"No, oddly enough she didn't. She simply appeared one afternoon with her luggage. She had a winter coat over her arm; I assumed she'd arrived on the afternoon flight."

"She was lucky to get a room. St. Chris is really jumping this season. I thought you were overbooked."

"I was. But I had one small room in the back I'd finished renovating a few days earlier. It sustained water damage from a leak in the roof during hurricane season last year. There's no ocean view, but she said she wanted quiet to write her book."

"So she'd been here about two months. Wow. She must have run up quite a tab."

"I gave her a discount on the rate. Now I wish I'd charged double."

"Oh?"

"Kelly, you have no idea how demanding she was."

"I think I do. I worked with her on the parade committee."

"You have my sympathy." We smiled in understanding as Victoria topped off our glasses.

"Do you remember when the power went out about a fortnight ago? She flew into my office demanding I install a generator for her room. That was over the top for me. I told her in no uncertain terms that she could learn to tough it out by opening the window and using battery-operated lights like the rest of us. I regret to say I also suggested that Harborview might have more suitable accommodations for her."

"What happened?" I loved the thought of Victoria giving Zena her comeuppance.

"She backed off. But the next day she was making life bloody hell again for my staff. Two of my maids threatened to quit without notice."

"What did you do?"

"Gave them bonuses and tidied her room myself."

"You're kidding."

"No guest is worth losing my staff. After my husband died—we used to come over from London for a month each winter—I emigrated and put every shilling I had into this hotel. The people who work for me have been here from the first day I took over. They're closer than family."

"What was her room like?"

"A shambles. She never picked up after herself. The only tidy spot was her desk. I never saw evidence of the book she said she was writing or any personal correspondence. She never received any mail that I know of. Perhaps it came to the post office by general delivery."

"Is the room still occupied?" I was itching to get a look inside.

"The police have it sealed pending further investigation and removal of her personal effects by her next of kin. I understand a daughter is arriving Friday. The funeral is planned for Saturday afternoon."

"Oh?" I said. "I hadn't heard. Why would Zena want to be buried here? It's not as if she had any ties to the community."

"That's what I was told when I asked when the room would be free. The police also took a half-dozen boxes of

Island Delights for analysis." Victoria sipped her drink. "They're not made here, you know."

"They're not? I always thought—"

"That I make them in my candy kitchen? That's what I led everyone to believe. It was easier to sell to tourists if they thought I made them on the premises. Actually, the concept is mine. But there's a famous chocolatier in Zurich who produces, packs and ships them to me."

She opened a desk drawer and produced an unopened tin of Island Delights. "This is how they're packaged in Zurich."

I looked at the familiar package. The peach-hued tin was shrink-wrapped in clear cellophane, the avocado ribbon tied in a floppy bow on top of the cellophane like a gift package. I could see the embossed lid, with a rendering of the Dockside Hotel viewed from the ocean and the words "Island Delights, a taste of the tropics from the Dockside Hotel, St. Chris, West Indies."

"If what killed Dr. Sheffield had been anything but manchineel, I would have thought someone had tampered with the candy in Zurich. But manchineel doesn't grow in Switzerland; it's strictly tropical. Whoever did it lives here and went to a great deal of trouble."

"What makes you say that?" I asked.

"Because Angelita told me there were no solid apple remains in Dr. Sheffield's stomach. Only Island Delights and manchineel."

"So, you're saying—"

Victoria finished the sentence for me. "Someone deliberately set me up by poisoning the sweets. This couldn't be happening at a more inopportune time. One of the networks is negotiating to tape a telly pilot here later this year. It could put Dockside over the top."

"Really? I hadn't heard about that." Visions of a glamorous walk-on part flitted through my head.

"Kelly, that information is strictly for your private ear. We haven't signed the contract yet. I swear to you I had nothing to do with Zena's death. Please help me, Kelly. Find the killer."

Chapter

16

ANGIE CALLED ME at the station Friday morning to ask if I'd come early for our turtle walk.

When I arrived at Leatherback Bay at five she was already at the point, talking to another woman. I did a double take. Had Zena risen from the dead?

"Kelly! I'd like you to meet someone. This is Zena's daughter, Catherine Sheffield. She arrived this morning."

"Lovely to meet you, Catherine," I said. "Catherine? With a *C*? Is your middle name Aragon?"

"It is. How did you know? Everyone calls me Kit."

Okay. Kit Cornell, Kitty Foyle? This Kit didn't resemble either of those. She was in her late thirties or early forties, looking so much like Zena it was uncanny. Same hairstyle, similar taste in clothes. Where did they find all that rumpled cotton? Yet there was something else familiar-looking about Kit. Something I couldn't identify.

Angie gave me a fish eye. "What is this, Kel? I thought you two hadn't met before. How did you know her middle name?"

Kit smiled. "It was Mother's private joke. Catherine of Aragon? Daughter of Isabella and Ferdinand, first wife of Henry the Eighth."

"Thanks for coming early, Kel," said Angie, neatly side-stepping Zena's historical obsession, which was obviously a family trait. "Catherine, er Kit, wanted to see the place where we found her mother."

We walked along the beach to the area near the twin palms. There wasn't much to see. Sand, trees, water. The sand had been smoothed by the trade winds. There was nothing to mark the spot where we'd found Zena's body.

"Do you think she died here?" Kit asked Angie.

"No. Definitely not. There was evidence that the . . . um, your mother's body . . . was brought here from somewhere else. We . . . er, the police . . . don't think she died in her hotel room, either. We . . . ah . . . still don't know where it happened." Angie talked like she was walking a verbal tightrope.

Tears slid down Kit's face. "Why would anyone want to kill my mother? She was the only family I had. I never knew my father. Mother said he died before I was born. She didn't talk about him very much, I never even saw his picture, but she must have really loved him because she never remarried and seemed obsessed by his memory. What did she ever do to hurt anyone?"

Oh, my. This topic was as tricky as quicksand. I avoided Angie's "over to you, Kel" gaze. Buying time, I fumbled in my fanny pack for a fresh tissue, which I wordlessly passed to Kit.

"I'm sure she was very respected in her field," I said. A lame but safe comment. So I thought.

Kit began to cry even harder. Loud racking sobs punctuated her next words.

"Mother. Was. Terminated. Before. Christmas."

I handed Kit another tissue, then passed over the entire package.

When Kit finally collected herself, we walked slowly back to the point.

"I don't get it," I said. "I thought tenure meant you couldn't be fired."

Kit looked at me as if I were speaking in tongues. "Tenure? What are you talking about? Mother didn't have tenure. She was a teaching assistant."

"What?" I tried to keep myself from shrieking.

"Kit, let me get this straight," Angie said, giving me a "shut up, Kel, I'll take it from here" look. "Your mother wasn't a professor of Renaissance history?"

"Oh, no. I'm the professor. Mother was a teaching assistant in the history department at a junior college. She was terminated after the fall quarter for not completing her master's thesis. She'd been working on it for over five years. But she told me when she finished her final paper she'd change the course of history."

"Where was this?" Angie asked gently, her tone quiet and conversational.

"Mother lived in Boston. I teach at Columbia."

Another illusion shattered. Did Kit also have something to tell us about Santa Claus or the tooth fairy? How had Zena managed to con us all?

It wasn't the only time residents of the West Indies had been taken for a ride. Columbus pulled the first con in February 1504 when he told the peaceful Arawak Indians an imminent solar eclipse was a punishment from God because the Indians had stopped supplying his ships. The Arawaks bought his act. They were so intimidated by his ability to blot out the sun, they immediately began stocking his stranded ships with food.

Any lingering sympathy I had for Zena was now ancient history.

Chapter

17

I BRIBED MARGO into attending Zena's funeral with a free lunch after the service at the restaurant of her choice.

Late Saturday morning on the way to the Isabeya wharf for the funeral, I left my car with the flashers blinking alongside the post office under the No Parking Zone sign while I dashed inside to grab my mail before the doors were locked for the weekend. The only item in my mailbox was a letter with a badly smudged postmark and no return address. I stuffed it into my purse to read after I found a legal parking place. I'm too cheap to risk a twenty-five-dollar parking ticket. I'd rather drop the money down a sewer grating than give it to the fiscally irresponsible St. Chris government for something as moronic as a parking violation.

Margo and Angie were waiting at the wharf. We all wore sunglasses and simple white dresses, our bare legs shod in low-heeled white pumps. St. Chris funeral attire. We looked like vestal virgins, a sixties singing group staging a comeback or an albino costumed version of the witches in the Scottish play.

We'd barely said hello when the hearse arrived from the mortuary. Reverend Cal and four mortuary employees serving as pallbearers, all dressed in somber black suits accented by white cotton gloves, emerged from the hearse. Zena's flower-draped coffin was moved on a wheeled cart to the wharf.

The funeral was set for noon. A sea burial, preceded by a dockside ceremony. My attention shifted to the Park Service launch, rising and falling in the gentle ocean swells, ready to transport the coffin to international waters.

Continentals who have lived in St. Chris for any length of time have severed their ties with the States and prefer to be buried at sea. Most of us don't have family here; a cemetery plot and headstone seem out of place if there's no one to care or care for it. The price of being an expatriate.

There were no black wreaths or ribbons hanging on doors to mark Zena's passing. When the service was over there would be no mourners following the casket down Isabeya streets to the cemetery, walking past windows and doors shuttered to keep the spirit of the dead from entering.

Kit arrived on foot from Dockside, dressed in ankle-length black cotton, her head covered with a wide-brimmed black hat Victoria might have worn at Ascot.

I tuned out when Reverend Cal began delivering the eulogy. I couldn't help thinking about the letter I'd just read. I was jolted back to the present by a subtle jab from Margo's elbow, then her hand pressing a freshly ironed lace-edged handkerchief into mine.

"Kel!" Margo whispered, "Why are you crying? I thought you despised that woman."

I hadn't felt the tears falling on my cheeks.

"Tell you later," I whispered back, dabbing my face,

then digging my fingernails into my palm to keep the tears from starting again.

The service was over almost before it began. The pall-bearers carried the coffin to the boat for the journey out to sea.

As the boat was preparing to cast off, I saw that Kit was making the journey to sea alone, with only the captain, Reverend Cal and two mortuary employees for company.

Angie swore softly under her breath. "Damn. I'd better go with her. Save me a seat at lunch."

She quickly shed her shoes, hitched up the skirt of her dress and nimbly jumped aboard. She sat next to Kit on the narrow bench running along the inside of the portside gunwale. I saw Kit squeeze Angie's hand in gratitude.

The low rumbling idle of the boat's inboard engines shifted to a higher pitch as the ropes were cast off. The boat headed slowly past Papaya Quay then out through the opening in the reef to the open sea.

Margo and I stopped at her condo at Sea Breezes to change into bathing suits and Java Wrap cover-ups. We strolled along the palm-lined path to Port in a Storm, the condo's oceanfront restaurant.

We made small talk while we waited for our Bloody Marys to arrive.

"At my funeral," said Margo, "I hope that someone who actually knew me will deliver the eulogy."

"What are you going on about?" I asked.

"Zena's eulogy. Get a grip, Kel. I knew you weren't paying attention during the service. Can't say I blame you, it was deadly dull." I groaned and Margo laughed. "You didn't miss much. Reverend Cal nattered on like he'd known the deceased forever. What a phony he is."

The waiter served our drinks in squat square glasses. I downed half of mine in one swallow and immediately ordered a refill.

"Slow down, Kel," said Margo. "We've got the whole

afternoon ahead of us. You'd better tell me what's going on."

I took the now crumpled envelope from my purse and slid it across the table. "This was in my morning mail. Jeff's getting married. To Perky. Or whatever her name is, he didn't really say."

Our waiter appeared with my fresh drink while Margo scanned the brief letter.

"Son of a bitch. Oh, not you sweetie," Margo said to the waiter, ordering another drink for me and one for herself. "Remind me to leave Mitch a big tip." I raised my hand in protest. "No, you're not buying lunch today. I'll pay, you deserve a treat."

Margo moved to the seat next to mine so we wouldn't be overheard. "How could Jeff do that to you?" She jabbed the note with a manicured nail. "What's this bit about 'you weren't there when I needed you'?"

"A crock of crap. He knew damn well I couldn't leave the station. Hell, I didn't even know where he was." Behind my sunglasses, tears began to well.

"What do you mean you didn't know where he was?"

"He wouldn't tell me. He called three or four times after the accident, but every time I asked where he was he changed the subject or we got disconnected."

"If we lived in the States, we'd all have caller ID. But that'll never happen on St. Chris. Island Ding-a-Ling thinks Touch-Tone phones are hot stuff," said Margo. "Do you want to get out of here?"

I nodded, not trusting myself to speak.

Margo cancelled our drink order. We retreated to the sanctuary of her living room. Being my own designated driver, I switched to iced tea.

Margo reread Jeff's letter before passing it back to me. "Kel, how do you know Jeff wrote this? He's got two broken arms, right?"

"I don't think he wrote it. I think he told Perky what to

write and she did the writing. Apparently she's been doing everything else for him since the accident. The little bitch."

Margo laughed. "That's the attitude, Kel. Forget him. He's too self-absorbed and not good enough for you. Why should he expect you to drop everything and risk losing your job? You have mortgage payments."

We were interrupted by Angie's return from the sea burial.

"Is there more of that iced tea? I'm parched."

"How did it go?" I asked. I really didn't care, but I was trying to make conversation.

"Interesting. In its own macabre way. I've never been to a sea burial before. Traditional cemetery plots are the rule in my family. No one said anything until we were three miles out in international waters. The boat idled as the men slid the coffin—did you know they drill it full of holes so it won't float?—into the sea."

Margo handed Angie a tall glass of iced tea.

"Reverend Cal muttered a few words. He looked pretty green the entire trip. I think he was seasick or dying of the heat in his suit and gloves. The coffin stayed on the surface for a few moments, then slowly slipped down through the waves until we couldn't see it any longer. Only the flowers remained afloat until they were caught up in the current and disappeared from view. Once we got back to shore Kit ran off to Dockside to grab a taxi for the airport. I'm glad it's over."

Angie swallowed the last of her tea and held out her empty glass to Margo. "Please, may I have some more?"

"That sounds like a cue from *Oliver!* Promise me you won't burst into song." Margo went back to the kitchen.

"I thought you two were having lunch at Port in a Storm. Mitch said you had a drink and split. How come?"

Margo reappeared with more tea and an 'it's up to you, Kel' expression.

"I got a Dear John letter from Jeff this morning."

"I was afraid of that," said Angie.

"What?" My voice hit a high note that would have made Pavarotti proud. "You knew and didn't tell me?"

"Kelly, I swear I didn't know you were getting a letter. The chief received a fax yesterday morning from Jeff requesting a six-month leave of absence."

"Angie, we were together for five hours last night. How could you know something like that and not tell me?"

Angie looked hurt and embarrassed. "Kelly, I'm sorry. I truly am. I didn't know what to say. Please understand, it wasn't my news to tell. God, this is so awkward. Living on a small island really sucks. I've gotta go."

A gust of wind slammed the front door shut behind her.

Chapter
18

I CALLED ANGIE as soon as I got home.

Pete answered. "I'll see if she can come to the phone. I don't know what you said, but she was very upset when she walked in the door. She really likes you. How could you do that to her?"

I didn't care for the tone of Pete's voice, nor did I have the patience to console anyone else when I needed a shoulder to cry on.

"Pete, I appreciate your concern for Angie's well-being, but this isn't about you. Spare me a sermon and ask Angie if she'll talk to me now, or have her call me later."

I waited while he put the phone down. What was this bull? Here I was, calling my ex-husband's present girlfriend to talk about getting dumped by her boss who was now my former boyfriend and getting flack from my ex-husband in the process. Angie was right about one thing. Life on a small island really sucks.

Angie finally came to the phone.

"Sorry, Kel. I was in the shower. Are you home? Can

I come over? We need to talk. I feel bad about what happened earlier."

When Angie walked in my house an hour later, she was dressed for an evening out in a raw silk suit, high-heeled shoes with panty hose, and carrying a beaded evening bag. I couldn't remember the last time I'd worn panty hose. Or a bra. The money I save on lingerie, I spend on books.

"I can't stay long. Pete and I are meeting Margo and Paul for dinner in town." She had the grace to be embarrassed by her gaffe. "I'm sorry. That was the wrong thing to say. I really came to apologize for this afternoon. I should have said something to you last night about the fax from Jeff."

"Angie, let's talk about what's really happening here." I poured her a glass of white wine and we went out to my gallery. "This isn't about Jeff and me. It's about you and Pete, isn't it?"

Minx came in from the kitchen to rub her face against my bare leg, then hopped into my lap.

Angie nervously rubbed her thumb on the stem of her wineglass. She looked very uncomfortable. "He told you?" Her voice was both accusing and questioning.

"Told me what?" Somehow I already knew what she was going to say.

She set her glass on the table, the wine untasted, and took a deep breath. "Pete's asked me to marry him. We're going to announce it at dinner tonight."

Minx fell from my lap with an irritated screech as I threw my arms around Angie in a hug. "What wonderful news! I wish you all the best."

"You really mean it, Kel?"

"You know I do." I could feign enthusiasm with the best of them.

The late-afternoon sun filled the gallery with a golden glow, making Angie's smiling face appear lit from within.

"I was so worried about telling you. Especially today."

"Today has nothing to do with your news. Have you set the date?"

"May Day, the second Saturday after the parade. Will you come to the wedding?"

"I'd be honored." I raised my wineglass in a toast. "To you and Pete. Many years of happiness."

We drank. Angie looked at her watch. "I've got to go." She squeezed my hand. "Kelly, thank you. You've been super."

Angie quickly departed. I sank back on the rattan love seat, the breath leaving my body in a whoosh. Minx glared at me through narrowed eyes, then scampered outside.

After my award-winning performance, my snug little house suddenly felt claustrophobic. I needed fresh air and the comfort of the sea.

I grabbed my kayak paddle and walked down my private dirt and gravel road, across the paved two-lane east end road, to the cove where Top Banana was moored, chained to a palm tree. Minx followed behind me, playing leapfrog and hide-and-seek in the bush, while I launched my kayak.

The sun was kissing the horizon when I shoved off. Earlier the wind had shifted from the east to the south, an omen of wet weather to come. Gentle swells instead of the usual crashing waves rolled in from the north and were broken by the coral reef a quarter-mile away.

The reef-protected bay was as calm as a millpond, a perfect time to paddle. I slowly stroked, the rhythmic figure-eight motion easing the tension in my back and shoulders, through clear water the color of pale green glass, pausing to look down at the sea grasses waving in the currents, watching tiny yellow-and-blue-striped fish dart between the blades. A school of minnow-sized fish made a sharp zigzag turn, flashing silver like a Calder mobile. On the ocean floor a starfish crawled toward a conch shell in search of a succulent feast.

I heard a soft sighing sound coming from the portside

and carefully turned my head to see a small green turtle rising for air a yard from my kayak. We maintained eye contact for a few seconds until it dove beneath the surface to reappear off starboard, then dove again and headed toward the reef cut to the open ocean.

I headed my craft in the direction of the uncharted cut. A rusty iron rod sticking a few feet in the air marked the entrance. Tied to the rod was a ribbon of Day-Glo orange plastic, the ends hung limply like overcooked pasta. I hooked onto the marker and sat, kayak paddle tethered to the boat and secure across my lap, rising and falling with the swells.

It had truly been a hell of a day.

What was I going to do about Jeff? Nothing.

I was angry and hurt. That feckless, faithless son of a bitch. There wasn't anything I could do about him. Nor did I care to. Something didn't smell right. But I wasn't going to make an ass of myself finding out what it was. I really wanted to punch Jeff out. Or make a wax doll and stick black pins in all the tender parts of his anatomy.

Angie and Pete? I wished them well. Even though, from a personal standpoint, the timing of their announcement was pretty lousy, I truly didn't want Pete back in my life.

I hadn't been a clinging wife or a clinging ex-wife. Pete and I never had children—we were too busy being yuppies to pursue the matter; nor did I take Pete's name when we married. It was important to keep my identity in an era when single women were credit-worthy in their own right while a married woman was judged by her husband's assets rather than her own net worth.

Being my own person holds me together. Stepping to the music of Thoreau's different drummer, I've been on my own since I was eighteen and I'm used to taking care of myself. I'm not the type to call for help when the water pump breaks down or my checkbook won't balance to the penny. After all, I was the one who divorced Pete. For a reason no longer devastating, but one I still did not care to discuss openly. My favorite handywoman fix-it book is subtitled "Did you marry for love or to get your toilet fixed?" I think that says it all.

I looked at my little schoolhouse tucked in the hillside, saw autotimed lights now glowing on the gallery. It was comforting and welcoming. Mine. All mine.

Somewhere in the distance one of my far-flung neighbors was hosting a barbecue. I smelled meat-scented smoke and heard laughter mixed with the faint strains of Cole Porter. A red-tailed hawk swooped and soared high above the valley.

Would I trade all this for the bustle of big city life I left behind a decade earlier? Not for a Chicago second. St. Chris was home. I could damned well hold my head high, put on a party face and make the best of being dumped. It was time to explore new options. I'd done it before and I could do it again.

The swells quickened, urging my kayak forward like a racehorse champing at the starting gate. I unhooked Top Banana, feeling poised atop a roller coaster ready for a swift heart-pounding ride.

With a mighty whoop and a hearty "Screw you, Jeff!" I joyously rode the phosphorescent swells back to shore.

I returned home from kayaking to finish the bottle of wine I'd opened with Angie. I now had a hangover doing a tap dance in hobnailed boots in my head and stomach. It was, as Shelley Berman once said, a "please God, don't fizz!" kind of morning. A morning I really didn't want to hear a ringing phone.

"I could strangle your ex-husband!"

"Top of the morning, Margo." I stifled a yawn, peering through the windows to see wall to wall grey skies and a fine mist of rain.

"Margo, what time is it, anyway?"

"It's late. Must be almost eight-thirty. Don't tell me you

were still sleeping. You always wake up the roosters."

"Of course I wasn't sleeping. I had to get up to answer the phone."

"Cute. Don't you want to know why I'm so angry?"

"Tell me." I knew what she was going to say and loved her for the friendship that roused her ire. I fumbled in the refrigerator for a wake-up Tab, and walked the phone back to bed.

"That snake asked us to join them for dinner last night. I thought it was going to be a casual snack at the Lower Deck or I would have said something to you earlier. I was dressed in slacks and a silk shirt for God's sake. Pete reserved a table at Posh Nosh and invited Jerry, Heidi and Angie's parents. How did I know Pete and Angie were going to announce their engagement? I almost walked out. I hope that son of a bitch had the balls to tell you first."

"Angie told me."

"What?" Margo shrieked. "When?"

"She came over here before she met you for dinner."

"You're kidding."

"Margo, it wasn't like that. She came to apologize for not telling me about Jeff's fax. I'm happy for them. I've even been invited to the wedding."

Margo replied, "You're probably lying through your perfect teeth, but I hope you're going. We can sit together. Pete asked Paul to be his best man. Her cousin Barbara is going to be the matron of honor."

It was my turn to shriek. "Son of a bitch."

"What's wrong? You don't want Paul to be in the wedding party?"

"Don't be silly. I just spilled Tab all over my brand-new sheets."

"Nice going, Kel. You've really had a crappy weekend."

"It's not one I want to press in my book of memories, but yesterday ended on a roll." I laughingly told her about my trip in Top Banana.

"Love it! I can hear you yelling, 'Screw you, Jeff.' Now get your buns in gear and come on over. You still owe me lunch from yesterday. We'll have an eggs Benedict brunch at Port in a Storm. Your treat. I'll buy the Bloodys."

Chapter
19

THE PARADE COMMITTEE was going down the tubes.

Angie was the only one who showed at the first meeting following our three-week hiatus. Thursday night we sat in the library until seven-thirty, longer than I waited for a full professor in my college days, then gave it up as a lost cause.

We were permanently short one member, but where were Mr. Daniel and Reverend Cal? I sent reminder notes in the mail, left follow-up messages on answering machines. Their unexcused absences would be noted on my attendance chart.

"C'mon Kel, let's get out of here and head over to Dockside," said Angie. "I'll buy you a drink. I need to talk to Victoria about the wedding reception."

I wanted to talk to Victoria myself. In the week since my birthday I'd done nothing about finding Zena's killer, but I had to begin somewhere. Dockside was a logical starting place. Victoria had once given me asylum, no questions asked or payment required; it was my turn to help her if I could.

While Victoria and Angie sat side by side at the bar busily pouring over possible menus and computing costs per head, I pushed the lime wedge in my Campari and soda back and forth with a swizzle stick. I felt twitchy and bored. There was no one in the bar I wanted to talk to, nor were the number of tiers on the wedding cake of monumental concern.

Angie's beeper sounded. She excused herself to use the bar phone to return the call.

Victoria moved to the seat next to mine. "Kelly, I was going to ring you in the morning. The police have removed the seal on Zena's room. Catherine asked me to pack and ship Zena's things. They're still in the room. You'll find the key to thirty-seven on the rack in my office. I'll keep Angelita busy while you have a look."

I used the dead bolt and chain to secure the door to Zena's room behind me. The plastic-covered mattress of the double bed was piled with knocked-down packing boxes.

I opened the armoire closet. Three ankle-length crinkle cotton dresses swayed in the breeze of the ceiling fan in a ghostly chorus line. A floppy brimmed straw hat rested on the closet shelf. Two pairs of shoes—no-brand tennis shoes and tan espadrilles—lay scattered like *Titanic* debris on the closet floor. I slapped the heel of each shoe against the floor to dislodge any centipedes napping within, then explored the interiors. *Nada*.

Nothing out of the ordinary in the loo, either. No false-bottomed cans of shaving cream ala Dick Francis, or hollow toothpaste tubes touted in Russian spy novels.

I didn't have a clue what I was looking for. I wanted to get a handle on the woman who irritated virtually everyone she met and in the end deceived us all.

Island Delights were her passion and her undoing. Peach

tins were in evidence throughout the room. They were holding pens, pencils and a blank Dockside notepad next to the telephone on the bedside table, a meager supply of cosmetics in the loo and a handful of sandy seashells on the desk. On a whim I stuck the notepad in my purse.

There was no sign of a purse or the Ivy League totebag Zena carried everywhere. I searched the dresser drawers and under the bed. Perhaps Kit had taken it home with her, or the killer had it. The tote had not been with Zena's body on the beach.

The only reading material in evidence was a tattered paperback of *Nicholas and Alexandria*—the choice of period surprised me—and a couple of recent true trash paperback best-sellers. For an author, she certainly traveled light. I remembered a comment she made to me the day of the power outage about not having time to type her notes properly. Another one of her fabrications. There was no typewriter in her room.

I was running out of time. Angie would soon wonder where I'd gone. The only article I hadn't examined was the straw hat. One I never remembered seeing Zena wear.

The woven beige straw was accented with an aqua background tropical print hatband and matching inside sweatband. I turned the hat around in my hands. There was nothing special about it; similar hats were for sale in every tourist shop on St. Chris.

My fingers stopped moving when they encountered a lump in the sweatband. I turned the hat over to explore the interior. I wiggled my little finger into the open end of the sweatband, then carefully eased the object through the opening.

A tiny brass key fell into my open palm.

Chapter
20

I THOUGHT ABOUT Zena while driving to work Friday morning.

Using her book-writing ruse as a cover, she'd come to St. Chris with a hidden agenda. But what had she hoped to accomplish? Winning friends and influencing people hadn't been high on her list of priorities. I'd never met anyone who seemed more determined to alienate everyone who crossed her path.

Zena struck me as a control freak the first night we met. Perhaps that was part of her plan; if she kept people from getting too close, they'd never uncover her secrets. It still rankled that I was one of those she'd duped.

I was blasted out of my reverie by the blaring horn of a car approaching me head-on in the left-hand lane. I swerved left toward the ditch and the tourist in the rental car headed to the right of me, almost running into a road sign reading Keep Left. The tourist shrugged an apology and kept on going.

I was in a thoroughly bad temper when I arrived at the station.

Resting on the stoop against the carved wooden door at the front entrance to WBZE was a brown paper-wrapped package bearing my name in press-on block letters. I carried it into the studio.

"Yo, Mama, what did you bring me?" When I cupped my hand behind my ear, Michael lowered the volume on Gene Krupa's "Sing, Sing, Sing" drum solo from *Benny Goodman's 1938 Carnegie Hall Jazz Concert* pounding through the studio speakers.

I slapped his outstretched fingers. "Hands off, big boy, this has my name on it. Maybe I'll share, and maybe I won't." I tore at the wrapping, then backed away from the contents in revulsion. Michael moved toward the box.

"Don't touch it," I snapped. "There may be fingerprints on it. I want to know who sent this to me."

Taped to the cellophane-wrapped tin of Island Delights was an unsigned index card with a typed message that read: "Hell hath no fury like a woman scorned." The letter *e*'s in the message were crooked and out of alignment.

"You're in a foul mood this morning, Mama."

"Damned right I am. I was almost run off the road by an effing tourist who can't read Keep Left road signs. Stupid fool. Why they let Statesiders rent cars down here I'll never know. And now this. It's too much for one morning." I choked back tears of rage.

Michael's face shed its usual merry grin. His blue eyes turned glacial as he studied the package and my stricken face. Then he made a very un-Michael-like gesture and wrapped his arms around me in a comforting hug. I closed my eyes and let his warmth envelop me. The moment ended in silence.

"Oh, shit, the track's over." Michael punched in a tape, and a commercial for Soup to Nuts filled the airwaves.

"Almost bought the farm that time, didn't we?" he said. We laughed in relief and said in unison like a Greek chorus: "There shall be no dead airtime. Amen."

I called Angie to tell her about the package. In minutes she appeared, dressed in workout clothes, to bag the evidence.

"I'll drop this off on my way to the gym. Who handled the package here?" She looked at Michael.

He raised his palms skyward. "*Pas moi*. Mama wouldn't let me get near it."

Angie turned to me. "Do me a favor. Stop at the police station for fingerprinting so we can eliminate your prints from any we find on the package. Will you do that?"

Behind Angie's back, Michael silently signaled, "not me," and stuck his hands in his pockets. I got the message.

"Sure, Angie," I said. "I'll do it when I get off the air at noon. I'll lay odds the only prints you'll find are mine. Anyone else who touched it probably wore gloves. Michael, will you cue my intro while I see Angie to the door?" He got my message.

When I returned to the studio Michael was standing at the plateglass window nervously stroking his moustache.

"Thanks for saving my butt."

I wanted to shrug it off with a smile and an airy wave of my hand, but couldn't. "Why did I do that, Michael? Is there something you want to tell me?"

There was no smile on his face when he replied, "Yeah, there is. We gotta talk. But not now. I need some *z*'s and you've got a show to do. Catch me here tonight."

"It'll be late. Probably after midnight. I'm on Friday night turtle watch."

"I'll be here." He picked up his helmet, wheeled his cherished Harley out the front door and was gone.

After the news break I treated my listeners to a new

recording of Dvorak's symphony *From the New World*, a perfect lead-in for a Navidad de Isabeya parade plug, then hightailed it to Mrs. H's office to check out Michael's personnel file.

Chapter

21

MARGO WAS LEANING against her bronze BMW—"It's the color of old money, honey, impresses the hell out of my high-ticket clients who don't know I bought it second-hand"—sipping a diet Coke when I shot into Leatherback Bay close to six-thirty.

I'd flopped for a brief afternoon nap. Thank God for Minx and her infallible stomach alarm.

"Chill, Kel. No one's punching a time card, not even the turtles."

"Where's Angie?"

"Doing her police woman shtick. She'll be here later. Let's lime and enjoy the sunset. The turtles won't start nesting until after dark."

We sat side by side on the point, digging our toes in the warm sand, our eyes focused west while the night crept in behind us. I told Margo about the package at the station.

Her reaction was what I expected. "That's horrible. Why didn't you call me?"

"I meant to, sweetie, but other things got in the way."

Like Michael's strange behavior and a disturbing phone call from Abby while I was feeding Minx.

Margo turned to face me. "Who would send such a thing? It's so mean-spirited. Do you have any idea?"

"I'm hoping Angie might have an answer tonight. She took the tin and wrappings for fingerprinting. Not that I think she'll find any prints except mine."

"Did you open it? Were there Island Delights inside? Were they poisoned? This really is too, too Agatha Christie. It's better than *Mystery!* on PBS."

"Margo!"

"Sorry. That was tacky." She had the grace to look contrite. "You know I care about you. But I can't help wondering who did this. And why? Jesus. You don't suppose it was Perky."

"Hell, no. The package was delivered in person; it didn't come through the mail. What's really strange is Island Delights aren't for sale right now. Vic said she won't sell them until Zena's murder is solved."

"Smart move."

We heard the slamming of a car door, then the thud of footsteps on the hard-packed sand.

"There you are!" Angie called out, but there was no warmth in her voice. She ran over to where we were sitting. "Kelly, I've got to talk to you. Now. Margo, do you mind?"

"Angie, it's okay. Margo can hear anything you've got to say."

Angie snapped, "You might be better off having your attorney present."

"Wait a minute," I said, my cool clipped tone matching hers. "What's going on?"

"You tell me. I'm about to have you hauled in for tampering with evidence in an ongoing investigation."

My mouth dropped open to my knees. "You've got to be kidding."

"I'm not. You're in deep guano, Kelly."

Margo dug her cellular phone out of her bag. "I'm calling Abby."

I put my hand on Margo's arm. "Let's hear what Angie has to say first."

Margo pushed my hand aside. "Get a grip, Kel. This isn't a social gathering."

Margo was right. My behavior was more like a Noel Coward drawing room comedy than *Law and Order* come to life.

Emily Post hadn't prepared me for this moment. I took a deep breath and said to Angie, "If you're here on official business, show me your badge and read me my rights."

Angie dug her badge holder out of her pocket while intoning the Miranda warning.

"That does it," said Margo. "I'm calling Abby. Kel, keep your mouth shut until she gets here." She pulled a voice-activated cassette recorder from a pouch on the front of her shoulder bag and smiled at Angie. A chilly little smile. "Abby warned me this might happen. I've got this entire conversation on tape. Your boss might be interested in hearing how you threatened Kelly before you Mirandized her. I believe Abby will call it coercion."

Angie scowled, Margo smiled, I stewed.

Offshore Eve wallowed fitfully in the shallows, disturbed by the strong vibrations emanating from her proposed nesting site. She backed into deeper waters, awaiting quiet.

Chapter
22

I HAVE A theory about lawyers.

Hire the meanest son of a bitch in the valley you can find. You can always make a bastard back off, but you can't turn a mouse into a tiger.

Abby was New England born and bred. Behind her proper Bostonian facade lay the heart of a pit bull and a razor-sharp brain that hummed even when she was asleep.

After five hours in the ring with Angie, Abby was deep into her closing argument mode. Even in jeans and a de-signer T-shirt she'd make a Supreme Court justice sit up and pay attention.

"Let's go over this again." Abby paced the length of the room, ticking off points on her fingers as she spoke.

"Kelly called you at home Friday morning at approxi-mately six o'clock to say she received a package at the radio station."

Angie nodded.

"The brown paper wrapping concealed a cellophane-wrapped tin of Island Delights and typed index card. The cellophane was intact and the tin had not been opened when you brought it into the police station for fingerprinting and analysis of the contents."

Angie nodded.

"After her air shift ended, Kelly—voluntarily, but at your request—came to the police station for fingerprinting so you could eliminate her prints from any you found on the package."

Angie nodded.

"You dusted the brown paper wrapping and found only partial prints that matched Kelly's. There were no prints on the index card. On the cellophane you found faint smudged partials from a second set of prints."

Angie nodded.

"Whose prints were those?"

Angie said, "Victoria Eaton's."

"Then you removed the cellophane from the tin. Were there any prints on the tin?"

Abby shook her head "no."

"You opened the tin and examined the contents. What did you find?"

Angie replied, "Island Delights."

"Had they been tampered with?"

"No. There were no traces of foreign substances in the pieces we had tested."

"Was the candy fresh?"

"It had a greyish cast. Victoria called it bloom and said it was caused by age and excessive refrigeration."

"Did she say anything else?"

"She said the candy and tin were from a limited edition Christmas assortment that sold out the week after Three Kings Day. She showed me the original invoices and her sales records."

"Was her attorney present when you questioned her?"

"No." A mottled red was creeping up Angie's neck to her face.

"Why not?" Abby answered her own question with another question. "Was it because you failed to warn Victoria Eaton of her rights?"

Angie's face was now the color of sorrel, a popular garnet-hued Caribbean Christmas drink. She responded with a curt nod.

"Did you have a search warrant?"

Angie paused, glaring at Abby, then shook her head, answering quietly, "No."

"Would you repeat your answer?" Abby asked.

"No, I did not have a damned search warrant," Angie shouted.

"Then you asked to reexamine the room occupied by the late Zena Sheffield. Victoria stated that Kelly had, with her permission, been in the room the previous evening and found a key overlooked during previous police searches."

Angie confirmed Abby's scenario.

"You then confiscated both the room key and the one Kelly found, threatening Victoria with prosecution and possible revocation of her green card for withholding evidence. Again I ask you: Did you have a search warrant?"

The question was rhetorical.

Abby stopped pacing, her blue eyes bored into Angie's brown ones.

"Twice in one day you exceeded your authority and used your personal relationships with parties involved to further your own interests. While some may admire your zeal and quest for promotion—it's no secret you're after Jeff's job—you're sinking in legal quicksand."

The final score was Abby: 2; Angie: 0. Victoria and I were both free on a technicality, but Zena's killer and my Secret Santa were still on the loose.

Chapter

23

A ROACH COACH is the closest St. Chris comes to an after-hours joint.

By the time I left the police station it was well after midnight. The restaurants and bars in Isabeya were shuttered and silent.

I headed for the waterfront parking area where the last of the Friday night revelers, mostly local boys-going-on-men in their late teens, clustered around a shiny aluminum-sided Grumman Kurbmaster step-van labeled in foot-high red letters, "Maubi's Hot To Trot." The *o*'s sprouted dancing yellow and orange flames, reminding me of the garish hair colors favored by MTV punk rockers, a hairstyling trend not yet seen on the streets of Isabeya.

Maubi is generally known around town only by his nickname. Osgood O'Reilly is the name on the baptismal record his mother keeps tucked in the family Bible. The old Bible is a cherished possession brought from Ireland by an ancestor who was part of a flock of Irish Geese, the emigration of children from Ireland during the height of a nineteenth-century famine to work as hired help in the Caribbean cane fields. The children sent most of their meager pay back to their parents in Ireland, but many were never able to save enough to return to their native land, so they stayed where they settled to marry and raise their own families.

Maubi is a construction worker forced into early retirement by an accident that shattered his left leg, leaving him with a permanent limp and occasionally dependent on a cane. He sells cold sodas, homemade ginger beer and maubi from ice-filled coolers, and takeout platters from the foil-lined containers of West Indian snacks and fried chicken kept hot under infrared lamps.

Maubi sat inside his van, elbows resting on the serving counter, chatting with his customers. Michael's voice crackled over the airwaves from an old boom box sitting high on a back shelf. Maubi ended a ribald story with a thigh-slapping belly laugh to greet me with a warm smile.

"Morning Lady! What carries you to town so late?"

"The memory of your wife's pates. Got any left?"

"Beef or saltfish?" I never ordered saltfish, but Maubi always asked just the same.

"Two beef, please."

"I got beef roti tonight."

"I'll take one. And two chicken legs."

"Something to drink?"

"Your specialty," I said, smiling. "Two large ones."

Maubi grinned. "Brewed it fresh myself this week in my big old enamel kettle. Best maubi batch ever." He kissed the tips of his fingers as a sign of his own approval.

"Are we going to see your Quadrille group in the parade?" I asked. I began digging into my fanny pack for cash, not really paying attention to his reply.

"It looks so. My band's been practicing every week with the dancers at the Legion Hall. We don't see you there, but the dead lady showed up one time spouting her fool-ishness."

He now had my full attention. "What dead lady?" I halted my money quest to stare at Maubi. "Do you mean Zena Sheffield?"

"That be the one. If she be the bossy person in a black wrinkle dress."

"When was this?"

"Two, maybe three weeks ago. She come with the vicar. Told us we were dancing what they used to dance in Spain in Columbus time, a gally something, but we were doing it all wrong. She show us how to do it right, she jump up and down like a rooster with the fits. Shorty, the Quadrille master, he say maybe Columbus prance like a fool, but we do proper Quadrille like we done here always, and maybe he teach she a t'ing or two. We don't need no tourist telling us our business, Shorty say. She take her huffy self and her Christmas candy box out of there mighty damn fast." Maubi chortled as he packed my food and drink in a card-board box.

"Where you parked?" he asked.

I pointed to my car a short distance away.

"That's too far to go by yourself. The jumbies—the mean spirits of the dead—could get you." He leaned to-ward me, lowering his voice. "It's not safe like the old days. We got drug dealers and lowlifes limin' around the fort. That's why I come to rest my van down here so late. Keep my boy and his friends out of trouble."

"You've done a good job," I said, putting the change in my coin purse. "He's a fine boy. He's graduating this year, isn't he?"

"First in his class." Maubi beamed with pride. "He got a scholarship to Cornell University to study hotel manage-ment. He's going to work full-time at Harborview this summer. Now he drives the parasail boat on weekends."

Maubi called to his son. "Quincy! You take this food and see Morning Lady gets to her car safe. Then come back and help me close up. It's time we go home."

Chapter
24

MICHAEL'S EYES WIDENED when I walked into the studio bearing the carton of food.

"What's in the basket, Little Red?" he leered.

"What big eyes you have, Big Bad Wolf," I responded, batting my eyelashes.

"I smell chicken."

"What a discerning nose you have."

He tore the foil from a paper plate, grabbed a chicken leg and began gnawing.

"And such fast fingers and sharp teeth! The chicken and roti are for you. Paws off the pates, they're mine!" I handed him a paper cup of iced maubi and sat down to enjoy my own snack.

Michael stopped eating long enough to change albums from a migraine-inducing rock group to something less volcanic. When we finished our food he gathered the wrappings to throw in the outside trash. We leaned back in our chairs, loudly slurping the last of our maubi through plastic straws.

I tossed my empty cup in the trash. "Michael, it's been a long night and I'm whipped. I've gotta go home and get some sleep. So, tell me. Why did I cover your butt this morning?" While I studied his face, his eyes slid away from mine to stare into the air above my head.

"I'm gonna have to plead the fifth on that one."

"Michael!" I wanted to slap him. "You owe me."

He dug in his back pocket for his wallet. "No sweat, Mama. I'll spring for dinner. How much was it?"

"That's not what I'm talking about and you know it. But as long as you're feeling so generous, your share was four-fifty."

He handed me a five. "Keep the change."

I pulled the coin purse out of my fanny pack, then slapped two quarters on the console. "I'm not your waitress, you don't need to tip me."

"Mama, I do believe you're pissed."

"You're damned right I am. It's almost dawn, I'm tired, I've had a night full of bull and I'm going home. You can keep your little secret, but don't expect me to cover your ass again. Ever."

I drove home, snapping my head from side to side in a nervous tic to stay awake. The digital clock on the dash read 3:00 when I pulled into my driveway.

Another vehicle was parked in my favorite spot.

Standing next to his Jeep was Pete. He followed hard on my heels as I ran inside to deal with a ringing phone. So far he hadn't said a word, but his face looked like a thundercloud about to burst. Minx slid under the covers on my bed, flattening herself to invisibility.

The red light on my answering machine was blinking like an accelerated heartbeat on the verge of a stroke. One more message would probably send it into cardiac overload.

I grabbed the phone before the machine kicked in. "It's late. Make it snappy or I'm hanging up."

"Mama, it's me."

"I don't have time for this now. Is there a problem I should know about?"

"No. I called to apologize."

"Too little, too late." I slammed down the phone and turned to Pete. "What fresh hell brings *you* here? Speak up or get out. My tolerance for crap ran out hours ago."

"Where in the hell have you been?"

"None of your damn business."

"Do you have any idea how long I've been waiting?"

"Pete, I don't give a rat's ass. This obviously isn't a social call, and I don't owe you any explanations. Tell me why you're here."

"Angie's been suspended for thirty days without pay. It's all your fault."

"You're still thinking with your dick. What happened to Angie was the result of her own actions, not mine."

"She blames you and so do I. I think you set this whole thing up to make her look bad and spoil our wedding."

"That's so far off the wall I can't believe it. And speaking of the happy day, what's the big rush? Sounds like a shotgun wedding to me."

The look on Pete's face answered my question.

"You didn't waste much time," I said. "You've known her for how long? Two or three months? You always were a hot-pants son of a bitch. What did you do? Knock her up on your first date?"

The veins popping in Pete's neck made him look as close to a coronary as my answering machine. "You've always been a jealous shrew. I couldn't even look at another woman without you running off to Dockside."

"That only happened once," I snapped. "It wasn't the looking I minded."

"Shakespeare was right about a woman scorned. You'll

pay for this. Watch your butt, Kelly. It's not safe out there."

Pete stormed out of the house, first slamming my kitchen door, then his Jeep door. I heard flying gravel pop like BBs against the trees as he sped down the driveway.

Chapter
25

DOWNSHIFTING TO SECOND, I crept along the rutted dirt road leading to the west end rain forest, reaching Miss Maude's house promptly at our agreed-upon hour of ten A.M.

Her rectangular one-story house was built of native stone, a clue to its age and a rarity in an era of concrete block construction, accented with mahogany window frames, doors and hurricane shutters. The matte white corrugated tin roof extended to cover the broad open gallery running across the front and sides of the house. Neatly clipped grass bordered the crushed blue bitch stone drive and parking area. Herb beds and vegetable gardens were laid out in neat rows in the side yard, and fruit trees dotted the property. Papaya, banana, mango and lime were species I easily recognized. Next to the driveway was a small palm frond-roofed stand where fresh fruits and vegetables were displayed for sale.

Miss Maude sat in a carved teak rocking chair on her front gallery, tying freshly cut herbs in small bunches for drying. On a low table at her side was a cobalt-patterned china tea set with four matching cups and saucers.

"In the days of sail, ships used to carry china in the holds for ballast," she said, pouring me a cup of tea. I held up one finger when she pointed to the sugar, and was handed a delicate cup and saucer graced with an antique silver spoon and small wedge of freshly cut key lime.

"This tea set has been in my family since Father came over from Denmark at the end of the last century to serve as the governor's aide. When we moved to this house after the transfer in 1917, my mother packed the good china in baskets cushioned with feather pillows. I was so proud when she let me carry the creamer and sugar bowl that I held my breath all the way from Isabeya, afraid I'd jostle the basket when the buggy hit a bump. In those days it took hours, not minutes, to make the journey from town."

"I wish I'd been here then," I said, cautiously sipping the scalding hot tea. "I love looking at old photographs of Isabeya. Seeing down-island schooners in the harbor, Danish officers in uniform and women in ankle-length dresses walking along Kongens Gade shading themselves with parasols."

"It was an exciting place for a small child to be," said Miss Maude, smiling in remembrance. "Especially on weekends when the planters would come to town with their families. When Isabeya was rebuilt after the fire in 1764, sugarcane was the main cash crop. The wealthier planters built homes in town—the same structures that house our tourist shops, offices and banks today—filled with handsome furniture created from the hardwood forests they destroyed to clear land for planting sugarcane. The merchants lived in town year-round in residences built over their ground floor shops."

"Where did you live?" I asked.

"At Government House," said Miss Maude. "There were parties there every weekend. And on very special occa-

sions, like the king's birthday, there would be evening
fireworks at the fort, and afternoon band concerts in the
gazebo on the adjoining green. During the festivities, the
men who were members of the colonial council would sit
with my father and the governor on the Government House
gallery discussing island matters over rum and cigars."

A car pulled into Miss Maude's driveway. A burly man
in his mid-thirties with a pleasant moon-shaped face
walked around to the passenger side to help a rotund elderly woman disembark. An image of a cerise-clad pouter
pigeon with plump feet in too-tight shoes flashed through
my mind.

"Kelly, of course you know Benjamin. Have you met
Lucy Smythe-Chadworth?" Miss Maude poured tea for the
newcomers.

I rose to greet Benjamin and offer my comfortable chair
to Miss Lucinda.

"Dear Benjamin occasionally drives Lucy on her errands
in his off-duty time."

Benjamin had been one of Miss Maude's students in the
last class she taught at the one-room school on Danish Hill
and was now the chief of the nearby police substation.
Miss Lucinda was the social columnist for the *Coconut
Telegraph* and honorary general chairman of the Navidad
de Isabeya festivities.

"Looks to me like we're having a tea meeting," said
Miss Lucinda.

"Lucy, these young people don't know about tea meetings. You came to St. Chris as a bride and have only been
to one," chided Miss Maude.

"My grandmother told me about them," said Benjamin.

"What's a tea meeting?" I asked.

"They were a form of evening entertainment," said Miss
Maude. "Held perhaps once or twice a year at various
places in the countryside. Families would arrive on foot

from nearby plantations to hear the church choir sing and watch set pieces."

"Like music hall entertainment or the Christmas panto-mimes in my native England," added Miss Lucinda.

"When the meeting ended, food would be served. Tea and slices of smoked ham with johnnycakes. The families would find their way home by lantern light," concluded Miss Maude. "But we're not here to reminisce about the past. We're here to help Kelly catch a murderer."

Three heads nodded in agreement.

"Kelly, you were very clever with that pesky tiefin' business on Papaya Quay last summer," said Benjamin. With a disarming smile, he set his teacup on the table. "Ladies, I must take my leave of you."

"What ears don't hear, the mouth can't tell," commented Miss Maude.

"Precisely." Benjamin grinned. "If I'm asked by my su-periors, I have no knowledge of your activities. For now my son's baseball game calls me."

We waited in silence until his car disappeared down the road toward town.

I stared at Miss Maude. "Why me?"

"You proved last summer that you have a very good head on your shoulders. Lucy and I are too old to go dart-ing about and Benjamin cannot risk his position. This mat-ter has not been assigned to his attention. We know the police are running short of clues. No one in an official capacity cares what really happened to an outsider no one liked."

Miss Lucinda chimed in, saying, "Murder is not good for our public image. We are, after all, 'the jewel of the Caribbean Sea.' It says so on our license plates. We have a reputation to uphold."

Miss Maude brought out a fresh pot of tea and a plate of homemade coconut cookies. Miss Lucinda's pudgy fin-gers edged toward the plate, but good manners held her

back until I'd put one cookie on my saucer. Then she
helped herself to a handful.

Miss Maude smiled fondly at her friend. "Lucy, there
are plenty of cookies to go around. I baked an extra batch
for you to take home. Now Kelly, tell us everything you
know about the murder!"

The women leaned forward in their chairs, glowing eyes
fixed upon mine in rapt attention. By the time I ended my
tale, telling them about the night on the beach but omitting
my excursion into Zena's hotel room, tiny yellow-bellied
sugar birds were snatching the last crumbs from the empty
cookie plate.

"I'm curious about two things," I concluded. "One. How
did Zena get on the parade committee? Two, where does
manchineel grow other than Columbus Bay?"

Miss Lucinda stole a look at the art deco design Cartier
diamond and platinum watch on her left wrist. "Maude, I
know I could think better if I had my elevenses."

"My thoughts exactly, Lucy. Kelly, will you join us in
a rum swizzle?" Miss Maude gathered the tea things on a
teak tray, returning a few minutes later with a plate of
cheese straws and three tall glasses filled with the ingredients that comprise a perfect swizzle.

Miss Lucinda took a preliminary nip of her drink:
"Lovely. One of sour, two of sweet, three of strong, four
of weak. Simply lovely." Then she quaffed like a camel
at an oasis after a three-day trek across the desert. A
pitcher was put on the table for "help yourself" refills.

I sipped my drink very slowly. I'm a cheap drunk on
rum, especially on an empty stomach. All that sugar zipping through my system goes right to my head. I would
have sold my soul for a Tab. Miss Lucinda was preoccu-
pied with her drink, so I staged a surreptitious assault on
the cheese straws. Forget sweets; I'll take savories any
time.

"Lucy, put down your glass and answer Kelly's question. I am also intrigued. How did Zena Sheffield get on the parade committee?"

Miss Lucinda tapped her cheek with her index finger, gazing skyward for inspiration.

"I do believe it was . . . no, that's not quite right. Perhaps it was . . ."

"Lucy! Stop dithering."

"Maude, I'm trying to remember. I know she came highly recommended." Miss Lucinda refilled her glass and settled back in her chair, her feet not quite touching the ground, acting as if her vague response concluded the matter to everyone's satisfaction.

"I'll check my parade committee notes," I said. "Perhaps Mrs. H left a clue in her file." I knew damned well she had done nothing of the sort, but there was little point pursuing the matter in present company.

Miss Maude handed me a slim volume printed in Danish. "My father trained as a botanist at the Royal Conservatory in Denmark. One of his duties here was to catalog island plant life. This book was published from the report he sent back to King Christian the Ninth as part of the St. Chris survey project." She proudly showed me her father's pen-and-ink sketches and watercolor renderings tipped into the book.

"Do you read Danish?" Not expecting an affirmative reply, she continued, "I'll translate his notes on manchineel."

"*Hippomane mancinella* . . . is recognized by its grey bark . . . and the small, yellow-green, pungent fruit . . . appearing like an apple . . . all parts of the tree are known to be of a poisonous nature, both to man and livestock . . . attempting to destroy the tree by fire will result in a smoke that is seriously harmful to the skin and eyes. The growth of manchineel is confined to the north shore of the island, with the largest concentration found in the area around Columbus Bay; smaller groves have been located along the shoreline extending westward from the far eastern side of Isabeya to the lighthouse on the western end of St. Chris."

Miss Maude presented me with an enlarged photocopy of the island map from the book detailing the areas where her father had located groves of manchineel almost one hundred years earlier. I had my work cut out for me. The best way to explore the north shore would not be on foot as he had, but by sea.

Chapter
26

Rosy fingers were streaking the eastern sky when I slid Top Banana into the shallows of the cove near my home early the next morning.

My kayak was loaded for an expedition. A coast guard-approved orange life vest was fastened to the top of a small cooler lashed in the well behind my seat. A laminated copy of Miss Maude's map secured on a plastic clipboard together with a waterproof marker was tethered to a braided nylon line clipped to the boat along with a small bottle of Evian cradled in a zipped neoprene beverage cozy.

I double-checked the contents of the O-ring-sealed plastic fanny pack strapped to my waist: house keys, Chap Stick, Kleenex, money, extra marker. All nestled inside individual snack-size baggies. When it comes to waterproof I opt for overkill.

I wriggled my tush into the molded seat, adjusted the nylon-covered foam backrest, braced my rubber-soled nylon surf shoes—protection from pointy rocks and those blasted sea urchin spines—against the footwell and prepared to shove off. I felt like Thor Heyerdahl launching a voyage of the *Ra*.

Destination: Columbus Bay, an easy five-hour paddle away. Margo would be waiting at the marina from noon on, lured by the promise of Sunday Bloodys and a free lunch in return for giving me a ride home.

The rising sun at my back illuminated the water ahead of me, making the shallows transparent as crystal. The sea was calm and smooth. I reluctantly took my eyes off my favorite little blue-and-yellow fish feeding in the sea grass to turn my attention to the shore.

Top Banana has a three-inch draw allowing me to stick close to the shoreline. I could easily beach my craft whenever I wanted to stretch my legs or find a clump of bush for a discreet pit stop. I would be in deep open water only when crossing the Isabeya harbor. Hugging the town shoreline would have added an hour to an already long trip.

The westward flowing current acted like a palm gently pressed against my back, urging Top Banana toward its destination.

A gurgle of happiness welled in my chest. I remembered early spring days in Chicago: childhood blizzards that cancelled birthday parties, watermarks of rock salt-laden slush on my boots, annual flu bouts that rendered me a pasty-faced vegetable, a chill that never left my bones until summer corn was ready for harvest. If I'd known of the eternal summer that awaited me in St. Chris, I would have flown the coop when I first learned to crawl.

I scanned the shoreline and discovered that time changes topography. Hurricane winds over the past century stripped previously existent sandy beaches down to volcanic rock, former creek beds now bore dense scrub. But the Danish-built landmarks that dotted the map Miss Maude's father had drawn were still visible.

In the days when sugar ruled the St. Chris economy,

thimble-shaped two-story-high sugar mills were part of every working plantation.

Isabeya was a heavy traffic port on molasses sector of the old slaves-molasses-rum triangular trade route until the Danish government abolished the importation of slaves in 1803. Forty-five years later, in a historic proclamation delivered on July 3 from Isabeya's Government House steps, all slaves were freed.

The old mills that formerly housed mule-driven machinery used to crush the cane stood as a charming reminder of a perhaps not-so-charmed past.

Plantation life continued until the market crash in 1929. Then lousy weather—hurricanes, droughts—and hard times hit St. Chris in a one-two punch. One by one, the sugar plantations were abandoned and sold for outstanding mortgages or back taxes.

The legacy of the planters survives in the estate names. When the Danes first mapped St. Chris in the early 1700s, the island was divided into five quarters: East End, West End, King, Queen and Prince. The quarters were further subdivided into matriculars consisting of 150 Danish acres each, the size of a working sugar plantation. Upper Love, Lower Love, Hard Labor, Palm Bay, Body Slob, Mary's Fancy, Whim, Little Profit, North Star, Diamond and Ruby were among the plantation names that are still used today to designate land areas. Land records are organized by estate names, then further subdivided into parcels and plots. Although my mailing address is an Isabeya post office box, the physical address shown on my property tax bill is Parcel 3, Estate Goat Hill.

I paddled slowly past Estates Jealousy and Solitude, Top Banana skimming over the water like a dragonfly, frequently drifting with the paddle resting in my lap while I tried to match the old map with the current shoreline. Cooling seawater sloshed over my feet through the self-bailing scuppers.

Sea grape leaves and palm fronds rustled in the soft morning breeze. I listened to roosters noisily crowing ashore and watched patrolling pelicans soar and dive kamikaze-style into the early morning fish breakfast special. They surfaced and swallowed, then soared to dive again. I once read that pelicans eventually go blind from salt water. Unable to spot the fish they need for sustenance, they die of slow starvation.

An hour into the trip, halfway to Isabeya, and no sign of manchineel. The plant is a shore hugger, so I had no need to look inland. The small easterly groves marked on the map had probably been eradicated by planters providing seaside recreational facilities for their families. Copies of old photographs in the fort museum show the planters at play: men in stiff collared shirts, the women in long-sleeved, full-skirted, wasp-waisted dresses gazing at the sea from under their parasols. I never see anyone swimming or looking like they're having a good time.

The Anglican church bells were tolling eight when I reached the WBZE tower on the eastern edge of the Isabeya harbor. The sun was becoming blistering hot on my back. I took a minibreak to rest before the hard paddling ahead, swapping an empty water bottle for a fresh one from my cooler.

Taking a deep breath, I shoved off again. So far I had the ocean to myself, but I was now entering a major boat traffic area. Ahead of me, barnacle-bottomed red-and-green channel markers swayed and bobbed in the water, the seafoam green calm of the shallows abruptly changing to churning deep water cobalt.

The noise level increased: cars of churchgoers on the Isabeya streets a quarter-mile away, motored dinghies ferrying day-trip supplies to moored sailboats, the familiar chug-chug of the ferry from Dockside to Harborview, a droning pair of jet skis circling the inner harbor. At the water sports pavilion on Papaya Quay, I spotted the parasail boat tied to a short dock.

Freed from the restraint of the protecting reef, three-foot northerly swells flogged Top Banana along its eleven-foot length. Strong northeasterly currents pushed my boat inland. To compensate and maintain a straightforward westerly course, I switched from my usual left-right, left-right figure-eight paddle to a one-left, two-right stroke, digging deep into the water for maximum forward thrust. Waves sloshed over my starboard side to flow through the self-bailing holes molded into the bottom of the boat.

My world shrank to the size of my craft and the task of getting across the harbor.

I never saw the jet skis coming.

One minute I was paddling alone, the next I was being attacked from behind by a pair of motor-driven sharks on a feeding frenzy.

They approached on a parallel course, then separated one to each side of me. They crisscrossed several yards ahead of me and began circling Top Banana in ever shrinking orbits, crossing in front of me and behind me. Their churning wake violently rocked my boat from side to side, up and down, like a fragile toy shaken in the jaws of a beast.

Blinded by salt spray, I couldn't see the faces of the drivers. I lowered my head, blinking furiously to clear my vision, and kept paddling with every ounce of strength I possessed, gasping for breath with each stroke.

I knew I'd never outdistance them. My greatest fear was being capsized and run over like roadkill. Left to drown in the deep blue sea, my paralyzed fingers still clenched to grip the aluminium kayak paddle.

One-left, two-right, I plunged blindly ahead.

The jet skis came closer and closer, the high-pitched screech of their engines reverberating in my splitting head like a thousand fingernails raking a blackboard.

One-left, two-right, water gushing over starboard and port.

I began choking from the jet ski exhaust.

One-left, two right, sheets of water drenching my body.

Two powerboats joined the fray.

One-left, two-right, Top Banana sluggish against the swells. My breathing reduced to a ragged wheeze.

An authoritative voice sounded over a bullhorn.

"Ahoy, jet skis. This is the harbormaster. You will go to shore immediately. I repeat. This is the harbormaster. You will go to shore immediately."

The jet skis peeled away from my kayak and shot off in different directions, each pursued by a powerboat.

My arms and shoulders throbbed; my legs were quivering. I had no choice but to keep paddling blindly.

One-left, two-right, over and over against the swells and current, until twenty minutes later I finally reached the western side of the Isabaya harbor and was back in the pale green reef-protected shallows. Only then did I let go of the paddle to clean my sunglasses and rub my stinging eyes.

I grounded Top Banana on the first visible sand spit and crawled out of the boat to collapse on the beach.

A powerboat sped into the area a few seconds later. The engine noise stopped abruptly and I heard an anchor plop in the water. A young man in a navy polo shirt and white shorts jumped from the boat and sloshed through the water to where I lay gasping on the searing sand, too exhausted to rise and take shelter in the shade.

"Morning Lady! Are you okay?" Quincy loomed over me, mercifully blocking the scorching sun.

Chapter
27

"SO THEN WHAT happened?"

Not waiting for an answer, Margo shifted into her Florence Nightingale persona. "Wait a sec, do you want another beer? Food. Let's get you some food. Medium-rare mushroom bacon cheeseburger and fries okay? You sit, I'll be right back."

She placed our order at the bar, returning with fresh cold bottles of Heineken and ice-frosted mugs. We were lunching at Columbus Landing, the open-air beach restaurant at the Columbus Bay marina. Palm and sea grape trees bordered an open deck where hatch-cover tables were shaded by a palm frond-thatched roof. From our table I kept an eye on Top Banana, temporarily moored at the visitor's dock, while chattering sugar birds table-hopped to steal grains of sugar, and small chameleons patrolled the wooden railing behind me, their quick tongues flicking no-see-ums from the air.

"There you were, gasping like a dying fish, when

Quincy O'Reilly appeared? I don't believe this. What brought him there?"

"He saw the whole thing from Harborview. He radioed the harbormaster, hopped in the parasail powerboat and raced to my rescue, arriving in a dead heat with the harbormaster."

"You get the guts and glory award hands down, or else you're vying for idiot of the year," said Margo. "I would have been scared to death."

"Sweetie, I was terrified. You know those really awful nature movies where panicked whales are being chased by harpooners in motorboats?"

"God, yes. You hear the plaintive cries of the whales when the poor babies are separated from their mothers. Those movies make me physically ill. How did you ever have the nerve to keep going after Quincy found you on the beach?"

"I had to. It was like getting back on a horse after being thrown. Look at my eyes. Are they still brown? I swear they turned blue."

Margo laughed. "That old joke about being full of crap up to your eyebrows, right?"

"Right. But you know the worst part? I kept thinking about what Pete said on Friday night—'Watch your butt, it's not safe out there'—and wondering if he had anything to do with what happened today."

"He wouldn't."

"I think he would. He was really pissed about Angie's suspension and said they both thought it was all my fault."

"Kel, that's bull. Angie did it to herself."

"You and Abby know that, I know that, but does anyone else?"

"Mind if we join you?"

We looked up to see Benjamin and Doug, the harbormaster, standing behind unoccupied chairs at our table.

"Benjamin and I wanted to make sure you were all right," said Doug.

I looked at Benjamin. "How did you know?"

"Miss Maude heard Quincy's radio call to the harbor-master on her scanner and phoned me," he said.

My eyebrows flew up several inches above my sun-glasses. Miss Maude monitored a scanner? Benjamin winked.

"We found the pair who chased you," said Doug. "The Ramirez twins. They've been in trouble before. Petty stuff."

Margo gave me a knowing look that years of friendship translated to "we'll talk later."

"There's no need for you to be involved any further," Doug continued. "We've confiscated the twins' jet skis and levied a hefty fine for reckless endangerment. They'll also be spending the next six weeks in water safety school be-fore we return the skis. Is that okay with you?"

"Works for me," I said. "But I want those kids warned that if they ever come near me or my property again I'll press charges. Also, I want to make sure Quincy is suitably rewarded."

"You got it, Kelly. By the way, you're one hell of a kayaker. That was some sprint across the harbor. I can't believe you stayed on the water for two more hours. I would have hitched a tow with Quincy." Doug smiled, slapping me on the back as he and Benjamin rose to leave.

I let forth an involuntary yelp when Doug's hand made contact.

"You okay?" Margo asked.

"Doug's a little heavy-handed." I leaned closer to Margo, lowering my voice to a whisper. "So? Dish."

Margo whispered back, "The Ramirez twins? They're Angie's cousins!"

"Why am I not surprised?"

"Kel, what are you going to do?"

"Watch my butt, that's for damned sure."

Our food finally arrived. Between bites, I asked Margo, "What do you know about Miss Lucinda? I met her for the first time yesterday at Miss Maude's. Is she all there?"

Margo swallowed most of a glass of water to keep from choking on her cheeseburger. "Really, Kel, you didn't know? Miss Lucinda's completely gaga. Has been for ages! I don't think she was ever the brightest bulb in the chandelier, but you should see pictures from her youth. She was beautiful. A real stunner. Rumor has it . . ." Margo paused for another swallow of water.

"Don't stop now. Tell me!"

"Did you see that scrumptious wristwatch she wears? The platinum and diamond number?"

I nodded.

"Guess who she claims gave it to her?"

"I give up. Who? Prince Charles?"

"Go back a couple of generations." Margo began softly singing "I Danced with the Man Who Danced with the Girl Who Danced with the Prince of Wales."

"You're kidding!"

"Well, it happened before that gold-digging Baltimore bitch Mrs. Simpson came along. The island scuttlebutt is that Miss Lucinda was quickly married off to someone else and came out here from England as the bride of one of the planters. Don't you love it?"

Still smiling over Margo's gossip, I leaned into the chairback and quickly sat up straight again. "Damn!"

"What's the matter?"

"Do me a favor," I said, putting money on the table to cover our lunch check. "Peek under my T-shirt and check my back. That sun was a real scorcher."

Margo took one look and immediately began fanning her face with her hand. "Honey, I've got news for you. Your back is the color of a Tab can. You're gonna blister and peel."

Chapter
28

MY BACK WAS hotter than a Texas sidewalk in July, and so flaming red you could have used me for a night-light.

Clothing felt like coarse sandpaper rubbing against my skin. I went to work Monday morning in a skimpy halter top that put me at risk of immediate arrest on a charge of public nudity.

Cans of Solarcaine rested in my cooler along with the usual Tab. Emily's mission, whether she accepted it or not, was to spray my back every fifteen minutes; otherwise I'd self-destruct in five seconds from heatstroke.

It was a morning for Handel and little chat. Forget the *Royal Fireworks*; I opted for the *Water Music Suite*, followed by Debussy's *La Mer*. Soothing and cool. I kept eyeing the studio wall clock, praying Emily would surprise me by showing up before her scheduled eight-thirty arrival time. Wishful thinking.

The studio door opened at seven-thirty. A disembodied white handkerchief fluttered in the air followed by a hand waving a McDonald's bag.

"Truce, Mama?" The aroma of Sausage McMuffins with cheese made me salivate. "Why is it so damned cold in here? You could hang meat in this room."

"What are you doing here on your day off?" I tossed Michael a can of Solarcaine. "As long as you're around, you might as well make yourself useful and spray me. But no touching. You touch, I scream, you die. In that order." I moaned with relief when the cooling spray bathed my back.

"The keelhauled sailor in *Mutiny on the Bounty* looked better than you do. Chow down, Mama. You need a carbo load. Then a skin graft."

I checked the remaining play time on Handel: 23:09. Long enough to enjoy my breakfast.

Michael popped the lid off his coffee. "I hear you tangled with the Ramirez brothers. They're bad-news bears, Mama. I'd steer clear if I were you."

"Very funny. You weren't the one paddling your butt off yesterday."

"What do you know about the twins?"

"What's to know?"

"Listen up, Mama. Those two have juvie rap sheets that make Al Capone look like a choirboy. So far it's all been petty stuff. Breaking and entering, joyriding in borrowed cars. But now they're getting in deeper. They're hanging around the fort with the penny ante drug dealers."

"How do you know all this?"

"I make it my business to know."

"Michael! What are you saying?"

"I'm not saying anything, Mama. You're the one trying to put words in my mouth."

"Am not."

"Are too."

We stuck out our tongues like little kids in a schoolyard name-calling contest, ending that round in a tie.

I used my hands to call time-out when I heard the final

part of the Handel suite, the four-minute hornpipe allegro. When it was over I cued *La Mer*, while sharing a few remarks with my listeners about Debussy's role in the impressionist movement. I shut off the mike when the new selection started.

"Mama, you blow me away. I'm always cribbing from liner notes on album jackets, but that intro stuff rolls right outta your head and off your tongue. Where did you learn to do that?"

"Northwestern, music minor."

"Berkeley, poli sci major."

I felt like we should shake hands and swap info on our sun signs. "Don't change the subject. Let's get back to the twins. They're in Quincy's high school class. Are they really dangerous?"

"Like a pair of angry centipedes under your bare feet. What did you do to piss 'em off?"

"That's like asking a rape victim what she did to provoke an attack."

"Your point. I'll rephrase. Why were they after you?"

A tricky question. I thought I knew the answer, but I wasn't sure I wanted to open up to Michael about the latest twist in my personal life. Mixing business with personal isn't my style, and I had a prickly feeling about Michael, that we were edging toward a line I didn't want to cross.

Michael smiled winsomely. "It's cool, Mama. I'm from the government, I'm here to help you."

"Yeah, right. And the check's in the mail," I retorted. "Get out of here. I've got work to do." I handed him the can of Solarcaine. "Spray me again before you go."

My back soothed to numbness, Michael placed a small manilla envelope on the console. "Sign this for me sometime, would you?" With a shy smile, he left the station.

Inside the envelope lay an old playbill. An ominous specter from my past.

Chapter
29

I SPENT MONDAY afternoon sitting cross-legged in my tiled shower stall sipping a frozen margarita, a spray of cool water pitter-pattering on my back, while listening to an old thirty-three lp recording of a Broadway cast album playing softly on my stereo.

Memories of Chicago in the waning sixties: Julian Bond and the Georgia delegation, Lincoln Park, Mayor Richard J. Daley, Grant Park, tear gas, Senator Abraham Ribicoff, the Democratic National Convention, a basement apartment off Rush Street, Oak Street Beach, the moon walk, Vietnam War protests, flower children. Heralds of the Age of Aquarius.

I never smoked dope, went to Woodstock, burned a flag, called a cop a pig or was arrested in Grant Park. But I stood naked on stage eight performances a week for six months in the original Chicago cast of *Hair*.

My parents were appalled when their only child landed a major role in the musical shortly after her eighteenth birthday. My father swore, my mother cried, then Mother swore and Daddy cried. When I wouldn't give up the part, I was legally disowned; cast out of suburbia—"We're so ashamed of you we can't face our friends. We didn't send you to acting classes at Goodman all these years for this"—with a high school diploma, an Equity card, rehearsal pay and a contracted six-month paycheck between me and starvation.

After *Hair* came *Hello, Dolly!* and the fateful closing night that turned me from a soprano to a tenor, with a husky voice that no longer matched my postadolescent face. I chopped my waist-length hair to the pixie cut I still sport, and went job-hunting.

Radio is one place where a face doesn't matter, only the voice. I was hired as a deejay at an all-female Chicago jazz station. On air I was known only as Morning Glory; my real identity was a closely guarded station secret. I moonlighted for tuition money doing freelance radio and TV commercial voice-overs, working my way through college in five years of afternoon and night classes to a business degree from Northwestern University with minors in music and theater.

Although I maintained my Equity membership, the resume I handed out began with my first deejay job. Pete never knew about my aborted professional acting career and thought my parents were dead. For all I knew they could be; we hadn't kept in touch.

So why was Michael taunting me with an old program from *Hair*?

I climbed out of the shower, leaving wet footprints on my plush bathmat and terrazzo floor, abandoning all thoughts of a towel in favor of air-drying my body under the kitchen ceiling fan.

I stopped to turn the cast album back to side one and the *Aquarius* overture. I still knew the lyrics to all the songs by heart.

Why, after we'd worked together for two years, was
Michael asking me to sign a playbill I'd previously auto-
graphed for a thirteen-year-old boy on his birthday?

I definitely needed another margarita to think it through.

Chapter

30

By Tuesday morning I was ready to buy stock in Solarcaine.

"Your back is really gross, Mama. Tomorrow we're gonna have to tie a bell around your neck to warn off the weekly cruise ship visitors. Have you thought about taking up residence in the old leper colony?"

"Cute, Michael, really cute. But here's a news flash for you: The St. Chris leper asylum closed for good in the early 1940s."

The asylum was located in an isolated area near a brackish salt pond, inland from Leatherback Bay. A hurricane destroyed the wooden buildings in the late forties, but the iron-fenced cemetery is still there. If you part the weeds you can decipher some of the weathered inscriptions on the old tombstones. Kids often sneak into the cemetery to make out.

Michael handed over the Solarcaine. I tossed it in my tote, digging inside for the small manilla envelope which I placed on the console.

"Got any caffeine in there, Mama? I don't mean that canned battery acid you drink."

"You're SOL. But there's a stale herbal tea bag in my desk drawer. Have at it."

The expression on Michael's face made a Mayan funeral mask look gleeful.

"Coffee, Mama, I need java. I'll fetch some chow. You want a McMuffin?" I handed him some money to cover my share.

Bernstein conducting the New York Philharmonic in a 1964 recording of Beethoven's Symphony no. 9 in D minor, "Choral" was still in the first movement when Michael returned.

I casually mumbled between bites, "Where did you get the playbill?"

"It's mine. A souvenir of the night I became the horniest teenager on the planet."

I felt my face redden then blanch. "But why show it to me? What do you want?"

"Mama! How could you think . . . ?" His eyes registered the apprehension flitting across my face. "You're serious." He put down his take-out cup, resting his warmed hand on top of my clammy one. "You've got it all wrong. Listen to me."

Michael leaned forward in his chair, his hand still on mine. I slid my hand away to fiddle with my pen, trying to maintain an emotional distance from whatever he was going to say.

"I waited two years to show you that program for one reason. To let you know you had a friend you could trust to keep a secret. I hoped, once you knew, I could trust you to keep a secret of mine."

"What secret?"

"Can I trust you?"

"Michael, put up or shut up. I don't want to play games."

"Mama, I can't afford to play them." He sat patiently waiting for my answer, as impossible to dissuade as Minx fixated on a kitty treat.

I felt myself slipping closer to the line. "All right. Yes! You can trust me. What's your goddamned secret?"

"This." Michael pulled his wallet from his hip pocket, reached under a flap into a secret compartment, then handed me an ID.

I stared at it, my eyes wide and mouth falling open. Wordlessly, I handed the laminated document back to him.

"Close your mouth, Mama, you'll draw flies."

"You've used that line before." I shook my head, trying to snap back to reality. "You really are . . ."

"Shhh." He placed a finger across my lips. "Let's just say I'm here to help you and leave it at that. Okay?"

I slowly nodded. "O-kay. Does Mrs. H know?"

"Hell, no. Does she know about you?"

I shook my head. "No one knows."

"You're kidding. Not even your ex?"

"No one."

"You were married to that guy for how long?"

"Fifteen years."

"He doesn't know that you were part of the greatest show on earth? Your performance was something to be proud of. When we first met here at the station after Mrs. H hired me, I thought you were doing a Garbo-type retirement number, traveling in disguise as the queen of the local airwaves. That's why I never said anything until now. I didn't want to blow your cover."

"Let's not go there, okay?"

"Your call, Mama. But I gotta tell you I'm honored to be in the same room with you. You were dynamite. I hocked my stamp collection to buy a matinee ticket so I could see you onstage again."

I smiled ruefully. "Michael, that's really sweet. It's nice to know after all these years I've still got a fan." The digital studio wall clock read 6:54:30. Time for business. "I've got to do the news. Are you going or staying?"

"Will you have dinner with me tonight?"

"That's not a good idea," I said.

"Why not? Because you're my boss or because I'm younger than you?"

"Younger by only five or six years. Chronologically. Mentally?" I made a waggling motion with my hand. "Is that why you call me Mama?"

"You never picked up on it?" Michael's baritone laugh boomed through the studio. "I call you that because you've got a husky voice like a great honky-tonk mama." He dropped his empty cup in the basket, laughing as he headed for the studio door. "Earn your bread, Morning Glory; I'm going for more coffee." He winked at me from the doorway.

Was there no end to Michael's surprises?

The last movement of the *Ninth* was building toward the nineteen-minute choral, Schiller's "Ode to Joy," when Michael came back, still chuckling to himself.

He settled in an armchair, feet propped on the console, eyeing me over the rim of his coffee cup.

"Let's get down to cases. Do you trust me enough to tell me about Sunday's run-in with the Ramirez twins?"

I crossed the Rubicon separating my business and personal lives when I replied, "I think Pete and Angie sicced 'em on me."

Michael let out a low whistle. "Whoa. Back up. Was Pete at your house when I called late Friday night?"

"Yeah. He was pissed because Angie'd been suspended without pay. He told me they thought it was my fault and to watch my butt."

"I'm still missing a chapter. Why was Angie suspended?"

I gave him sketchy details.

"Shit. I'm sorry if anything I did Friday morning got

you in trouble. But who knew you were going kayaking Sunday?"

"Several people. Margo, Miss Maude, maybe Miss Lucinda."

"Miss Lucinda's a walking fruitcake. She thinks it's still 1928 and every man is the Prince of Wales trying to get in her knickers."

"So Margo said. Am I the last to find out?"

"Mama, you gotta get out of St. Mary Mead."

"I didn't know you read Agatha Christie."

"I don't, I read Ludlum or Clancy. But I got bored and picked up a Christie you left behind. What I'm saying is this. For a hip lady, you walk around with your head in blinders. Did anyone else know you were going out?"

"No. But I didn't say it was a secret. Margo told me the twins are Angie's cousins."

"More like second cousins, but still family. They're hustlers who'll do anything for a buck. I'll put the word out they're to leave you alone. But walk with your street smarts from now on, okay? So, are we on for dinner?"

"I can't. We work together. I'm not ready for this."

"Are you still mooning over Jeff?"

I held up my hand like a crossing guard signaling "stay." "Michael. Don't. Just don't."

Michael backed toward the door, his open palms raised chest-high. "Don't shoot the messenger, Mama. But here's a reality check for you. Jeff's not coming back. Not now, not in six weeks, or six months; not ever, unless it's in irons. He's on the lam for drug dealing."

"How do you know that?" My voice had turned to cold steel.

"I was one of the guys who nailed him."

Chapter
31

MICHAEL'S PARTING SHOT blew my mind.

It also explained a lot of things I'd been too starry-eyed to question when Jeff and I were together. The dates he didn't keep, sudden trips off island, the last-minute urge to go spring skiing in Colorado. I should have smelled a rat the first time he refused to give me a number where he could be reached. Color me stupid.

I really wanted to talk to Margo about Jeff's defection.

But if I did, I'd have to tell her how I found out, and it would mean compromising Michael. I couldn't do that, because I'd given my word. Trust weaves a very tangled web.

Victoria called to invite me to lunch at Dockside, giving me an excuse to avoid Margo temporarily by skipping lunch at the Watering Hole.

We lunched on lobster salad, tiny herb croissants and iced tea in Victoria's blissfully cool shuttered office. We talked about the key I found in Zena's room.

"I spent the morning making inquiries," said Victoria.

"I've been to the post office, every bank in Isabeya and finally the locksmith's, but no luck. I had a letter in the morning post from Catherine, reminding me to ship her mother's belongings. I really shouldn't put it off any longer; I need the room for paying guests. Let's have one more look while I do the packing."

Zena's room was as I'd left it five nights earlier.

Victoria and I formed a relay team, beginning with the armoire closet. We carefully examined every seam, pocket and hem of each garment before Victoria folded it for packing.

We finished taping the last box at four-thirty.

"Have you time for a drink?" Victoria and I went to the Posh Nosh bar where dinner setup was in progress. The bartender stop slicing limes to fix each of us a large Tanqueray and tonic.

"Vic, I don't get it. We went over every inch of that room, every scrap of Zena's belongings. We even turned the mattress and checked the box spring. Nothing. I don't understand about the key. I certainly don't think it came with the hat."

"You have a point. However, it's the one item I didn't pack." Victoria reached inside her collar to show me the brass key hanging from a beaded chain around her neck. "I can always send it along later."

We sipped our drinks in thoughtful silence.

"Vic, maybe we're approaching the key problem from the wrong angle."

"What are you getting at?"

"We've assumed all along that the key belonged to Zena and unlocks something she owned or had access to. Like a safety-deposit box."

"Right you are. But the banks all deny having ever seen that type of key."

"What did the locksmith say?"

"He didn't recognize it. He did say there were no markings on it that he could trace."

"Vic, what if Zena stole the key from someone else?"

"Brilliant. I never thought of it that way."

"It doesn't put us any closer to discovering its purpose, but we do know it's not tied to anything she had in her room."

Victoria looked at her watch. "Kelly, I really must get ready to hostess. We'll talk more later. I can't thank you enough for your time and trouble. Please be my guest for dinner any evening—with a companion, of course."

"May I use the bar phone?"

Victoria handed me her office key. "My office line is more private."

I was tired of eating alone every night with only Minx for company. I dialed Michael's number, hoping I wouldn't wake him. His machine picked up on the second ring. I started to leave a message when his voice cut in.

"Don't hang up, Mama, I was in the shower. Change your mind about dinner?"

"Yes. But it's my treat—actually, Victoria's. Are you up for Posh Nosh?"

"Not tonight. Let's save it for Saturday when we're both on weekend hours. I'll meet you at the Lower Deck at seven."

I asked Victoria to make a reservation for two, Saturday night at eight.

"You and Michael? Lovely. He's such a dear. He went to a great deal of trouble for your birthday surprise party. Everything had to be perfect."

"Vic, I thought Margo organized that."

"Oh, no. It was all Michael's doing. Perhaps I've let the cat out of the bag. You won't give me away, will you? I believe he's quite smitten with you."

"Mum's the word." I drove home to feed Minx and change for dinner, smiling all the way. Minx bounded out the kitchen door after scarfing down her dinner, while I stood looking in my closet for something to wear. My back was at the blistering stage, too repulsive for public scrutiny. I grabbed an old long-sleeved East Indian cotton white-on-white embroidered tunic-length shirt, laundered so many times it felt like a whisper of gauze against my back, tossed on a pair of jeans, and found my favorite blue-and-green-striped thong sandals. I closed and locked the sliding glass doors that opened onto the gallery, flipped on the outside light illuminating my driveway, locked the dead bolt on my kitchen entrance door and headed back to town.

Michael roared up to the Lower Deck on his Harley a few minutes before seven. I was already seated at a small round table for two, drinking an iced tea, looking at the twinkling lights of Harborview. The sun had set seconds earlier, and a not-quite-first-quarter moon rode high overhead.

He chained the Harley to a lamppost, walking toward me with his helmet tucked under his arm. A fleeting image of Ichabod Crane made me snicker. A shorter, younger, bearded Ichabod in khaki Dockers, a blue oxford cloth shirt, Bass Weejuns on his feet. A preppie type who reminded me of the guys I'd known in high school. The spicy scent of his cologne tickled my nose when he bent to kiss me on the cheek.

"What's so funny? Haven't you seen a man in long pants before?"

"Never mind, Michael. It was a silly thought."

"No secrets, Mama. This is us. We have no more secrets between us."

It took a minute for that to sink in. I nodded slowly, my smile growing broader until I began to laugh. I suddenly felt freer and lighter than air. Michael laughed too and grabbed my hand.

"Leave your drink," he said. "We'll be right back."

We ran along the boardwalk toward the Watering Hole, stopping at a darkened part of the waterfront where the shops had already been shuttered for the night. He pulled me into his arms and kissed me.

"I've wanted to do that since I was thirteen," he murmured, gently kissing my eyelids, nose, and throat, then moving back to my mouth, his lips warm on mine. "I used to fantasize about this while listening to you on the radio in Chicago when I was supposed to be getting ready for school. After seeing you on stage, I recognized your voice the first time I heard you on the air."

"Oh, Michael," I purred, "where have you been all my life?"

"Waiting for you, Mama," he said, "but you need a better script. That line's older than you are." He kissed me again, taking his time to do it properly. We walked slowly back our table, heads together, arms wrapped around each other's waists. We fit like fraternal twins.

Victoria was waiting, a twinkle in her eye, with a Heineken for Michael in her hand. "We're going to have a limited number of prime rib dinners Saturday night. Shall I reserve two for you?"

We nodded in agreement, saying "medium rare" in unison.

"That's set, then. Carole will be here in a minute to take your order. Enjoy your evening." I heard Victoria chuckle as she went upstairs to hostess at Posh Nosh.

After English-style chips with malt vinegar and freshly caught deep-fried fish at the Lower Deck, we had enough time to stroll over to Maubi's van for coconut ice cream before Michael had to leave for work.

"Hey, Michael. Long time. You with Morning Lady?"

"Looks that way." Michael put his arm around me and squeezed my shoulder.

"Well, don't that beat all." Maubi nodded several times, slapping his thigh, grinning his approval. "Don't that beat all." Handing us each a double-dip cone, he asked, "Morning Lady, you makin' out okay after Sunday?"

"I'm good. How's Quincy? I want to thank him again." I reached out to clasp Maubi's hand. "You've got a great son. I owe him big time."

"Quincy doing just fine. He studying tonight. But I tell him you asked. He be pleased to know that."

Michael chimed in, "You see the twins around?"

"They be lyin' real low since Sunday. Like snakes hidin' in a hole."

"You spread the word. They mess with Mama again, they mess with me."

"That news go 'round fast." Maubi turned to a new group of customers clamoring for his attention.

Michael tossed the remnants of his soggy cone in the trash barrel. "Where are you parked? I've gotta split for the station."

We walked briskly to my hatchback, parked between two cars under a streetlight a few yards from Maubi's van.

I wouldn't be going anywhere soon.

All four of my tires had been slashed.

Chapter
32

MICHAEL AND I ran back to question Maubi.

"I been here since eight," he said. "There be people around, but I can't say for true I see any messing with your car."

Michael looked at his watch. "Mama, come with me to the station, then you can ride my bike home and bring it back in the A.M."

I shook my head. "I've never driven a bike; I don't think that's an option."

Michael zoomed off to sign on and phone the police while I remained close to my crippled car.

I knew the odds of getting a tow truck to come after seven P.M. on St. Chris were on par with winning the local lottery. Or getting home delivery on a pizza. All gas stations and garages were already closed for the night. I also needed more than a tow. First I needed two new tires so the wheel rims wouldn't be ruined when the car was hauled to the garage.

Maubi commiserated. "This be bad business, meh son.

Bad, bad business. Soon I may not be safe in town myself."

The police arrived to take down the particulars. I had no choice but to leave my car where it was until the next morning, knowing as I did so that I ran a big risk of coming back to find it stripped.

"We'll keep watch on it when we patrol, but that's the best we can do. We'll give you a lift home."

But once home, how would I get to work in the morning?

I ended up spending the night with Michael at the radio station.

"Why didn't you call me?" asked Margo the following noon over a chef salad lunch at the Watering Hole round table. "You know I would have come immediately; you could have borrowed my car. Or spent the night at my place."

"It seemed like too much hassle," I replied. "If you'd come I would have had to drive you home, then go home myself, then drop the car off at your house before six, and you'd have to get up early to drive me to work. All around, a giant pain."

"You got that right. Especially the getting up before six A.M. part," said Margo. "But Paul could have driven you. He's usually up for an early flight. What did you do all night?"

"Michael and I talked for a while, then I crapped out on Mrs. H's couch." I couldn't hide the little smile playing on my lips, remembering how Michael had awakened me for my morning air shift.

"Wait a minute, Kel. I see that smile. What are you not telling me? And what were you doing in town on a school night?" Margo sat back in her captain's chair, arms folded across her chest, waiting for my answer.

"Having dinner with Michael."

"Yes!" She slapped the table with her fingertips. "He's

such a cutie. How long has this been going on?"

"Since yesterday."

Margo signaled the Watering Hole waitress for refills on our iced tea. "Back up, Kel. Start at the beginning and don't leave out even one teensy detail. I'm all ears."

In truth, I left out quite a few details. But I was so used to lying about my past by omission that beguiling my best friend about the present came quite easily.

"So Michael asked you out to dinner, you turned him down, then when Victoria offered you a free meal, you changed your mind and Michael met you at the Lower Deck. Have I got it straight so far?"

"To the last detail." I sat with my fingers crossed in my lap.

"I love this," said Margo. "Before your birthday I thought Michael was sort of a flake. Do you remember his centipede weather forecast?"

"Remind me."

"Typical weather thing. But Michael ended with, 'Waves near one foot, and you better watch out because there's a big centipede next to the other one.' I thought then, who *is* this nutcase? But he grows on you."

"That sounds like Michael. A few weeks ago he said 'pissable showers' during a weather spot." I shook my head. "What made you change your mind about him?"

"Your birthday. Don't tell, but he set up the whole surprise party."

"Really? I thought it was your doing."

"I would have, you know that, but Michael beat me to it. He was really sweet. He wanted you to have a good time."

"Why didn't you tell me?" I asked.

"Jeff was still in the picture. That poop. You needed him like—how did Gloria Steinem put it?—'like a fish needs a bicycle.' You were just a notch on his bedpost. Sorry, sweetie. But it's the truth."

"Amazing what can happen in two weeks." I couldn't help smiling.

"Kel, be happy. You deserve it." Margo reached across the table to squeeze my hand. "I'll tell you how I knew that Paul was right for me. Because I could put my life in his hands and he wouldn't drop it. I think Michael's the same kind of good guy. Give him a chance to prove himself."

Jerry trotted out of the Island Palms real estate office, zigzagging through the weekly throng of bargain-hunting cruise ship passengers, to join us at the round table. He looked like he had canary feathers permanently embedded in his mouth.

After ordering his usual rum and water—"I'll have a white on white on the rocks"—he gloated, "I just heard some hot gossip."

Margo and I leaned forward in our chairs. "What?" we asked.

Jerry smiled slyly, savoring the moment.

Abby waved as she passed by, briefcase in hand, heading toward her law office above the toy store.

"Abby, get over here," called Margo. "Jerry's got fresh dirt."

Abby declined an invitation to sit and ordered iced coffee to go. "Talk fast, Jerry. I've got a client coming in five minutes."

Jerry stalled by clearing his throat, milking the suspense.

Barbara, Abby's secretary, yelled from the landing in front of the second-story office: "Your client called, he's running twenty minutes late."

Abby put down her briefcase, settling herself in one of the battered captain's chairs to enjoy her coffee.

Margo snatched Jerry's drink, holding it out of his reach. "Dish or die of thirst."

"Pete called from Phillipsburg in Sint Maarten. He and

Angie got married in Marigot on the French side Monday afternoon."

Jerry always did know how to steal the show. The old ham. He was really typecast when he played the Old Actor in our community theater production of *The Fantasticks*. He stretched a one-minute death scene into a five-minute production number, leaving an audience standing on its feet at every performance stomping, cheering, clapping and begging for an encore. He brought down the house every night.

Margo and Abby turned to see how I was taking the elopement news. I was a little surprised, but certainly not devastated. In my heart of hearts, I didn't give a damn. The real reason for the quickie wedding wasn't my news to tell. This wasn't a performance of *Cats*.

I raised my glass in a smiling toast. "To the happy couple."

"The happy couple," echoed Margo, Abby and Jerry. We all sampled our drinks.

"Guess that takes care of the wedding present," said Jerry.

Margo poked him with her elbow. "You're so cheap, Jerry."

"No reception, no present," said Jerry. "I read it in the Miss Manners column."

A passing middle-aged tourist, sporting a Carnival Cruise Line tote bag hanging from her shoulder, halted in midstep to stare at Jerry.

"Excuse me," she said excitedly. "Are you Sander Vanocur?"

Jerry preened. "Would you like an autograph?"

"Oh, no. I wouldn't trouble you when you're with your friends." She put down her six-bottle box of duty-free liquor to pump Jerry's outstretched hand, gushing, "I'm so honored to meet you."

"Good night and good news," Jerry replied solemnly.

The tourist scurried off to catch up with her friends. She kept pointing back at our table, reliving the glorious moment.

The rest of us were wiping tears from our eyes.

"Get it right the next time, Jer," said Margo. "Sander Vanocur did not say 'good night and good news,' that was Walter Cronkite."

"Wrong," I remarked. "Cronkite said, 'And that's the way it is.' Edward R. Murrow said 'good night and good *luck*.' I don't think Vanocur said anything."

"Whatever," Jerry snapped.

"Jerry, you're such a fraud," said Abby. "There are laws against impersonation."

"Did I actually say I was Sander?" Jerry asked in injured innocence.

I felt hands gently squeezing my shoulders and looked up to see Michael's smiling face.

"Your car's ready, Mama. I came to give you a ride to the garage."

"What happened to your car?" asked Abby.

"Her tires were slashed last night on the waterfront," said Margo.

Abby ordered another iced coffee. "Any idea who was responsible?"

"Probably the Ramirez twins," said Margo. "Didn't you hear what they did to Kel on Sunday?"

"What happened? I left early Saturday for a seminar in San Juan, flew back today. I got the last seat on the only morning flight coming over from Puerto Rico. The plane was loaded with tourists. I think I was the only local resident on board."

"I saw the whole thing from my front gallery," said Jerry. "They tried to run Kelly down in her kayak with their jet skis."

"You actually saw it happen?" said Michael.

"Heidi and I were having breakfast. She spotted Kelly

starting across the harbor—Kelly has the only yellow kayak on this island, it's an easy target—then the jet skis charging after her. Heidi kept watching through binoculars while I called the coast guard. All I got was the damned recording, so I called the police. They said the harbor-master was already on it."

"Would you testify to what you saw in court?" asked Abby.

"Sure. Heidi will, too," said Jerry. "Kel, I would have called you, but Margo said you were all right except for a bad sunburn."

"Kelly, may I talk to you for a minute? In private?" Abby and I walked a few feet away from the table. "Did Sunday have anything to do with Friday night's session with Angie?"

"I think so, but I can't prove it. Pete was waiting for me when I got home late Friday night. He was furious about Angie's suspension and shooting off his mouth. Told me to watch my butt. Maybe it's coincidence that the twins are related to Angie. Barbara, too?"

"No. Different branch of the family. There's no love lost on either side. Do you want to file a complaint?"

"I told Doug and Benjamin I wouldn't unless the twins came after me again."

"Call me if you change your mind. Nothing would make me happier than getting those terrorist punks off the street before they kill someone."

Chapter

33

MICHAEL INSISTED ON waiting with me at the garage.

"Have you had any sleep today?" I asked, digging in my purse for my checkbook. "You look like you've been up since Korea."

"I know that line, Mama. You stole it from a Willie Nelson movie. But the real thing was before my time."

"Vietnam?" Having found the checkbook, I continued digging for a pen.

"Missed that one, too. It was over before the draft got me. I had a student deferment."

"You still look like you need a nap." I kissed Michael's cheek to the snickering amusement of the young garage mechanic waiting for my check. "Thanks for spending your day getting my car fixed."

"I'll follow you home," said Michael.

"I'd like that," I replied. "Call me paranoid, but I can't help feeling my slashed tires were a setup to keep me away from the house. I'm afraid of what I'll find when I get home."

"Don't sweat it, Mama." Michael squeezed my hand. "I'll wait outside while you settle up."

"When will my car be ready? I was told two o'clock and it's still up on the rack. How long does it take to put in a new starter?" The sound of a familiar voice made me look up from my check writing to see Reverend Cal standing in the doorway.

"We missed you last Thursday at the parade committee meeting," I chided. "I mailed a reminder to your post office box and left a message on your home answering machine. We're having our final meeting tomorrow night at seven. I hope you can make it. I need your list of donors for the school floats for the parade program."

"I turned over the donations to Eli Daniel before I went to Puerto Rico for medical treatment," Reverend Cal replied. "I didn't fly back until this morning."

"Oh? I hope it's nothing serious."

"A little flare-up of skin cancer on my hands," he said, pausing for a dramatic sigh. "Too many years outdoors toiling in the fields of the Lord."

That probably explained why, on the hottest day of spring with temperatures pushing the mid-nineties, Reverend Cal was bareheaded but clad in a long-sleeved clerical shirt instead of his regular short-sleeved version. The hands mopping his dripping brow were bandaged like a prizefighter about to enter the ring.

"Have you considered prayer?" I asked. "I hear it works miracles. See you tomorrow night. Remember, I need that donor list." I waggled my fingers in his direction and skipped outside to where Michael was leaning against his bike. I heard Reverend Cal bartering for a clerical discount on his repair bill.

"Let's get out of here," I said to Michael, heading for my newly shod car. I called over my shoulder, "You can nap while I feed Minx and fix us some dinner. I'll make sure you're up in time to get to work."

Caravan style, with me in the lead, we headed east.

We arrived at my house to find my worst fears confirmed.

Chapter

34

NAILED TO MY front door was a letter-sized piece of paper.

Printed in block capitals under a crudely drawn picture of a cat hanging from a noose were the words "you got off easy this time."

Minx was nowhere to be seen.

I ran around the yard calling to her like a crazy woman.

I went back to the front door to have another look at the note, praying it was a mirage.

My stomach cramped, my breath came in wracking heaves. I thought I was going to lose my lunch.

I reached out to rip the obscene paper from my door.

Michael grabbed me around the waist from behind, burying his face in my shoulder. I struggled to free myself.

"Mama, don't. We need the note for evidence. Turn around and look at me."

I totally lost it.

I pounded Michael's chest with my fists, screaming in his face, "This has gone too far. I don't care who killed that damned woman. This has gone too far. M-i-n-n-n-x!

My baby! Oh, God." Tears gushed from my eyes, coursing down my cheeks.

Michael relaxed his grip. I slipped through his arms, sinking to the gravel where I sat, knees drawn to my chest, my head buried in my arms, sobbing. Michael crouched beside me, gently stroking my hair, murmuring softly until my tears subsided.

I stared sightlessly at the sea while Michael walked around the perimeter of my house looking for signs of intrusion.

He completed the circle to sit at my side, patting my arm, talking quietly as he would to a small frightened child. "Sweetheart, I'm going down to the main road to call the cops from the fire station. You stay here. I'll be back soon." He kissed the top of my head. "Everything's going to be all right."

I slowly shook my head. Without Minx, nothing in my life would ever be all right again. I blindly clutched Michael's hand, chewing my lower lip to keep fresh tears at bay, then turned back to stare blindly at the sea.

The Harley's roar faded to nothing. The afternoon droned around me. A rising thermal shimmied through the bush behind my house, rattling the desiccated seedpods on the Mother Tongue trees. A tiny chime on my gallery tinkled twice, then hung silent.

A while later I heard Michael's bike heading toward my house from the east end road, a siren-wailing police car in close pursuit.

Benjamin scrutinized the note on my door. "Kelly, I'm truly sorry," he said. "We should have arrested the twins Sunday instead of letting them off with a tap on the wrist."

It took half an hour to dust my wooden door for prints, secure the note for evidence, and check the yard for signs of disturbance before I was permitted to enter the house.

The interior was exactly as I had left it almost twenty-four hours earlier.

Benjamin departed to test the note for prints. "I'll call when we know anything. A patrol will pass by every hour to check on you."

Michael held me close. "Can I have a raincheck on the nap and dinner? I want to tag along with Ben and see what turns up. I'll call you by ten at the latest, okay?"

"Works for me." I hated to see him go.

"Will you be all right by yourself? Should I call Margo to keep you company?"

I shook my head.

"Do you want to spend the night at my place?"

"No. I want to be here in case Minx turns up. I can't believe she's gone." Fresh tears welled in my eyes.

Michael continued to hold me, stroking my hair. "I don't want to leave you."

"Go. Do what you have to," I said.

Michael took off at a run, pausing only to blow me a kiss from the kitchen doorway before he sped down the dirt road on his bike.

I looked down at the dishes on the grey vinyl paw-print mat on my kitchen floor. The brown stoneware water dish with a blue glazed interior I bought at Harrods in London, and the ceramic food bowl mail-ordered from Neiman Marcus was inscribed "Go ahead, make my dinner." In a special spot on the counter was a newly opened canister of Minx's favorite Haute Feline fish-shaped kitty treats I special-ordered from the States.

I couldn't bear to look at those dishes any longer. I went outside to continue calling for Minx, remembering all the times we shared. Discovering with a shock one morning when she was still a small kitten that the fur was completely gone from the top of her head. Scaly scabs were crusted on the thin skin covering her skull. The vet diagnosed it as ringworm.

"It's very expensive and time-consuming to treat," he

said. "And highly contagious to humans. You might want to think about having her put down."

That was not an option. I didn't care what it cost to cure her. If I had to, I'd eat hot dogs in order to pay the vet bill.

For six weeks I wrapped Minx in a beach towel twice a day to squirt yucky pink medicine down her throat. Every time she squirmed frantically, yowled like she was in excruciating pain and tried to spit it out.

The vet was absolutely right. It was contagious to humans. I sprouted atoll-shaped, dime-sized welts on my inner wrists, upper chest and shoulders. They itched like crazy. The vet wrote two more fifty-dollar prescriptions. One for me and one for Minx.

At the end of six weeks, we were both cured. I stroked the soft ebony and copper fur on the top of her head, knowing in my heart that my money hadn't been wasted.

I called to Minx until I was hoarse, finally going back into the house at dusk.

I sat listlessly picking at cheese and crackers for dinner, wishing Minx were sitting opposite me to steal bits of cheese off the tray as she always did, when Benjamin phoned shortly after seven.

He didn't pull any punches.

"We found the Ramirez twins' prints on the note, but we can't locate the twins. We've got an APB out on them. I've got an unmarked car parked across the bottom of your drive. Lock your door. Don't open the door or leave the house for any reason without calling me first."

"Where's Michael?" I asked.

"He went home for a quick sleep before work. He'll call you shortly. I promise you we'll find the boys if it takes all night."

I was too scared even to think about sleep. The house felt so empty.

I flopped on my bed and tried rereading my favorite

Agatha Christie, *A Murder Is Announced*, to pass the time. But I couldn't stay focused on life in Chipping Cleghorn.

Then I heard a faint meow that sounded like "Mommy" coming from the hillside behind my house.

I jumped to my feet, ran to the door, calling out, "Minx! Mommy's here, where are you?"

Silence. Then Minx answered, louder this time.

I dashed toward the sound, stumbling on loose shale in the dark, clawing my way upward through the bush, oblivious to the needle-sharp cassia thorns scratching my hands and face.

Minx was huddled in the crook of a tamarind tree halfway up the hillside, her head scrunched turtlelike into her shoulders, lemonade eyes squeezed shut.

I coaxed her trembling body into my arms and held her, rubbing my cheek on her soft mottled fur. She nestled her head in my neck and purred.

Holding Minx close to me with my left arm, using my right for balance, I gingerly sidestepped down the hillside.

Halfway down the hill I slipped on a loose rock. Minx's ears flattened. She let out a low growl, tearing through the thin gauze tunic I'd worn to dinner the night before at the Lower Deck to dig her claws into my bare shoulder. I winced but clung to her as she tried to wriggle free.

When we reached level ground I sprinted into the house, locking the dead bolt on the kitchen door behind me.

Safe on her home turf, Minx leapt to the top of the refrigerator. Hunched and glowering like a gargoyle, she loudly demanded dinner. I shoved a bowl of food on top of the refrigerator to placate her.

Benjamin called to check on me. "I phoned five minutes ago, you didn't answer. Where were you?"

"I went outside. I heard Minx meowing."

Benjamin was furious. "Damn it. I told you to call me first. Kelly, the twins are dangerous. They may be armed." His voice softened. "Is your cat all right?"

"She's fine. I'm relieved she's safe."

"Listen to me," he said sternly. "Don't go outside again for any reason without calling me first. My deputy has orders to disable anything that moves. I don't want you hurt."

Minx ambled out to the gallery to torment the resident lizard populace. I could hear her faint growls from time to time. I went back to my bed to try focusing on my book.

Except for Minx and a faint breeze rustling the uppermost leaves of the tamarind trees on the hill outside my bed area window, all was quiet.

I'd unwittingly nodded off when I was suddenly wide-eyed awake. But didn't know why. I listened intently but couldn't hear anything. I quickly doused my bedside lamp.

I wanted to make a quick run to the loo, but was afraid to pass in front of the uncurtained windows.

My body felt riveted to the bed.

A silent leap brought Minx to my side where she squeezed next to me, trembling in the dark. I still didn't know what had wakened me and spooked Minx.

Then I heard it.

Soft crunching sounds coming from the bush behind the house. The same hillside where I'd rescued Minx.

Crunch. Crunch. Silence.

Again, crunch, crunch. Then silence.

I was scared spitless.

Now I really needed to get to the john, but was too frightened to move. If I stayed where I was much longer I'd wet the bed.

I also had to get to the phone to call Benjamin.

Cautiously, I rose to my knees and peered through the open glass louvers of the jalousie window above my brass headboard.

The first-quarter moon put the trees half in shadow, half in light.

My overstimulated imagination was making me crazy.

Had the twins come back to finish what they started?

Again, a single crunch. Silence.

A faint rustling of leaves.

Then, crunch, crunch.

I bit my finger to keep from screaming.

A dark shape emerged from the trees.

I bit down harder.

A beautiful island deer, a legacy from the mid-seventeenth century when the Knights of Malta ruled St. Chris, came into view. The dry weather had driven him from the hilltops in search of an evening meal.

I watched the buck in silence as he made his painstaking way down the hill toward my house, tasting some leaves, ignoring others as he drew closer.

I dashed to the loo, then grabbed Minx, threw her over my shoulder and whirled around the living room, laughing hysterically with relief.

The ringing phone startled me so that I dropped Minx. With an angry yowl she ran to the gallery and began scritching her claws against the nubby cushions on the rattan love seat.

"Minx, stop that!" I commanded. She ignored me.

Benjamin said, "Calling to check on you."

"I'm fine, but you might want to warn your officer there's a large deer heading his way *now*. It scared the devil out of me."

"Call you right back."

Benjamin phoned again in less than a minute. His message was terse.

"We've had several reports sighting the twins in various parts of the island. Separately and together. Some reports may be false, but we can't take any risks. Again I caution you, keep your door locked and stay inside. Call me immediately if you require assistance."

I double-checked the dead bolt on the kitchen door, made sure the gallery screen door was fastened shut, turned on every light in the house, the gallery and the outside floodlight illuminating my driveway, then assembled the ingredients to make bread.

Michael called a few minutes before ten.

"How are you doing?" he asked. "Ben said you found Minx. Where was she?"

"Hiding in the crook of a tree about halfway up the hill behind the house."

"That's really cool, Mama. Everything else okay?"

"I had a scare about an hour ago, but it was only a deer. And you? Did you get some sleep?"

"A little. Not enough. What are you doing?"

"Baking bread."

"From scratch? I'm impressed."

"I use a machine. Want fresh bread for breakfast?"

"I'd like chocolate chip muffins even better."

"I'll see what I can do," I replied, knowing I had a stash of semisweet chips in the refrigerator.

"I miss you. I wish you were here."

"Me too," I said with a sigh. "But I don't think I could take another night on that lumpy office couch."

"I've got a better idea. Call me later and I'll tell you about it." Michael ended the call with a seductive chuckle.

With Michael's *Midnight Madness* show for company, I cleaned the kitchen, did several loads of laundry, put fresh sheets on my bed, hosed out Minx's litter box, swept up the skeletal remains of her dead lizard collection from under the bed and watered the plants on the gallery, even taking time to pick off the dead leaves. Anything to keep busy. And awake.

By four A.M. two loaves of bread were cooling on a wire rack, a tin of chocolate chip muffins was baking in the oven and I was exhausted. I brewed a pot of Earl Grey tea and plopped on the gallery to wait out the night. Minx snuggled next to me on the love seat, as close as a shadow.

At five I showered and dressed for work. Despite the

long night and earlier trek through the bush, I didn't look too bad. A few scratches on my arms and face, Rocky Raccoon circles under my eyes—nothing eight or ten hours of sleep wouldn't cure. My back itched and was starting to peel like a birch tree.

I called Benjamin at five twenty-five to let him know I was leaving the house, put Minx in her wicker carrier and headed for work.

The twins were still at large.

Chapter
35

"HEY, MAMA, WHAT'S in that big wicker basket? Breakfast?"

"Forget it, Michael. That is definitely not breakfast. Minx is here for career day. She's training to be the first feline deejay."

"Okay by me. I'm getting too old for night duty. She can have my shift. We'll call her show the *Midnight Meow*."

"Are you serious? You're not quitting, are you?"

"And leave show business? Mama, get real. It's an April Fool's joke! Grab a Tab and wake up. Where are those chocolate chip muffins you promised me?"

I tossed him the bag of still warm muffins and put the cat carrier in a secluded corner of the studio. Minx yawned, made a nest in the bath towel liner, and fell asleep, hugging her red satin catnip mouse.

The phone rang a few minutes before six.

"It's still your shift, Michael. You do the honors."

Benjamin had news.

"We found the twins' car. They ditched it near a cluster of fishing shacks at a cove on the west end. A fisherman called half an hour ago to say his boat had been tiefed. It's not much of a boat for true; an old dinghy with an outboard, but it's his only means of support. He wants it back. There's a full can of gas missing, as well. The coast guard's been alerted. They're joining the hunt by sea and air."

Michael continued talking to Benjamin while I went to grab the news copy.

"Ben fixed it so I'm going out with him on the chopper. You hang tight, Mama, and keep the troops entertained. Lock the front door after me."

Grabbing the unopened bag of muffins, Michael departed with a hearty "Hi, Ho Silver."

I went back into the studio to launch the morning show.

After the news I put on a Jean-Pierre Rampal recording of Mozart and Telemann. I needed some bouncy flute music to keep my eyes open. Operating on less sleep than usual for two nights running left me feeling like a zombie.

I popped open a Tab, then called Margo at six-fifteen.

"Kel, this better be good. If you're calling before seven to crow about your sex life, call me later."

"Would I be so gauche? Plug in the coffee and call me back."

"I lied. I'm on my second cup. Have they caught the twins yet?"

"Not yet. How did you know?"

"Michael called late yesterday afternoon. He was really worried about you. I hate to ask this, but is there any sign of Minx?"

"I found her last night hiding in a tree."

"Oh, Kel, I'm so relieved. I know how much she means to you. I would have come if you'd called me."

"I know, sweetie. But there was no point putting you in danger. I was freaking out enough for both of us. Wait until you hear about this." I replayed the deer story and we both had a good laugh.

Margo was quick to see beyond the humor. "I would have been scared out of my wits. Your house is so isolated."

"I've never been safer. Benjamin was a phone call away, there was an unmarked cop car parked across the bottom of my road. Michael and I talked once an hour throughout the night."

"I told you Michael was a good guy. You two really look good together. Jeff was always trying to hog the spotlight. Kel, I gotta go meet a big buck prospect for breakfast. Promise me you'll call the office as soon as you hear anything."

I played Dave Grusin's Gershwin album, followed by the classic Cleo Laine and Ray Charles recording of *Porgy and Bess*, deciding to follow it up by airing the complete London cast recording of *Cats* for Minx.

The morning wore on. I stared at the phone, willing it to ring. Emily had the good sense to keep busy at her desk.

Michael opened the studio door at eleven-thirty.

Before I could utter a word he wrapped his arms around me and kissed me in a way that made Rhett and Scarlett on the bridge look like spin the bottle.

"It's over, sweetheart. Let's haul ass. I'm so whipped I'm comatose."

"I'm not through with my shift for another half-hour. Tell me what happened!"

"Ben wants to be there. It's his collar. He's waiting for us at the Lower Deck." Michael paused on his way out of the studio. "I ran into Quincy last night. He asked when you were going parasailing. The boat's going in dry dock for an overhaul the week after Easter, so I booked you for Easter Sunday morning."

"Without asking me?"

"You'll get a rise out of it, Mama. It'll be a real blast."

The dubious look on my face made Michael change the subject very quickly. "What are we doing tonight to celebrate?"

"It's Thursday, Michael. I've got a parade committee meeting at the library at seven."

"Can't you bag it?"

"I wish I could, but it's our final meeting. Next week is Easter. Government offices, including the library, will be closed from Holy Thursday through Easter Monday. The Saturday following Easter is the parade. I've lost half my committee. I need to be sure Reverend Cal and Mr. Daniel, the only members I have left, did what they were supposed to do."

"I get the point," said Michael, his voice tinged with irritation, "you don't have to draw me a picture. Tonight is out."

"You're coanchoring the parade broadcast, why don't you come to the meeting with me?"

"Whoa, Mama. I told you before. I don't do committees. Scary stuff. Whew!" He shuddered in mock revulsion. "I'll meet you at the Lower Deck in a few minutes."

Benjamin and Michael were drinking Heineken and eating plantain chips with mango salsa when I joined them after settling Minx in Victoria's cool office.

"Same for me," I told the waitress. "And another round for my friends. This party's my treat."

"Are you trying to bribe a police officer for information?" asked Benjamin, a merry smile tugging at his lips.

"Whatever works," I quipped.

"Ben, it's your story," said Michael. "Remember, I was only along for the ride."

"We were up in the air for an hour when the chopper spotted the fishing boat adrift about two miles out," said Benjamin. "The twins ran out of gas and forgot to carry oars with them. The swells were kicking up. That boat was bucking something fierce, meh son."

Michael put his hand over mine, lightly stroking my wrist with his thumb. "Tell her the best part."

Benjamin guffawed as he swapped his empty bottle for a fresh full one. After a long, cold swig, he continued his story.

"We tell the chopper pilot to go low, low, low. We must be sure, of course, that it is really the twins in the boat and not some innocent fishermen." He winked at me, pausing for another swallow of beer. "While we hover over the sea, we radio the police boat our location. 'Ten minutes away,' says the captain. We stay low. The downdraft from the chopper rocked that poor little dinghy like it's a school yard teeter-totter. Back and forth, up and down. The twins were hanging on tight, meh son, and they weren't wearing life jackets. Finally that little boat rocked so hard it flipped them right into the ocean. You never saw such thrashing about. Those two were begging to be rescued. Jail looked mighty good to them after being dunked in the sea."

Benjamin ended the story with a hearty laugh, then added a postscript. "What goes around, comes around."

Chapter
36

THE LAST TIME I saw Mr. Daniel he was in a full-body wet suit being read his rights.

I decided it would be prudent to overlook that encounter when our paths crossed again.

"We missed you at the meeting last week," I said, trying to keep a scolding schoolmarm tone out of my voice.

"I had more important business to attend to off-island," he replied. "An educator's conference in Boston."

"I wasted an evening," I said. "You might have let me know ahead of time."

"The commissioner was unable to attend. I was sent in his place," Mr. Daniel replied with his usual lack of warmth.

"I'm pleased you could make it tonight," I said. "We'll try to keep this last meeting brief."

In response, Mr. Daniel raised his wrist to view his digital watch.

I read somewhere that Americans are compelled to

breach any conversational gap exceeding four seconds. I let this one drag out to six.

"Reverend Cal should be here very soon," I chirped. "Why don't we begin with your report. We'll finish the lineup of parade entries when he arrives."

"I feel it is incumbent on all of us to be present when final reports and preparations are made," said Mr. Daniel. He settled against the laddered chairback; adjusted his collar, jerking free a loose thread that once anchored a button to the neck of his black golf shirt; then folded his arms across his chest in stolid silence.

That was one conversational gap I wasn't going to breach even if the building caught on fire.

I busied myself with the parade lineup. Despite an afternoon nap, I was exhausted and wanted to hurry home for at least eight hours of sleep.

"Follow me, and I will make you fishers of men," Reverend Cal said airily as he bustled through the open double doors, appearing much the same as he had the previous day at the garage.

If looks could kill, Mr. Daniel would have turned Reverend Cal to stone or a pillar of salt on the spot.

"Beware of false prophets, which come to you in sheep's clothing, but inwardly they are ravening wolves," Mr. Daniel muttered, his glacial stare unwavering.

"Gentlemen, I believe Bible class meets on Tuesday," I said, rapping on the table to call the meeting to order. "Cal, you're late. Let's get down to business so we can get out of here. Where's your donor list?"

Reverend Cal fumbled through his papers. "I must have left it at home. I'll get it to you tomorrow."

"Don't forget. I need to get the program copy to the printer ASAP. You're the one holding me up."

I turned to Mr. Daniel. "Cal said he turned the donations over to you last week. Is that correct?"

"Yes, and they have already been put to good use," Mr. Daniel replied. "The children were most appreciative."

"Good. Then let's move on to the last order of business," I said, handing each man a list of the registered parade entries. "By the way, special places have been reserved for each of you on the Government House reviewing stand. Please try to be seated before the governor arrives at ten forty-five. We want the parade to begin at eleven sharp."

We completed the parade lineup in under an hour.

Every St. Chris parade is spearheaded by a freshly washed police car, light bar flashing, siren on mute. Then comes the color guard bearing the St. Chris flag, accompanied by a drum and bugle corps. After that, Miss Lucinda in her role as the Navidad de Isabeya grand marshal, wearing a frilly hat and waving from the wrist like the queen mother, would be paraded down the street in an open convertible.

Then the good stuff. We alternated school floats with steel band entries, interspersed with troupes of drum majorettes, followed by adult floupes. The mocko jumbies—gaily dressed dancing figures on stilts, a highlight of every St. Chris parade—would strut and weave through the parade at their own pace.

Michael would be anchoring his part of the parade broadcast from the Government House reviewing stand, while I did my broadcast on foot, roaming the length of the parade route from the Anglican church down Kongens Gade past Government House to the fort. That way I'd be able to keep an eye on the entire parade and hopefully spot any disasters in the making.

Michael's main duty was to keep a running tally of the road march competition, noting which song was being played whenever a band passed the reviewing stand. The composer of the song performed by the most live steel bands, reggae or calypso groups in the parade—canned music didn't count—would win a trophy. Competition for this award was always fierce. Rumors of bribes abounded. I remembered the year "Fire, Fire" won. I couldn't get that song out of my head for weeks.

We saved Maubi's band and the Quadrille dancers for the final entry. They were a particular crowd pleaser, stopping often to perform intricately patterned old-world dance routines to continual applause.

Barring any unforeseen calamities like drivers tossing truck keys down sewer gratings, the parade would run for about two hours. After the Quadrille dancers reached the fort, awards would be presented from the reviewing stand to be erected two days before the parade, further cutting down available town parking.

Every bar and restaurant in Isabeya was stocking up for Navidad de Isabeya parade day. Paradegoers usually arrived in town early in the morning to get a good parking place and bar hop before the parade began.

The church ladies would set up their card tables on both sides of Kongens Gade to sell home-baked cakes and pastries; food vendors would be hawking iced beer and hot dogs. Every restaurant would have a special for the day, many would erect sidewalk grills to serve hamburgers on the spot. Maubi's wife would be working the Hot To Trot van, earning more in one day than he made in a slow season month. Isabeya would be one big block party from dawn to dark.

While Mr. Daniel and I gathered our papers, preparing to depart, Reverend Cal handed each of us a flier promoting an Easter morning service at Columbus Bay.

"I will be camping at Columbus Bay Easter weekend," said Mr. Daniel, dropping his flier on the table. "But I will be assisting in the celebration of this most holy day at my own church where I have been a deacon for the past twelve years."

Reverend Cal turned to me.

"I've already made plans," I said, handing back the flier without visible regret. "I have reservations to go parasailing. A belated birthday gift."

"Be sure your sin will find you out," Reverend Cal said piously.

"Judge not lest ye be judged," I snapped.

For once Reverend Cal didn't have a rebuttal.

Chapter
37

MINX BOLTED OUTSIDE immediately after breakfast Friday morning to escape spending a second day confined to her carrier.

I arrived at the station to find Michael in rare form. He was wearing a new flowered shirt, this one with a puce background, and sporting a bright green baseball cap with gold lamé wings puffing out from each side. He looked like a tropical version of Mercury. Or a rogue FTD messenger.

"Morning, Michael. You look like a Polynesian outcast from Olympus." I couldn't hide my smile.

He grinned back at me. "Knew you'd like it, Mama. Where's the feline?"

"She thinks she's too pretty for radio. Now she wants to be on television. The announcers dress better."

"You're mean, Mama." Michael pulled me onto his lap as I tried to pass him to pick up the news copy.

"Let's work on the good morning part again," he said, planting a long slow kiss on my mouth.

"An afternoon nap perks you right up," I commented.

"Nice euphemism," he retorted.

I swung off his lap. He caught my hand to keep me from leaving. "What are we doing tonight?"

"I've got a date with Margo at six for our weekly turtle walk," I replied with a regretful shrug. "But we have Posh Nosh reservations for tomorrow night, remember?"

"Tomorrow night's a long way off."

I thought I detected a peevish undertone to his voice.

"Michael, don't pull the pouting bit, it makes me crazy. When Pete did that I wanted to scream."

"Don't compare me with that asshole," he snapped.

"Your point," I said. "That wasn't fair."

"It wasn't kosher of me to give you crap. Truce?"

"Truce." We did a nice take on a kiss and makeup scene, but I could tell he was still miffed.

"Tell you what," he said, "I'll call you at home when I get up. If you feel like it, stop here on your way home after the turtle walk. Or I'll buy you breakfast in the morning if you're up that early." Michael left the station, being very careful not to slam the front door on his way out.

I stewed over Michael's attitude during lunch with Margo at the Watering Hole round table.

"I don't get it, Margo," I said, shaking my head. "I really don't understand."

"Men, Kel," she replied. "It's still the same old bull. They want what they want when they want it. Michael wants you. He's jealous of your other activities." She patted my hand. "It's a male power thing. He'll get over it. Get on with your life."

"I suppose you're right," I said, signaling our waitress for a refill on my iced tea.

"You know I'm right," said Margo. "Kel, you've been out of circulation for a long time. You went through a social drought after the divorce from Pete before you met

Jeff. Now Michael's in the picture. He may be a prince, but he's still a man. Don't be stupid."

"What?" I stared at my best friend.

"Don't be a doormat. Stay your own person. Men haven't changed since they walked out of the cave. They still want their own way all the time and they pout when they don't get it. They also want what they can't have, so don't be so available. Make him work. Let him miss you a little."

"I'm running late," said Abby, sliding into a chair next to Margo. "Long morning in court at the Ramirez twins' arraignment. Kel, I'll tell you about that later. What's this I hear about Jerry?"

I looked at Margo. "What did I miss?"

"Jerry logged the first turtle last night," said Margo.

"You're putting me on," I said.

"How did he ever pull it off?" asked Abby.

"With his usual dumb luck," said Margo. "He fell asleep on the beach, the turtle started digging a nest and woke Jerry by flipping sand in his face."

"Are you sure that report wasn't Jerry's idea of an April Fool's joke?" said Abby with a broad grin.

"For crapping out on the beach he wins a bottle of Perrier-Jouët?" I said.

"Those are the rules, Kel. The first one to log a turtle wins." A smirk appeared on Margo's face. "But we get to help him drink it."

"I'm taking my lunch up to the office," said Abby, rising with a foam take-out carton in her hand. "Kel, come on up when you're finished."

Abby pulled the frilly topped toothpick out of a triangular wedge of her club sandwich. "Forgive me if I eat while we talk. I didn't have time for breakfast. I'm famished."

"I wonder what the twins are eating?"

"Crow," said Abby, pausing to sip her iced coffee. "But not on toast."

"How did this morning work out?" My fingers gripped the ends of the chair arms.

"Better than I hoped. No bail because they pose a flight risk. They're being held separately. For whatever that's worth. They're probably plotting something by Morse code or mental telepathy even as we speak. But they turned eighteen a few weeks ago, so they'll be tried as adults. You can stop worrying on that score, Kel."

I ran around the desk to hug Abby. "Thank you. I'll sleep well tonight."

"Not before ten if the rumors I've been hearing are true." Abby smiled. "Michael's a nice guy. I'm happy for you."

My response was a broad grin.

"You'd better sit down again, because there's more." Abby stopped eating her sandwich to give me her full attention. "The twins admitted they were paid to harass you. But they say they don't know by whom. They claim a blank envelope was slipped into their car late last Friday night while they were limin' around town. Inside the envelope was two hundred dollars in cash, mostly tens and twenties, and an anonymous message, 'Give that trouble-making bitch Kelly Ryan a taste of her own medicine' typed on an index card."

My hand flew to my mouth.

Abby nodded. "It's a match. The same typewriter with the broken *e* that was used to type the card on the box of Island Delights you received that Friday morning. But it doesn't prove that it was the same card the twins claim they received. I don't know why they kept it. I never said they were rocket scientists. Hell, they could have typed the card themselves as an alibi for their reprehensible actions. They're not ones to take responsibility for anything they do. There were no prints on the card and envelope but their own. Kel, we'll try to find the typewriter, but I don't think we're going to have much luck. This is a small island, but it would take a house-to-house search and the police don't have the time or resources."

"What do we do now?" I asked.

"You go home and get some sleep," said Abby. "I'll handle the Ramirez twins. I promise they won't bother you again. With the case against them for stealing the fisherman's boat, not to mention the previous charges of reckless endangerment and harassment, they'll be cooling their heels for a long time."

Abby leaned toward me. "Kel, I've got to tell you something else. Something you might not want to hear. I don't think Pete or Angie were involved in setting the twins on you, and I'm not saying this because we're all friends. I've got a sneaky suspicion that someone else was the instigator, but I have no idea who or why. Please continue to be very careful and don't let your guard down."

Before I left Abby's office I had a final question, one that had nothing to do with her work, about a comment she'd made on Tuesday. Her one-word response gave me plenty to think about.

Chapter

38

I WOKE FROM a brief nap a few minutes after four, feeling groggy, grumpy and generally out of sorts.

My mood didn't improve when my purse fell to the floor, spewing its contents. I scrambled across the terrazzo on my hands and knees gathering the jetsam of my life.

Minx thought it was great fun to bat my strawberry-flavored lip balm around the floor like a hockey puck, ultimately scoring a goal under my wicker living room couch.

Get your act together, I growled mentally while picking up keys, pens, checkbook, old grocery receipts, loose change, wallet and a tattered paperback of Agatha Christie's *Evil Under the Sun* which I hauled around to reread in spare moments.

Wedged in the pages of the book was a small Dockside notepad, the top page creased and grimy.

I stared at the notepad, wondering how and when it had gotten into my purse. Of course. I'd taken it from Zena's bedside table the first night I explored her room. The impressions on the top page stood out against the dirt-speckled background like pale scars on a tanned arm.

I poured a glass of iced sun tea, flavored with spearmint breath mints, from the two-quart clear plastic pitcher that occupied a permanent spot on the top shelf of my refrigerator, then walked out to the gallery to scrutinize the notepad in the direct light of the late-afternoon sun.

It was like trying to read the sand-scoured ancient Egyptian hieroglyphics on the walls of the open-air temple on the Nile at Kom Ombo.

I turned the notepad to the horizontal to gain a fresh perspective.

The impressions weren't made by words, but by a drawing.

I ran to the phone to call Victoria.

"Vic, it's Kelly. Is Zena's room still unoccupied? Oh? When are they arriving? That flight lands about now. Don't let anyone inside the room until I get there. See you in twenty minutes."

Victoria sat with her legs properly crossed at the ankles on the edge of the freshly made bed in Zena's former room. She watched intently while I fiddled with the base of the free-standing armoire.

A section of wood came loose in my hands. On the carpeted floor, shoved against the back wall, was a flat metal box. The box was locked but opened easily with the tiny brass key Victoria still wore on a chain around her neck.

Victoria's photocopy machine hummed in the background while we stood in her office. The metal box lay open on her desk.

"I think that's the last of it, Kelly. We'll put the originals back in the box and I'll store it in my private safe. By rights the box should go to Catherine."

"But not until we've studied the contents," I said with a smile. "Vic, I've got to run. I promised to meet Margo at six at Leatherback Bay and I'm running late."

"My hotel guests will also be arriving by taxi at any moment. Here are your copies." Victoria handed me a legal-sized manilla envelope. "We'll talk again tomorrow. Come by for elevenses if you're in town."

Margo and I were sitting on the point, getting ready to make our first patrol of the beach. The sun had set moments earlier behind a large, dark cloud bank, the early evening air felt damp and chilly. I wished I'd brought a sweatshirt and worn long pants.

"What do you think is in those papers?" asked Margo.

"I don't know. I haven't read them yet," I said. "But they probably explain what Zena was doing here and may tell us why she was killed." I shivered in the rising trade winds, watching waves pound the beach in quick succession. "Did you happen to check the marine weather forecast before you left home?"

"I was out with that megabuck prospect I had breakfast with yesterday and didn't have time. Why?"

I licked my index finger and held it aloft to test the wind, then sniffed the air. "There's a front moving in. I think it's going to start pouring buckets any second now. I vote we get out of here and go to my house. We've got some reading to do."

We sat snugly inside while the rain pounded against my red tin roof, flowing into the gutters, gurgling through the downspouts, gushing into my cistern. Life on an island without a fresh water supply means we're dependent on Mother Nature for every drop of drinking water. A good rain is always a blessing.

My living room was awash in paper. The photocopies Victoria had made earlier were scattered on the floor along with Caribbean history books, Spanish and Italian dictionaries and an open world atlas. My bookshelves looked like they'd been ransacked by marauders.

Minx dozed in her favorite spot, curled against the pillows on my bed, the tip of her striped tail draped across her pepper-freckled pink nose like a blanket.

Margo flopped against the pillows on my couch, her arm flung over her eyes. "Kel," she mumbled, "are you still awake?"

I marked my place in the Caribbean history book I was skimming. "Barely. My eyes are about to bug out. I'm hosting a memorial service for my brain." I glanced over my shoulder at my antique schoolhouse wall clock. "It's almost eleven-thirty. Do you want to spend the night?"

"No, I'd better go when the rain lets up. If your damned phone hadn't gone out, I'd call Paul and camp out here. But if I don't show up at home fairly soon he'll think I've been in an accident. I don't want him to worry." She pulled herself to a sitting position, rubbed her eyes and yawned broadly like Leo, the MGM lion. "Is there any coffee left?"

"I'll make a fresh pot." I left the open book on the arm of my chair and walked barefoot across the cool terrazzo floor to the kitchen. "Do you want a slug of brandy to go with it?"

"Got any Baileys?"

"Coming right up. I've got a fresh bottle in the refrigerator."

We moved to the bar stools at the tile-topped island in my kitchen.

"Zena was certifiably crazy," I said.

Margo nodded in agreement. "Completely bonkers."

I sipped my Baileys. "I remember reading a book about a man who faked a solo sailing trip around the world by hanging out in the Atlantic away from the shipping lanes and radioing false course positions. What was his name? Donald something."

"What prompted him to do such a fool thing?"

"A race. It was a race and the first prize was quite substantial. The poor bastard was declared the winner. The race committee was eagerly expecting him to sail back into port the next day and collect his prize. But he never showed."

"What happened to him?"

"No one knows," I said. "His empty boat was found adrift. He vanished without a trace."

"Do you suppose Zena read the same book?"

"It wouldn't surprise me," I said. "What does surprise me is that Zena thought anyone would take her cockeyed views seriously."

"Kel, I can't imagine what she hoped to gain."

"Notoriety, for starters. Her fifteen minutes of fame. Geraldo would have eaten her up with a spoon." I topped off our small stemmed liquor glasses.

A devilish gleam appeared in Margo's eyes. "Imagine Zena's face on the cover of *People* magazine."

"More likely the *National Enquirer*," I retorted. "Right next to another story about an alien baby."

"Kel, think of what would have happened on parade day if she'd gone through with her original plan."

"I can picture it now," I said.

Margo added, "Can you imagine the reaction when Zena announced her theory from the reviewing stand while she presented her historical award?"

"Everyone on St. Chris would have wanted to kill her."

Chapter

39

MICHAEL AND I were finishing an early Saturday sit-down breakfast in a booth at McDonald's. We were the first customers of the day.

"I could crash at your place," he said.

"I'm going to be in and out all morning," I replied. "You wouldn't get much sleep."

"Sleep isn't necessarily what I had in mind," he retorted with a leer.

"Hold the thought, Michael. Tomorrow is another day."

"I think I've heard that line before, Scarlett. What's on your dance card this morning?"

"The usual Saturday morning chores and errands. Grocery shopping, taking trash to the dump, picking up the mail. Then I want to stop at Dockside for elevenses with Victoria. She's not going to believe what I found in Zena's notes."

"What are you going to do with the box?"

"Vic said she'll ship it back to Catherine, Zena's daughter. If I were Kit, I'd burn the contents on the spot. It won't do her academic reputation any good to disseminate her mother's shoddy scholarship."

"Mama, you sound like a lockjawed pedant."

I balled my used napkin and threw it at him. "Let's go. You need some sleep. You're getting testy. If you're awake by one, come over. We'll spend the afternoon at the beach. Bring your snorkel gear."

The rain ended before dawn, leaving behind a clear blue sky and morning air smelling fresh and clean. The hillsides were lush and green. The yellow trumpet blossomed Ginger Thomas, the official St. Chris flower, was beginning to bloom and soon the orange-red blossoms of the tulip trees would be in full flower against dark green leaves. The sweet scent of purple, scarlet and white frangipani now wafted through my gallery screens. By May St. Chris would be ablaze with orange and red flamboyant.

I walked from McDonald's over to the supermarket where I'd parked my car as close to the front door as I could get, conscientiously avoiding the handicapped spaces with their one-thousand-dollar parking tickets.

When the supermarket doors slid open at seven, I was ready for action. With my grocery list in hand, I snagged a cart and prepared to join the Saturday morning early bird shoppers in supermarket roulette.

Living in a place where almost everything is brought in by boat or plane makes shopping for specific favorites a game of chance. Most of us adopt a bunker mentality, stocking up and hoarding nonperishables. I don't feel comfortable unless I have at least four cases of Tab stashed in my pantry to ward off impending Tab famines.

I began my shopping in the produce section and was looking for my favorite bleu cheese salad dressing in a screw-top jar when I heard the crash of shattering glass one aisle over in bottled juices.

A woman yelled, "You mess wit' my man and I cut you

for sure," followed by a second high-pitched female voice screaming, "She gonna kill me."

A lanky woman in her mid-twenties, dressed in cutoff jean shorts and a paint store giveaway T-shirt cut at the neck into a V and cropped to her midriff, flew around the corner heading straight for me waving a two-foot-long machete over her head. The newly sharpened edge glittered in the overhead fluorescent light.

"Where dat bitch go?"

I ducked for cover behind the lettuce bin.

The store manager ran for the security of the glass-enclosed office at the front of the store. Shoppers abandoned their half-filled carts in the aisles to flee the store or hide behind displays.

I heard a pyramid of cans destruct in a low rumble like an avalanche, followed by a crash and the clattering sound of large tins rolling across the linoleum floor like bowling balls.

The two women ran shrieking up and down the aisles, knocking over displays, crashing metal shopping carts into fully stocked shelves. Three aisles over, a baby wailed.

Two police cars with screaming sirens screeched to a tire-burning stop at the store entrance.

In minutes the subdued women were slumped behind the grilles on the backseats of separate police vehicles.

The store manager mopped his brow, straightened his tie and walked out of the office with as much bravado as he could muster.

"Are you finding everything you need today?" he asked me.

I giggled as I replied, "I must have overlooked live entertainment on your list of weekly specials."

He smiled wanly and went to soothe the remaining shoppers.

I finished my biweekly shopping, breezing through the checkout line in far less time than usual. The clerk was still laughing so hard she scattered my change on the floor.

On the way home I passed the baseball field on the eastern edge of Isabeya where tables were being set up for a flea market fund-raiser. Benjamin was helping another man hang a banner reading "The Team Needs Your Green" on the cyclone fence. I parked my car, nimbly dodging traffic to cross the busy east end road, and approached the tables to bargain hunt.

I ignored boxes of mismatched kitchenware, children's clothes and used toys to concentrate on paperback books.

"Kelly, come over here. I'll give you a sneak peak at the good stuff," said Benjamin, motioning me to a table at the end of the row. "Some of these things are practically new."

"Where did all this come from?" I asked.

We don't have basements or attics in our houses so storage space is always at a premium. What doesn't rust or rot in the humid salt-laced air is often tossed or tiefed.

"Donations," said Benjamin. "We set up boxes at the Anglican church. We've been collecting since Christmas."

I looked through the assortment of small kitchen appliances. A compact electric juice extractor in its original box with the price sticker still attached caught my eye.

"I had an eye for that myself. That came to us late last week."

I examined the juicer carefully. It would fit nicely on my kitchen counter. Although it looked brand new on the outside, the interior was discolored and stained.

"How much?" I asked.

"For you? A bargain for true. Give me ten dollars."

I handed Benjamin a ten-dollar bill but left the box in his outstretched hands.

"You pay for the item, but you don't want to go with it?"

I leaned across the table to whisper in Benjamin's ear. His eyes grew wide. He nodded several times, then walked to the parking area to lock the box in the trunk of his car.

Chapter
40

MICHAEL WAS HAVING a drink with Margo and Paul at the Lower Deck when I arrived at Dockside a few minutes before eleven.

"Hi guys, fancy meeting you here," I said, pulling up a chair next to Michael. He leaned over to give me a quick kiss.

"Kel, did you hear?" said Margo. "A woman was shot to death by a jealous lover at the supermarket this morning."

"No kidding," I said, flagging the waitress to order a drink. "What happened?"

Margo launched into a salacious tale of a love triangle gone wrong that only the St. Chris rumor mill could have fabricated.

"She died right there in frozen foods? I don't believe it." I kept a straight face while stirring my Bloody Mary with a crisp celery stalk. "Sweetie, I was at the market. Wait until I tell you what really went on. There was a woman with a machete—"

Victoria came flying down the outside steps from her second-floor office.

"Kelly! I heard you were shot at while shopping at the market this morning. Are you all right?"

Four people convulsed with laughter.

Victoria ordered a fresh round of drinks while I finished recounting the true story of the morning's events.

"Did you have a chance to read the papers we found?" Victoria asked.

Margo and I took turns relating what we'd discovered.

"That poor, poor deluded woman," said Victoria, clucking sympathetically. "I regret the times I was rude to her."

"Vic. Don't waste your pity. She wasn't worth it," I said. "She came here with malicious intent to destroy this island. She wanted to make fools of all of us."

"But in the end she only made a fool of herself," replied Victoria. "I still feel sorry for her. She must have been very lonely."

"Did she have any kind of social life?" I asked. "What did she do every night?"

"For the first month or so she ordered room service or ate by herself at the Lower Deck, went for walks along the boardwalk, then retired to her room with a tin of Island Delights. After she joined the parade committee she socialized more often."

"With anyone special?"

"I wasn't keeping a strict tally, but I do recall seeing her with Reverend Stowe on at least one occasion. There was, of course, the evening she had an argument with Mr. Daniel."

I held my glass in midair, halfway to my mouth. "Do tell, Vic! I hadn't heard about this. What were they arguing about?"

"I haven't a clue. I was upstairs and couldn't hear what was being said," Victoria replied. "Mr. Daniel was having a snack at the Lower Deck. Zena—one really can't call her Dr. Sheffield any longer, can one?—was sitting by herself, busily writing in a notebook like the ones we found yesterday. Mr. Daniel went over to speak to her, and seconds later a row ensued. He went back to his table, threw down some money and left immediately. Zena watched him go with a very smug smile on her face."

"I wish I'd been a chameleon on the wall for that little scene," I said. "When did this take place?"

"The evening before Stamp Day. I remember it well because a short time later it began to rain and some people left the Lower Deck without paying their checks. I wondered at the time if the rain would affect the next day's festivities at Columbus Bay."

The evening before Stamp Day was the night after the disastrous meeting of the parade committee. Zena's last hurrah.

"I must prepare for my luncheon guests. Your drinks are on the house." Victoria rose to go back to her office. "I noticed you all have reservations upstairs tonight. May I seat you at a table for four? We're booked to capacity because of the pre-Easter Jump-Up."

Margo and Paul decided to join Michael and me for an afternoon at the beach. A noteworthy event for all of us.

When I moved to St. Chris I thought I'd be eating fresh seafood every night and spending every weekend at the beach. Neither fantasy proved true. The lobsters were flown in from Maine; locally caught fish were occasionally tainted with ciguatera, a form of fish poisoning; and some weekends it rained.

We stopped at Soup to Nuts, a gourmet deli on the east end of town across from the ballpark and one of my biggest advertisers, for a take-out picnic.

The flea market fund-raiser was still going on, but the tables were mostly picked over. I looked for Benjamin's car, but it was no longer in sight.

After a quick detour to my house to change into our

swimsuits and fill a cooler with ice and drinks, we drove to the beach.

We had the cove to ourselves. After lunching on thick deli sandwiches with all the trimmings, we swam and snorkeled in the clear tepid ocean. I spotted a school of my favorite tiny electric blue-and-yellow-striped fish clustered around a clump of coral. I hovered on the surface, like Gulliver observing the Lilliputians, watching the fish dart between the sea grasses.

Michael and Paul snorkeled toward the reef while Margo and I paddled back to shore.

"It doesn't get much better than this, does it, Kel?" said Margo, rummaging in the cooler for a snack and a cold drink. We sat in the shade of the palm trees, using plastic forks to finish the potato salad we bought at Soup to Nuts.

"What do you know about Mr. Daniel or Reverend Cal? I never spent much time with either of them before chairing the parade committee." I lay back on my towel, pulling my visor over my eyes to shield them from the sun.

"I don't know much about Mr. Daniel, except he likes to see his name in the paper. He's always writing long-winded letters to the editor. They're usually about trying to get Columbus Bay declared a national historic district and sticking the feds with the tab for upkeep. Anything to get his name in print and pump up his ego. The man has a mania for blatant self-promotion."

"Right." I sat up in order to think more clearly. "I remember he was also on a kick to have the marina condemned by the local government and all boat traffic banned in the bay. Fat chance. Columbus Bay is the only hurricane hole we've got. I signed a petition against that one."

"Reverend Cal is another story. He makes my teeth ache," said Margo. "He's like a mosquito you can't get rid of, always buzzing in your ear. He's constantly in our office hitting us up for donations for one cause or another.

Last time it was for school floats for the Navidad de Isabeya parade."

"Oops. Mea culpa. That was my doing. I told him to call the chamber of commerce."

"Kel, get real. Who do you think funds the chamber? I'll give you a hint: it's not the tooth fairy."

"Sorry, sweetie. I told him to get material donations like lumber and chickenwire, not cash. How big a bite did he put on you?"

"I think we got off for twenty bucks total. And a Bible verse in lieu of a receipt. That's what frosts my cookie. He never gives receipts and he never has change, but he's always got a quote."

Paul and Michael sloshed through the shallows to the beach, bragging about the size of the barracuda—"the damned thing was as big as a house and it tried to eat us"—they saw hanging around the reef. We finished the food we'd bought—"Who ate all the potato salad?"— dumped the water from the cooler around the trunk of a thirsty palm tree and headed back to my place.

There was a cryptic message from Benjamin waiting on my answering machine.

"Kelly, call me. I'll be at home until seven."

Margo and Paul went home to Sea Breezes to change for dinner. Michael headed west to his own place to shower.

I quickly fed Minx, then called Benjamin.

"Your hunch this morning about the juicer proved absolutely correct," he said. "How did you know?"

I had to be honest with him. "It was a lucky guess."

"I called the hardware store where it was purchased. They sold out of that particular model the end of February and are presently awaiting a next shipment. The manager is going to check his sales records, but I don't hold out much hope. Some stores are very lax in their accountings."

"At least we're on the right track," I said.

"True," replied Benjamin. "Where are you going to be this evening?"

"Michael and I are having dinner with friends at Posh Nosh at eight."

"A fortunate coincidence. My wife and I will also be dining there this evening to celebrate her birthday. Let us briefly continue our discussion then."

I showered, then stood staring at my closet, fluff-drying my short hair with my fingers, trying to decide what to wear.

The formal-length black I'd worn to Mrs. H's bon voyage party was too dressy; jeans and a top were strictly Lower Deck and far too casual for Posh Nosh. It was difficult to drive in high-heeled shoes, but flip-flops wouldn't do. Decisions, decisions.

I settled for a sleeveless jade silk tank top to cover my blotched, peeling back. True to Margo's prediction I blistered and peeled to baby skin; my back still looked very ugly. I hoped the blisters wouldn't leave permanent marks. I dug through my shoe bin for a pair of jade thong sandals to match the top. A blue-and-green print cotton sarong wrapped and tied at my waist made an ankle-length skirt with an easy walking side slit.

From the floor safe in my closet I layered Burmese jade and gold bracelets on my arm and chose a simple pair of jade drop earrings and a plain gold link necklace. I was ready to roll.

St. Chris is very laid-back and provincial. It's a big deal that the supermarket stays open past five P.M. during the week and is open a half day on Sunday; everything else shuts down tight at night and on Sunday, except for the Isabeya pharmacy, open from nine A.M. 'til noon to accommodate readers of Sunday papers. During the slow summer season the Isabeya merchants take half-day holidays on Thursday and Saturday afternoons.

Jump-Up is an exception. Every shop in Isabeya was

brightly lit and filled with browsing customers. I heard the strains of a steel band coming from the small gazebo on the waterfront green next to Fort Frederick, and saw the brightly costumed mocko jumbies parading on their stilts through the town streets to the delight of squealing children. The smell of meat pates, fried chicken and johnnycakes coming from the food carts made my mouth water.

I circled the block around Government House three times looking for a parking place, finally settling for a "five minutes only for postal patrons" spot across from the post office, a block away from Maubi's van. The post office was shuttered for the weekend, I hoped that would count in my favor if the police were writing tickets.

"Morning Lady, look at you!" Maubi whistled in approval. "Looking good. You out for an evening with the man?"

"We're having dinner. Have you seen him?"

"He hasn't passed yet. Where you parked?"

"At the post office." I grimaced. "In the five-minute zone. Why?"

"I got something for you, to keep your house safe from jumbies." He called to Quincy, "Walk with Morning Lady back to her car and take this box with you." He handed Quincy an open case of Heineken, while saying to me, "When you come back I tell you what to do with the empty bottles. I already scrub them clean and soak off the labels."

I couldn't wait to hear what Maubi had to say. Along with the family Bible from Ireland, his ancestor had given his descendants the fabled gift of gab bestowed by the Blarney Stone.

"Jumbies be frightened of two things," said Maubi in all seriousness, "salt and green glass. You hang some green glass in your yard and I guarantee they won't trouble you ever again."

"Green glass? You can't be serious."

He smiled. "Trust me, Morning Lady. I born here and

I know so. Green glass wards off jumbies, I'm telling you for true."

I thanked him for the gift.

"I keep watch on your car so no one mess with you like before," Maubi added. "It sure is pleasant with the twins put away. People glad to come to town tonight. Jump-Up is good for my business."

"And I must be about my Father's business," said Reverend Cal, emerging from the shadows. "But I thirst. As Coleridge penned: 'Water, water everywhere nor any drop to drink.' May I prevail upon you, good sir?"

Wordlessly Maubi handed Reverend Cal a small paper cup half filled with tepid water but no ice.

Reverend Cal's hands were free of bandages. The palms and hairless backs looked like mottled baby skin.

"It appears your prayers were answered," I remarked. "By the way, I'm still waiting for your donor report."

Reverend Cal avoided my gaze, pretending he hadn't heard me, melting into the crowd of passengers disembarking from a taxi van.

"That vicar vex me," said Maubi. "He too cheap to pay, but not too proud to ask."

"He does this often?"

"Every night. Every night he spout the same stupidness. Maybe he get a pulpit one time, he be a preacher for true."

The Harley rumbled beside me.

"Mama, you are a vision." Michael patted the seat behind him. "Hop on."

I sat sidesaddle with my arm around Michael's waist. We waved to Maubi, slowly making our way through the throngs of revelers to Dockside.

Margo and Paul arrived as Michael and I were waiting in line for Victoria to show us to our table. Margo looked elegant in a simple black, sleeveless A-line dress and Audrey Hepburn-type midheel black sling-back sandals. Her long sun-streaked blond hair was done up in a neat Grace

Kelly French twist. We casually eyed the other's jewelry and smiled. Margo had gone the less-is-more route, with bezel-set diamond studs and a diamond tennis bracelet worn next to her gold Rolex watch.

The men were dressed in slacks, open-collared long-sleeved shirts and polished loafers with no socks. In St. Chris a man wears a jacket and tie on three occasions: going to court, getting married or going to a church funeral. The rest of the time they get as much use as my winter coat.

Benjamin and his wife were already seated at a table for four. I excused myself to talk to Benjamin.

"Kelly, have you met my wife? Camille, this is Kelly. Camille is the assistant principal at the high school. She works with Miss Maude's granddaughter, Amelia, the school principal. Kelly is a friend of Miss Maude's."

"It is a real pleasure to meet you," I said, clasping the slim, cool hand Camille extended to me. "Many happy returns."

"Thank you. It's also nice to meet you at last. Benjamin speaks quite highly of you. I enjoy listening to you in the morning," Camille said warmly. "I trust you've recovered from your ordeal of the other evening."

"Thanks to Benjamin and his officers," I replied with a smile. "Enjoy your birthday celebration."

"I see our guests," Benjamin said to his wife. "I'll show them to our table."

Benjamin spoke quietly in my ear as we walked back to the reception area.

"There has been an unfortunate development since we spoke earlier. Please keep this to yourself for now. We will talk more tomorrow. I was informed that last weekend Catherine Sheffield was the victim of a hit-and-run driver. She died this afternoon without regaining consciousness."

"Where did this happen?" I asked. "New York?"

"Catherine Sheffield was in Boston settling her late mother's affairs."

Chapter
41

MY LIVING ROOM was a disaster area verging on condemnation.

Amidst a sea of paper, coffee cups, drink glasses, and snack plates, Michael, Benjamin and I tried to make sense of the life and death of Zena Sheffield.

Miss Maude arrived, backing her Land Rover snugly next to Benjamin's Blazer in my limited parking area. When Miss Maude entered the house Minx jumped from the bed, sprinting and sliding across the terrazzo to rub her face against Miss Maude's tennis shoes.

"I was working in my garden this morning," Miss Maude explained. "Tending the catnip plants. I've brought you some cuttings for drying." She bent to scratch Minx's head. "What a sweet little cat. As lovely as you described her."

Minx purred shamelessly, following Miss Maude to the couch to climb on her lap, where she began kneading Miss Maude's thigh with her front paws.

Miss Maude looked around the room. "You have made

a charming home out of a ruin. I remember the days when this was the only school on the east end. It closed during the depression when sugarcane ceased to be a viable cash crop and the few children still living out here were sent to school in town. Those were hard times; this island was sadly referred to as the 'poorhouse of the Caribbean.' We had no tourists or outside industry then, only a few beleaguered souls seeking a climate to cure tuberculosis, and some poor lepers seeking refuge from their scandalized families in our asylum. History is not all glory and triumph, or parades."

Michael carried the dirty dishes to the kitchen. He began brewing a fresh pot of coffee.

"Mama, run Zena's theory past me again. Miss Maude hasn't heard it yet."

"Here's the bottom line," I said. "Zena concluded that Columbus never landed here on his second voyage. Therefore, the history of St. Chris is founded on myth."

"Have you ever heard such foolishness!" exclaimed Benjamin. "That woman was crazy for true. How did she come to believe that stupidness?"

"Her reasoning was convoluted." I grabbed the atlas and Zena's notes. "It's sort of like the dog that didn't bark."

"Ah, Sherlock Holmes," said Miss Maude. "Holmes was once able to solve a case because of something that didn't happen. Very clever."

Benjamin nodded. "Good reverse psychology."

"Please continue, Kelly." Miss Maude sipped her coffee, her attention focused upon me as if I were one of her former students delivering a social studies report in front of the class.

"Zena's theory was based on three main points." I counted them on my fingers. "One, the journal of his second voyage was lost. Two, the longitude problem had not yet been solved. Three, the inaccuracies in translations of handwritten documents."

"We know Columbus returned to St. Chris in 1502 on his fourth and last voyage," said Miss Maude. "That has been well documented, as was the earlier visit in 1493."

"Zena discounted the 1502 return as well. Also on the premise of a missing journal from the fourth voyage."

"There are maps based on his accounts and those of the men who sailed with him," said Miss Maude. "My dear departed father was an avid collector of maps. You recall he worked on the mapping project of St. Chris, cataloging the botanical species for the Danish King. In my home is one of my father's most cherished maps. A very fine copy of a map prepared after the second voyage by one of Columbus's shipmates, a highly esteemed cartographer named Juan de la Cosa. It very clearly shows St. Chris. How did Zena get around that?"

"The longitude problem," I replied.

"Ah," said Miss Maude, a smile playing on her lips. "Do explain."

"Zena believed Columbus was a lousy navigator and his journals were full of inaccuracies. Since a reliable method of determining exact longitude was not developed until the mid-1700s . . ."

"The famous navigational clock invented by John Harrison of England," added Miss Maude.

". . . Columbus could have been anywhere east or west of here. She cites his latitude error regarding Iceland in a letter Columbus supposedly wrote to his son Fernando, describing a purported voyage to Iceland in 1477, as proof that most of the time Columbus didn't know where in the hell he was. East, west, north or south."

"An interesting point," said Miss Maude. "However, given that the maps made after his voyages show the islands in relative proportion and distance from each other with distinguishing features like the prominent bay and harbor of our own island, I don't suppose it matters that he may have been off a few degrees."

She smiled at Michael, handing him her empty coffee cup for a refill. "After all, Columbus did think he'd found a new route to Asia."

"If Columbus wasn't cruising around this neighborhood in 1493, then where did Zena think he was?" asked Michael. "I'm still not clear on that."

"She thought he was limin' back in the Bahamas," I said. "She claims the journal was lost on purpose, then a few maps were drawn up with imaginary islands sketched in to impress the Spanish monarchs, any resemblance to actual land masses being mere coincidence. She says the second voyage was mostly an act enhanced with smoke and mirrors."

"Stupidness for true," said Benjamin.

"That sounds like *The Strange Last Voyage of Donald Crowhurst*, a book about the guy who faked his trip around the world by hiding out in the Atlantic," said Michael.

"You read that one, too?" I said.

Michael winked and smiled.

The lightbulb finally went on in my brain.

"Now I know what Zena meant on Stamp Day when she shouted, 'He was never here,' " I said, barely able to contain my excitement. "At the time I thought she was referring to King Ferdinand, who was depicted on one of the stamps. I wonder who else heard her?"

"Most people were trying to avoid her," said Benjamin. "I doubt anyone was paying close attention."

"Everyone on your parade committee was in attendance that morning," said Miss Maude. "I saw each of them as they passed the table where I was selling my ginger beer and johnnycakes."

"Are you sure?" asked Benjamin.

A look and a nod from Miss Maude affirmed her statement.

"Why was this so important to her?" asked Benjamin.

"According to Catherine, before coming to St. Chris in

early January, Zena had been working as a teaching assistant in the history department of a junior college. She was fired before Christmas for not having completed her master's thesis."

"It sounds like she came here in an attempt to save her professional ass," said Michael.

"But why come to St. Chris?" asked Miss Maude. "Columbus is part of the history of many of our Caribbean islands."

"Columbus blasted through these islands like a hurricane dumping Christian crosses and Spanish flags," I said. "He reminds me of a cat marking its territory."

"There were certain rituals to be observed," said Miss Maude. "Accounts of instructions from the Spanish monarchs speak of oaths to be administered and rites to be performed. A secretary of the fleet was to witness and record these events in explicit detail. The Spanish were very fond of ritual."

"We have not yet ascertained why Zena came to our particular island," said Benjamin. "I cannot believe she came here purely by chance."

"Who would have known what she was planning to do?" I asked. "In her notes is a draft of the speech she was going to give from the grandstand when the parade awards were being presented. Can you imagine the reaction?"

"A melee for true," said Benjamin.

"Quite a fuss," said Miss Maude.

"A real scoop," said Michael.

"I think she hinted to Mr. Daniel what she had up her sleeve," I said. "Vic said Zena and Mr. Daniel got into a real tiff at Dockside the night before Stamp Day."

"That will bear looking into," remarked Benjamin.

"What will become of Zena's notes?" asked Miss Maude.

"Vic has the originals," I said. "She was planning to ship them to Catherine, Zena's daughter and only heir."

"A wise decision," said Miss Maude. "Surely the daughter has a more rational mind than the mother."

"But Catherine is dead," said Benjamin. "Who will take possession of them now?"

Miss Maude's hand flew to her mouth, upsetting her coffee cup. I ran to get a towel.

Benjamin related the facts of Catherine's death. Repeating what he'd told me the night before at Posh Nosh about the hit-and-run, he added that Catherine had been hit crossing the street near her mother's Boston apartment late on a grey, rainy weekend afternoon. A witness said the car was a dark sedan, possibly a rental, and may have been parked facing oncoming traffic before pulling onto the road in the wrong lane.

Miss Maude was visibly distressed. Michael kept shooting questioning looks in my direction.

"Mr. Daniel told me at Thursday's parade committee meeting he was off-island last weekend at an educator's conference. In Boston," I added pointedly.

Benjamin looked at me with raised eyebrows. "This will also bear looking into," he said. "If you will excuse me, I have inquiries to make. Thank you for your hospitality."

"Don't forget the time change," I called after Benjamin. "The Statesiders set their clocks ahead this morning."

On St. Chris it's always Atlantic Standard Time, or Greenwich Mean Time minus four. We never spring ahead or fall back. The only time we reset our clocks is after one of our frequent power outages.

Miss Maude also prepared to depart. I walked with her out to my driveway to say good-bye.

"Are you feeling all right?" I asked. "You look upset."

"I wasn't prepared for the news of the daughter's death," replied Miss Maude. "It brought back painful memories of my only child's death. My daughter was also the victim of an automobile accident, while on holiday with distant relatives in Denmark. I am blessed to have my granddaughter Amelia residing here with her family. When I see my dear friend Lucy I am reminded of how lonely it can be to grow old without family around you."

I put my arms around Miss Maude's thin frame in a gentle hug.

"You have become very precious to me in the time we have known each other," she said, getting into her car. "I hope you will come to feel you're part of my extended family." She waved good-bye as she headed down my driveway.

I went back into the house. Michael and I were alone at last.

"Did you know about Catherine's death?" he asked.

"Yes."

"Why didn't you tell me?"

"We were otherwise occupied," I replied, smiling.

"Mama, I thought we had no secrets."

"Michael, I was told about it in confidence. If you expect me to keep your secrets, then I'm honor bound not to divulge what others tell me." I tapped his nose with my finger. "Even to you."

"You're tough, Mama." He wrapped his arms around my waist. "But fair. It's one of the things I like best about you."

I put my arms around his neck, feeling the heat of his body meld into mine. "Let's clean up this mess, then take a nap. Entertaining wears me out."

Michael kissed my ear, murmuring, "You are a shameless manipulator."

I kissed him back. "Everything I know I learned from my cat."

Chapter
42

THE NEWS OF Mr. Daniel's arrest didn't appear in the *Coconut Telegraph* until Tuesday; by then it was old news, as Mr. Daniel had already been released pending further questioning. But it was the hot topic of Monday's gossip.

"Kel, that's some committee you're chairing," said Margo over Monday lunch at the Watering Hole. "It's like Agatha Christie's *And Then There Were None*. You're losing members left and right. Mrs. H skipped off on her cruise, Zena was killed, Angie ran off to marry Pete, Mr. Daniel was arrested. That leaves you and Reverend Cal. You'd better watch your step."

"The parade's a week from Saturday. I can take care of myself until then."

"Wasn't Mr. Daniel charged with Zena's death?"

"Yes, but he was released after questioning. He was poaching lobsters at the time. So he said."

"But why Kit?" asked Margo. "I don't get it."

"He had opportunity," I said. "He was in Boston at the time." I caught the dubious expression on Margo's face.

"I know, I know, opportunity isn't means or motive. Mr. Daniel is so closemouthed, I haven't any idea how his mind works."

"Let's talk about something more pleasant," said Margo. "I'm showing condos to snowbirds this afternoon. There may be a fat commission involved. What are you up to?"

"Going out to the marina to collect Top Banana. It's been there for over a week. I thought I'd paddle around Columbus Bay for a while. It's a good day for kayaking; there's not too much wind. I may have a snack with Michael at the marina bar if he's up in time before work."

"You two are becoming quite an item," said Margo with a twinkle in her eye. "Are you happy?"

Memories of the previous weekend made me smile, wanting to stretch and purr like Scarlett the morning after Rhett carried her up the stairs. "I'm happy. But more than that, I'm content. With Michael I can be myself. It's nice."

"Kel, I'm glad. Don't forget, Paul and I are expecting you and Michael for our Easter Sunday pig roast on the beach at Sea Breezes," said Margo.

"That's at two, right? I should be recovered from parasailing by then."

"Para what? Have you slipped your trolley?" Margo began to laugh. "Aren't you the one who has an acrophobic fit reaching for items on the top shelf at the supermarket?"

"Sweetie, I'd rather push an Easter egg up Kongens Gade from Government House to the Anglican church with my nose, stark naked at high noon, than do this."

"Then why are you doing it?"

"It was a birthday present from the gang at WBZE. I got roped into it."

"I'm going to forget you said that. Kel, you don't have to do this. Wimp out."

"It's too late. Michael set it up with Quincy for Easter Sunday morning. I want to get it over with so I won't ever have to do it again. I think it's going to be like riding the little train from hell at Disney World. I hated every minute of that bloody ride."

"I'll tell Jerry and Abby—they're gonna love this. We'll all be there to watch. I'll bring champagne, but you don't get any until it's over. Gotta go, Kel, I see my clients waiting at the office." Margo tossed some money on the table to cover her share of the lunch check, striding toward Island Palms with a bright welcoming "I'm going to show you the condo of your dreams" smile on her face.

I drove to the marina at Columbus Bay, changed into my kayaking clothes—bikini top, nylon shorts, rubber-soled nylon surf shoes, sun visor, sunglasses fixed on a nylon cord around my neck—grabbed a bottle of water, paddle and backrest from my car, then shoved off into the calm of the bay.

Fingers shoot off from Columbus Bay forming isolated pockets back in the mangroves, good moorings during hurricane season.

One of my favorite spots, an inlet east of the marina, I'd dubbed "the bowl." It reminded me of a bulb at the bottom of a flask or the base of a turtle nest, accessed by a narrow channel of water opening into a pond surrounded by tall greenery. Being in the bowl made me feel like Henry David Thoreau in the solitude of Walden Pond.

I decided to save the bowl for last. Heading due west, I crossed Columbus Bay, then turned south to explore the mangroves where five hundred years earlier the Caribs had come forth in their canoes to encounter the Spanish invaders. Zena be damned, I was sticking with history as I knew it.

In the mangroves the shallow water was tinted brown from the tannin in the bark. The roots prevent erosion, provide nursery and feeding areas for fish and birds, and act as a filtration system. The further back I got, the more the limbs entwined overhead, forming a cool green canopy. I drifted in the slight current, using my paddle to push off when I grounded. I listened to chirping birds and watched tiny fish meander through the roots.

Streisand's rendition of "Lazy Afternoon" echoed pleasantly in my head on an endless loop.

When the no-see-ums became too pesky I turned north, leaving the mangroves to hug the coastline curving toward the oceanfront beach where the Brigadoon post office had been erected for Stamp Bay. Protected from the pounding surf and high seas by the reef a quarter-mile out, I completed the expedition I'd begun a week earlier.

On a Monday work and school day the beach was deserted, but by Wednesday night it would be a tent city of Easter weekend campers. I saw crabs scuttling sideways along the beach popping in and out of sand holes, shore birds hopping through frothy remnants of waves at the watermark, overhead a flock of pelicans headed for the easterly feeding grounds of Columbus Bay. I continued slowly paddling west.

Above the high tide line on the western end of the beach was a grove of manchineel, its distinctive grey barked wind-twisted limbs stretching sinuously upward.

I considered beaching Top Banana for a shore excursion when I spotted a lone figure kneeling near one of the trees.

This was no ordinary beachcomber.

I backpaddled on the port side to maintain my position against the westerly flowing current, my eyes firmly fixed on shore.

The figure rose to a standing position, its back still toward me.

My eyes widened in shocked recognition.

The figure slowly turned toward the sea.

I executed a fast U-turn to starboard. Hoping the trade winds would mask the sound, I paddled like hell against the current to a place around the point where I was completely out of sight.

There was only one car in the parking area close to

where Miss Maude and the church ladies set up their food tables on Stamp Day. I'd seen that car before. I quickly memorized the license plate number.

I scooted southward down the coastline away from the high rolling swells, then cut quickly across the bay to the channel leading south toward the bowl.

Fifteen minutes of hard paddling later, I was safe inside the bowl. Only then did my heart stopped thumping and my breathing slow to normal. I slumped against the backrest, draining my small bottle of Evian in four swift gulps. While I caught my breath I watched a small brown-and-white mottled jellyfish silently pulsing through the water next to my boat.

My capacity for self-delusion and rampant stupidity made me shake my head in rueful wonderment. Michael was right. I needed to get my head out of the mannered environs of St. Mary Mead and into the real world. I had just seen a killer. But how could I prove it? And how could I use what I'd seen to set a trap? I was batting two out of three: I had opportunity and means, but I still needed a motive to hold it together.

My waterproof watch read four o'clock. If I hauled ass I could get back to the marina and call Benjamin before he left for the day at five.

I put my back into it, heading up the channel, around the peninsula then south to the marina in a brisk left-right stoke. I glanced across the bay as I coasted into the marina. The car was gone.

Benjamin and I met in the deserted Columbus Bay parking lot. I filled him in on my afternoon excursion.

"This astounds me," he said. "You saw this person for true?"

"For true," I replied. "Of course I can't prove it, you have only my word, but here's the license plate number. Check it out." I handed him a napkin I'd filched from marina bar.

Benjamin tucked the napkin in his uniform pocket.

"I think I also know what happened, why Zena came here and why she was killed. We're dealing with two ego-driven people with very private agendas."

Benjamin leaned forward, his bright eyes fixed on mine. "Can you prove it?"

"Not yet," I said, "but you can supply the missing pieces. You're in an official capacity and have access to sources I can't tap. Here's what I think we need."

I made a list on another bar napkin. Benjamin watched while I wrote, nodding in agreement.

"We must act fast," said Benjamin. "We have only two more days before the government offices shut down for the Easter holidays."

"Are you camping this weekend?" I asked.

"I'll be on duty some of the time," he said, "but we're setting up our campsite Wednesday afternoon. If you're in the area this weekend, come by. We always have drinks and snacks for our friends. Now kindly show me where you saw this person."

We walked along the hard-packed sand at the tide line. As we turned south to approach the manchineel grove, the cloying sweet smell of overripe fruit filled the air. On the ground were yellow-green apples about an inch in diameter.

"Now I know what the phrase 'fruit of the poisoned tree' means," I said, sticking my hands in my pockets to resist even the slightest temptation to touch the fruit.

Benjamin pointed to some apples that appeared half-eaten. "Poison to humans and most animals, but a delicacy to our land crabs. However, the meat from those crabs will be tainted and should not be eaten unless carefully purged. But our bees make a most delicious nontoxic honey from the nectar in the flowers."

I shivered, feeling I'd walked into a malevolent part of Eden.

"If you will stay where you are, I will see if I can find any traces of our visitor." Benjamin stepped gingerly through the small grove of trees, his head lowered, eyes scanning the ground. He stopped at the area where I saw the kneeling figure.

I watched as he carefully picked up something from the ground, hidden among the rotting fruit.

He walked toward me, his palm outstretched.

In his hand was a small black button.

Benjamin shook his head sadly. "I also found a used syringe lying in the leaves. I am very distressed that our young people are falling victims to the greed of drug pushers."

As we strolled back to the parking lot, we heard Michael approaching on his Harley.

"I leave you in good company," said Benjamin. "I must commend you. Like last summer's episode at Papaya Quay, you have been very observant." He smiled warmly, patting his shirt pocket. "I will call you as soon as I have results. We will keep these developments to ourselves until we are ready to act."

I mimed zipping my lip. Benjamin laughed, stopping on the way to his patrol car to chat with Michael.

When I finally got home I made good use of Maubi's gift of green glass, thinking I should start by hanging a bottle around my neck like a talisman.

I made a game of it. First I hung a few bottles in the bush behind my cottage. They clinked together in melodic harmony with the wind chimes. The rest I buried in the ground, neckdown, tops above the dirt, around the perimeter of the yard. The glass glinted in the setting sun, making my yard look like an outpost of Oz or an exotic bottle garden. I hoped Maubi was right and the jumbies would now leave me alone.

Chapter
43

BENJAMIN CALLED ME at the station late Tuesday morning as I was getting ready to leave for the day.

"Wheels are turning," he said, "we should have some answers very soon. As you are aware, no one is anxious to take on extra work with the holidays approaching, but I have stressed the need for urgency. Information will also be coming by fax and express mail."

Jerry was holding court with Abby and Margo when I arrived at the Watering Hole round table for lunch. They burst into a rowdy chorus of "Up, Up and Away" when I took my seat.

"Give it a rest, guys."

Abby giggled. Most unlike her. "Kel, the thought of you dangling in the air had me laughing in court this morning. Aren't you the one who paid two hundred and fifty dollars to go hot-air ballooning in Egypt's Valley of the Kings and sat huddled in the basket with her eyes tightly closed the entire time?"

"Not true," I said. "I only sat down for a few minutes when the ride got a little bumpy."

"I'm going to sell tickets," said Jerry, "and take advance orders for the video."

Margo had the good sense to keep her mouth shut.

"Traitor," I snapped. "I'll get you for this. Remember, paybacks are hell."

Michael sauntered up to the table. "What's so funny?"

"It's the middle of the night," I said in a vain attempt to change the subject as he bent down to kiss me, "what are you doing up at this hour?"

"I couldn't sleep. What's the joke?"

Jerry and Abby laughed themselves into speechlessness.

"Hush, you two," said Margo, glaring at Abby and Jerry. She turned to Michael. "They're giving Kel a hard time about her upcoming parasailing adventure." She began to laugh uncontrollably.

"Why? I don't get it," said Michael innocently.

By now Margo was in danger of falling off her chair, and even I had a smile on my face.

Margo managed to spit out, "Kel is terrified of heights," before she ran off to the ladies' room.

Michael turned to me with a look of surprise on his face. "You are?"

"You got it in one," I said, feeling sweat beading on my palms. Jerry wiped his eyes while Abby dashed off to the loo on Margo's heels.

"Kel," said Jerry, "how did you put it? You'd rather sweep Kongens Gade with your tongue than go up in the air?"

"I said I'd rather roll an Easter egg with my nose."

"Same difference," he remarked.

Michael took my hand. "You could irrigate a desert with that palm." He handed me a napkin, then gently stroked my cheek. "You don't have to do this, Mama. I had no idea you had a phobia about heights. We wanted to give you something fun for your birthday."

"I know, Michael. I really appreciate the thought."

"I'll call Quincy and cancel. We'll do something else."

I took a deep breath. "No, don't."

"Are you sure?"

"Margo promised me champagne after it's over. That's a promise she's going to keep."

Michael smiled. "You'll be as safe as sitting on the beach. I'll be in the boat with Quincy, we won't let anything happen to you. Scout's honor."

"I don't believe you were ever a scout, but I'm holding you to it," I said.

Reverend Cal dropped one of his Easter Sunday fliers on our table in front of my plate. "I'm still praying you'll be joining my little flock," he said to me with a smarmy smile.

"I'll be around," I replied. "When are you going to the beach? I may need to get in touch with you this weekend about last-minute parade details."

"I'll be back and forth." Reverend Cal backed away from the table.

"I'm still waiting for your parade donor report," I said sharply.

"I'll get the report to you this afternoon or tomorrow morning." He moved swiftly to paper the rest of the Watering Hole tables with fliers.

"I need to get the program copy to the printer by noon tomorrow," I called after him, "don't let me down."

Michael insisted we take the ferry over to Harborview after lunch.

The beachview terrace was overflowing with tourists and residents finishing late lunches. The beach was dotted with sand chairs, large towels and oiled bodies carefully angled to catch the best rays. Children laughed as they jumped up and down in the sun-dappled wavelets.

We walked over to the parasail boat tied to the short dock at the water sports pavilion.

"C'mon, Mama, we're gonna do a dry run for Sunday," Michael said as he helped me into the boat. "Think of it as a dress rehearsal for Peter Pan."

He got me with that one. It's a part I always wanted to play. Except for the flying thing. I put my hands on my hips, threw back my head letting out a raucous "caw-caw, caw-caw." Heads on the beach snapped to stare in our direction.

"Mama, what in the hell was that racket?"

I smiled like Meg Ryan at end of the *When Harry Met Sally* restaurant scene. "I was crowing, Michael. You never saw Mary Martin play Peter Pan?"

We sat in the boat. Michael pointed out the rope coiled neatly around a winch.

"You'll be in a body harness, like a butterfly in a cocoon, with a sling seat under your rear end. The harness will be attached to the parachute and this rope. We'll take off from the dock, you'll be sitting on the back of the boat like a homecoming queen, and as we pick up speed the wind will gently lift you into the air. Okay so far?"

"So far so good." I forced a small smile. Theory is one thing, practice quite another. I was doing okay as long as I was sitting safely inside a boat tied securely to the dock.

"I'll be manning the winch. I'll let the rope out slowly and you'll go only as high as you want to go. We'll arrange hand signals, okay?"

"Okay." My smile became a little more relaxed.

"When you're ready to come down, I'll start hauling in the rope and you'll float back to the boat as easily as a bird settling on a nest. You won't even get wet." Michael put his arm around my shoulders and kissed my cheek. "Keep smiling, Mama. Come on, I'll buy you a drink, then I gotta go home and crash."

I really wish he hadn't said the final *c* word.

Chapter
44

A SCREW-CAPPED MASON jar filled with an amber substance rested against the edge of my front door like a doorstop.

"What the hell?" I muttered as I got out of my car. I was tired of having my privacy invaded the minute I left the house. Forget the hot tub, my next home improvement was going to be a chain-link fence and an electronic gate. So much for Maubi's theory about the protective qualities of green glass. He probably made it up and was getting a big laugh out of my gullibility.

Minx bounded around the corner from the hill side of the house, her quivering tail held high with the tip curled forward like a shepherd's crook. She sniffed at the jar, then sat patiently waiting for me to unlock the dead bolt. I reached down to pet her.

"Who brought us a present?" I asked. Minx concentrated on licking her right front paw.

A faint rustle made me look over my left shoulder. I gasped in horror.

My pink blossomed frangipani tree looked like a vision from a sci-fi nightmare.

I picked up the jar, threw open the door and rushed inside, Minx on my heels batting playfully at my bare ankles, to study the tree from the security of the gallery.

My lovely tree was crawling with hornworms. Fat, ugly, leaf-crunching hornworms. Six-inch-long hornworms with matte black bodies striped with yellow, topped with scarlet heads. Hornworms pooping all over the ground beneath the tree.

Like locusts, hornworms appear to spontaneously generate in an internally regulated cycle known only to Mother Nature.

I welcomed them with far less enthusiasm than the residents of Hinckley, Ohio greet the annual mid-March pilgrimage of buzzards.

Once hornworms have stripped a tree to bare branches, they disappear like the Cheshire cat's smile to resurface wherever another frangipani blooms.

I tried to ignore the ghastly sound of their crunching and reminded myself not to walk barefoot near the tree until after they were long gone and we'd had several heavy rains.

Minx grew tired of play and swatted my ankle with serious intent to draw blood. Food was obviously uppermost in her mind.

I opened a can of her favorite tuna with cheese bits, mixing a quarter can with dry crunchies. When her bowl was placed on the paw-print mat, she scrunched her body to the floor to consume her feast.

I put a tray of Italian seasoned chicken in the toaster oven to bake for an hour, poured an iced tea, and went to listen to my phone messages.

Margo: "Hey, Kel, if I spring for an early movie tonight, will I be back in your good graces? Call me at home."

Benjamin: "Kelly, we've come up empty in two places.

If you have any more ideas, call me before five."

I skipped over the hang-ups, then I heard:

". . . the fruit of that forbidden tree, whose mortal taste brought death into the world, and all our woe . . ."

Say what? I played that message three times, trying to identify the voice. I already knew the origin of the quote. Milton's *Paradise Lost*. But who would call me to read poetry? Someone who used the oldest ploy in the world for disguise—a handkerchief over the phone. Was this a practical joke?

I called Benjamin at the police station and played the message for him.

"Most mysterious," he said. "Why would someone do that? Can you relate it to anything?"

"Wait!" I yelled, tucking the phone into my shoulder to run to the kitchen for the jar I'd left on the counter. "When I got home there was a mason jar leaning against my door."

"I suppose you've put your fingerprints all over it," he chided.

"Well, Minx wanted dinner and the hornworms were eating my frangipani."

"What's in the jar?" he asked.

"Hang on, I'll tell you." I opened the jar and sniffed, but definitely did not taste. "Honey."

"Excuse me?"

"Benjamin, as much as I treasure your friendship, that was not a term of endearment. I'm telling you what's in the jar. Honey."

"Oh, ho," he laughed. "My dear wife will be pleased to learn of the distinction."

"Please give her my best. Now, who would have done this?"

"You might telephone our friend Miss Maude. I seem to recall she keeps several hives in her fruit orchard."

"Benjamin, that definitely was not Miss Maude's voice on my answering machine."

"Of course not."

"I'll call Miss Maude and get back to you."

Miss Maude confirmed she had indeed been the donor of the honey jar. "I left one of my calling cards tucked under the jar," she said. "The wind must have carried it away. Or perhaps your dear cat removed it with her claws."

I thanked Miss Maude for her generosity.

"I keep the hives near my lime trees," she said. "The honey is quite nice in a hot cup of morning tea."

"I'll try it tomorrow morning," I promised.

"Lucy and I would welcome your company for a Saturday morning swizzle. At our ages we're too fond of our creature comforts to camp out on the beach as we did in our younger years."

I promised to join them Saturday morning at eleven o'clock. Miss Lucinda and I needed to review the final parade arrangements. With the parade only ten days away, Saturday would be the perfect opportunity to get that out of the way.

I reminded myself to deposit my paycheck at the bank Wednesday before three, after I went to the printer with the parade program copy; otherwise I'd be cash-poor until Tuesday when the banks finally reopened on a normal schedule. I didn't want to wait for the half-day bank opening Saturday morning when the lines would stretch out the door onto the sidewalk.

I called Benjamin. "You were right. The honey was a gift from Miss Maude. But I still don't understand the phone message. I wonder if someone overheard us yesterday on the beach and then came snooping around my house today while I was gone. This is too coincidental for my taste."

"I suggest we file the phone message away under 'unexplained' for the time being," he said. "We have more pressing matters facing us at present."

We talked about the news he'd received earlier in the afternoon, the dead ends, and a new avenue that required further investigation: something I thought of while flipping through the ads in the back of a magazine I found lying around the station.

"I think we're dealing with someone whose ego is totally out of control," I said. "Someone who needs to be noticed and is playing us for suckers in a game of cat and mouse."

"I could not agree more," he said. "I'll phone you tomorrow morning if I have any news. I'm taking personal leave in the afternoon to help my family get settled at the beach."

While I waited for the chicken to bake, I went outside to look for Miss Maude's calling card. I had a horrible vision of one of those fat ugly hornworms falling on my head, so gave the frangipani a wide berth.

I saw a white card lodged between the blades of one of the Spanish bayonet plants bordering my yard. Spanish bayonet leaves are tipped with needle sharp points, resembling an aloe plant with broad leaves growing in a rosette pattern around a thick stem. Spanish bayonet grows like a weed, sending underground runners to propagate new shoots. I used it as a natural perimeter defense system.

I carefully leaned over the plant, cautiously sticking my hand between the blades. I jumped when a leaf point jabbed the tender flesh of my underarm. Using kitchen tongs, I finally extracted the card. There were no claw marks on it.

Written in fine script on the back of the engraved card was the message, "Wishing you a joyous Easter season. Affectionately, Maude."

Not far from where I found the card, an ant-encrusted plastic spoon lay on the ground.

Who's been littering in my yard? Probably a meter reader stopping for a snack break, I thought. Annoyed at having to clean up after other people's piggyness, I went back into the house for a plastic grocery bag to cover my hand and keep it from being bitten by fire ants, picked up the spoon and disposed of it in my outside trash can.

I called Margo to take a pass on the movie. I really didn't feel like going out on a school night.

"I'll buy you lunch tomorrow," she offered.

"That's a deal," I said. "But you don't have to bribe me, I'm not mad at you."

"I'm only doing it because you need your strength for Sunday," she chortled, hanging up on me with an audible click.

I called her right back. "Where's Paul today? Jetting off to some exotic destination?"

"No, he's on standby at the airport. Why do you want to know?"

"I need to talk to him. Nothing special."

I called Paul at the airport and asked if he could do me a big hush-hush favor. He said he would and called me back within half an hour. I promptly called Benjamin, but he'd already left for the day. It could wait until morning.

When the chicken was done I put two pieces on a plate for my dinner, leaving the rest to cool in the closed toaster oven. I went out to the gallery to eat, with Minx in close pursuit. She sat opposite me, alert for any opportunity to snag a piece of chicken.

"Wait, Minx, it's too hot, you'll burn your mouth. I'll put some in your bowl later when it's cool."

After several abortive attempts to swipe food from my plate, Minx left the gallery.

I went back into the kitchen to dispose of my dirty dishes, to find the toaster oven door pulled open and chicken bones on the floor. Minx was nowhere in view.

"Minx!"

She crawled out from under my bed, a picture of innocence.

I picked her up and walked back to the gallery, holding her in my arms, stroking her rounded tummy. How angry could I be with a cat clever enough to figure out how a toaster oven worked? Perhaps I could teach her to wash windows.

We sat on the gallery enjoying the night air, watching the lights play shadow tricks with the trees. When Minx had had enough of lap sitting, I let her out in the yard where she yawned and stretched with the grace of a T'ai Chi artist doing warm-up exercises, then lay languidly on her side washing her face in the moonlight. A few moments later she darted into the bush.

I spent part of the evening at my desk doodling on a yellow legal pad. I felt like Hercule Poirot compiling the list of clues he would later spring on a group of suspects gathered to hear his brilliant deductions.

My list read: Island Delights, manchineel, juice extractor, Ramirez twins, typewriter with a bad *e*, black button, brass key, Zena's notes. Ending the list was one other item Benjamin had mentioned. It could be a major clue to solving the entire mystery.

But I couldn't make those disparate items coalesce. I felt like someone had taken random pieces from several jigsaw puzzles and tossed them all into one box on the white elephant table at a jumble sale.

Was it merely coincidence that five people were all off-island the same weekend?

Perhaps it was time to return to Chipping Cleghorn for inspiration. I'd read the book several times, but Agatha Christie has a way of surprising me every time.

I crawled into bed to read. One vital clue early in the book concerning the identity of the villain was a real eye opener. Why hadn't I thought of that possibility before? I added it to the list of things I wanted to discuss with Benjamin. I looked at my bedside battery-operated alarm clock. I was already an hour past my bedtime. I turned off the light and went to sleep.

On Wednesday morning I began my day at the usual early hour with a cup of eye-opening Irish breakfast tea, sweetened with a generous dollop of Miss Maude's lime honey instead of my regular no-cal sweetener. Hot tea and honey had always been part of a preshow ritual in my theater days to soothe my throat before a performance.

I sat on the gallery, my knees drawn to my chest, hands wrapped around the cup, a beach towel around my shoulders to ward off the morning chill, deeply breathing the comforting steam from the tea. A pleasant contrast to the salt-laced sea air.

I wished I had time for a second cup, but I was running late as usual.

I never got around to calling Benjamin.

Less than three hours into the morning show my lips and tongue began to swell. My throat exploded in burning, searing pain.

I punched Emily's extension on the intercom.

"Emily!" I gasped, "call an ambulance, get someone to cover for me. I think I've been poisoned."

I slid from my swivel chair to the carpeted studio floor in a dead faint.

Emily ran into the studio, took one look and screamed, swallowing her gum. She grabbed the phone and dialed 911.

Chapter
45

THE ANGLICAN CHURCH bell tolled noon as Benjamin paced in my small hospital room.

"Miss Maude is devastated," he said. "She's in the waiting room and insists on seeing you when you're allowed visitors."

"Please tell her it's not her fault," I croaked. The swelling had receded in my lips and tongue, but my throat felt like someone had used a belt sander on it. My stomach ached from undignified treatments I shuddered to recall.

"I've assured her of that, but she still wants to see you."

"When can you get me out of here? I want to go home." I knew I was whining like a spoiled brat, but I couldn't help it. I'm a hospitalphobe. When I was five years old I had pneumonia and spent a horrible week in a Chicago hospital. I remember being wakened at all hours and hating every minute I was there. When I left I screamed at a nurse that I hated it and was never coming back. The feeling was probably mutual. To this day I can't even walk into a hospital as a visitor without feeling queasy.

"Be patient for a few more hours," he replied.

"Benjamin!" I groaned. "I can't believe you said that!"

"I wanted to see if you were paying attention," Benjamin grinned. "The doctor wants to keep you here overnight, but as soon as your pressure returns to normal he'll release you."

"My blood pressure is always low, he knows that."

Benjamin sat in the chair next to my bed. "We had the honey tested. It came up positive for manchineel. Not as much as was found in the Sheffield woman, but you had only tea in your stomach so a smaller dose had a strong effect."

"Did you test the plastic spoon?"

"We couldn't find it."

"I put it in my outside trash barrel, wrapped in a plastic grocery bag."

Benjamin shook his head. "It wasn't there, I looked for it myself. The only thing we found was a clump of melted wax near your frangipani."

I suddenly remembered that I wanted to phone Benjamin and why.

"I was going to call you this morning," I said. "I was reading a book last night, an Agatha Christie mystery, and something occurred to me about those dead ends you mentioned yesterday afternoon. Try this on for size."

Benjamin listened intently while I shared my ideas with him. "You are very clever! So Zena might not have been a widow after all. I'll get right on it."

"Wait, there's more." I told him about my conversation with Paul, beginning with my earlier chat with Abby in her office the previous Friday.

"Most interesting," said Benjamin. "Why do people tell silly lies that can easily be proven false? I will follow up on this. I applaud your persistence."

The doctor stuck his head in the door. "How are we feeling this afternoon?"

"I don't know about you," I grouched, "but I'm feeling better and I want to go home."

"We'll see about that," the doctor said. He put a blood pressure cuff around my arm and pumped the little squeeze ball. I focused on my breathing.

"You're almost back to your normal level. If you're stable when I do afternoon rounds at four you can go home, otherwise you're stuck here for the night. You had a very close call, young lady."

"Young lady? Doc, you're such a flatterer."

He smiled, then grew serious. "This is the second time in my forty-five years of tropical medicine that I've come across manchineel poisoning. The first was the autopsy on the late Zena Sheffield. If I hadn't read up on it then, we might have lost you. You were lucky to be at work and not at home when the poison took effect. It was vital that we act quickly."

"I always thought poison worked instantly," I said.

"You've been reading too many mysteries," the doctor said, smiling and wagging his finger. "You're thinking of cyanide, where the victim gasps and falls to the floor dead on the spot, and the smell of bitter almonds is present. Manchineel acts in several ways."

Benjamin and I listened in rapt attention.

"First there is the tree itself, with a poisonous sap in its veins. The milky sap will cause an instant blistering of the skin. That's why we caution people not to sit near the tree, especially during a rainstorm. The Caribs used the sap to poison the tips of their arrows. They cut a shallow slit around the tip of the arrow and filled it with sap. Burning the tree will create smoke immediately irritating to the skin, eyes and respiratory system."

"But what about the fruit?" I asked.

"The fruit itself contains a different toxin, one that is slow-acting. It may be several hours—almost four in your case, possibly longer if you'd consumed solid food with your tea—before the effects are felt. You fainted because of the rapid drop in your blood pressure. You might have died of suffocation from the swelling of your lips, tongue and throat if we had not treated you in time."

Tears welled in my eyes. I reached for the doctor's hand, mumbling, "Thank you."

He patted my hand reassuringly. "In a day or two you'll be fine. But until then I'm going to prescribe rest and a bland diet. Cold soups, ice cream, cool drinks. Foods that are easy to swallow and gentle on your system. Here's my home phone number if you need to reach me at any time. Is there someone who can stay with you tonight?"

Benjamin said, "I'll see to it she's not alone."

"Very well, I'll look in on you again at four. For now young lady," a twinkle appeared in the doctor's eyes, "I want you to get some rest. Doctor's orders. You have ten minutes for visitors."

Miss Maude entered the room, deep lines of worry etched in her normally smooth face, followed by Margo and Michael.

"Hi guys," I said, "would you two mind waiting outside? I need to talk to Miss Maude for a minute." I clasped Miss Maude's trembling hand in mine.

"Oh, my dear," she said, "I am so very, very sorry. I insist on paying your hospital bill. I swear to you . . ." Her voice faltered, tears coursed down her cheeks.

"I know it wasn't your fault," I replied gently. "My insurance will cover the bill. But I need to ask you something."

Her blue eyes looked questioningly into mine.

"How did you seal the honey jar?"

"With melted paraffin poured on top of the cold honey," she replied. "I always do that to prevent spoilage and mold."

"That proves someone tampered with the jar," I said to Benjamin. "There was no paraffin inside when I unscrewed the cap, which accounts for the melted wax you found under my frangipani."

I sent Benjamin off on his planned half-day holiday at the beach with his family. Miss Maude departed, looking much relieved, the worry lines slowly fading from her face.

A limply starched but crisply efficient nurse stuck her head in the door, pointing at the watch on her wrist. "Five mo' minutes, the doctor say."

Margo and Michael brushed past her to enter my room.

Margo smothered me in a hug. "Kel, here's your purse. I went and got it from the radio station. If the doctor lets you out of this clip joint—do you realize you could have the bridal suite at Harborview for less than you're paying here?—I'll take you home at four and stay with you tonight. What do you want for dinner? Name it."

"The doctor has me on a bland diet for a couple of days," I rasped. "I'm only allowed cold soup and ice cream."

"Tough luck, kid," said Margo. "I wish someone would put me on an ice cream diet. What's your favorite kind?"

"Anything Häagen-Dazs, except chocolate. And no scratchy nuts."

"Three mo' minutes," said the nurse. Margo smoothly edged the nurse into the hall as she left the room, shutting the door firmly behind her.

"Yo, Mama." Michael's smile looked shaky.

"Yo, yourself." I tried to smile and couldn't.

Michael wrapped his arms around me, his cheek pressed to mine. I felt water droplets fall on my shoulder.

"If anything had happened to you . . . ," he murmured.

"Honey pie, I'm much too mean to die." I handed him the key ring from my purse. "Why don't you sleep at my house this afternoon. Minx would love the company. I'll see you there later, okay?"

"Time's up," said the nurse. "Everybody out. Now."

Chapter

46

THE DOCTOR RELEASED me from the hospital at four P.M.

"I want you to go straight home and stay in bed," he said. "Your system has suffered quite a shock and needs time to recover. Call me if you need to."

Margo was waiting at the hospital entrance in her bronze BMW.

"Your car's at home, Kel," she said. "Michael and I ran a shuttle service this afternoon. He drove your car home, I followed and drove him back to town so he could get his Harley. But first I stopped at the market for ice cream. Wait 'til you see what's in your freezer! How are you feeling?"

"Woozy. Poison is nasty stuff. I don't recommend it."

"Gee, Kel. I was going to bake you a manchineel pie for dessert," said Margo. "I thought you'd like apple pie à la mode."

"Bite your tongue and go to your room," I quipped.

"Kel, do you have any idea who did this?"

"Yes," I replied. "I'm fairly certain I know who it was."

"Who?" Margo turned to look at me.

"Keep your eyes on the road, sweetie."

A horn blared. Margo slammed on the brakes, swerving to avoid an accident.

"If it's all the same to you, I just got out of the hospital and I don't want to go back there."

"Smart-ass." Margo's eyes were firmly fixed on the road ahead of us. "Tell me who did it."

"Sweetie, I can't tell you now. Let's not play twenty questions about it, okay? For the time being, I've got to keep this to myself. Forget we even had this conversation. I don't want you telling Abby, Jerry or Paul. Or anyone."

"Are you going to tell Michael?"

"Nope. Loose lips sink ships," I said with a smile. "Promise me you'll keep your mouth shut."

"Promise, Kel. Cross my heart. If you don't know it already, Michael really cares for you. I've never seen a man as visibly shaken as he was this afternoon. I take back what I said before. Go easy on him. He deserves it."

I felt my face flush. "When we get to my house, go slowly up the drive. If Michael's sleeping I don't want to wake him. The poor guy's been burning the candle at both ends."

Michael was fast asleep on my living room couch snoring softly, Minx curled next to him. She yawned, stretched, leapt nimbly to the floor and came to me for a head scratch. While I was feeding Minx, Michael woke with a start.

"They let you out," he said, rising to give me a welcome home hug.

"Time off for good behavior," I replied.

"How are you feeling?" He caressed my cheek.

"I've been better but I'll live. Do you want a drink?"

"I'd rather have a shower first."

Margo shooed me onto the gallery. "You're supposed to be resting, Kel. If you don't want to go to bed, at least stretch out on the love seat while I take care of dinner. I stopped at Soup to Nuts for gourmet take-out. You're having cold lobster bisque, Michael and I are having fettucini Alfredo and we're all having ice cream for dessert."

"Isn't Paul joining us for dinner?"

"Didn't I tell you? He's stuck on the ground in Antigua. Mechanical problems. He won't be home until tomorrow. Are you allowed to have a glass of wine?"

"The doctor said no booze until Saturday."

"Go sit on the gallery and I'll bring you a Tab."

I was back on the job at usual time Maundy Thursday morning, but I didn't feel much like talking.

At nine o'clock Dahlia delivered a large Easter basket filled with candy and flowers.

Emily quietly opened the studio door and I motioned her inside. Bach's *St. Matthew Passion* filled the airwaves.

"No one's ever sent me flowers before," Emily said with a shy smile. "Thank you, Kelly. Are you really all right?"

I got out of my chair to give her a brief but heartfelt hug. "I owe you my life. Thank you for acting so quickly. Do you have plans for the holiday weekend?"

"Some friends of mine are camping at the beach, I'm going to join them when I get off work today."

"You're on paid holiday right now," I said. "I don't want to see you back here until Tuesday morning."

"Really?" Emily was so pleased and surprised she forgot to chew.

"Go," I said. "Have fun. I'll take care of the phones. Lock the front door behind you when you leave."

Emily skipped out of the studio.

The phone rang a few minutes later.

"Good morning, WBZE," I said.

"Kelly, why are you answering the phone after eight-thirty? Have you been demoted? And how are you feeling?"

"Good morning, Benjamin. I gave Emily the day off. And I'm feeling much better, thank you. What's up?"

"I received a very interesting fax this morning. Your hunch of Tuesday was right and tied in with what you told me yesterday. By the way, the license plate checked out, too."

"Come on over, I'll be here alone until noon."

A short time later I handed the fax back to Benjamin. "I didn't want to be right about this, but from the comments people were making, I knew I had to be."

Benjamin shook his head. "What is it about our island that brings unscrupulous people to our shores?"

"I think it's the illusion of fantasyland," I replied. "That this isn't the real world and whatever happens here is as temporary as footprints on sand."

"We take too much at face value," he said sadly, then brightened. "But we also attract people like you, who are an asset to our little community. One must consider the balance."

"Benjamin!" The lightbulb in my head was flashing like a strobe. "I think I know how the poison got in the candy. Do you still have that item you found on the beach Monday afternoon? Is there time to get it to the lab for testing?"

Benjamin grabbed the phone, and after a brief conversation, he said to me, "They will cooperate. But only if I get there within the hour."

"Are we ready to act?" I asked.

"Not quite. There will be no mail delivery tomorrow because of the day-long Good Friday holiday, so we must wait until Saturday morning for the rest of our proof to arrive."

"But we'll have it in time for Sunday?"

"It looks so. Are you feeling well enough to go through with your part of the plan?"

"Absolutely. I'm going home to rest this afternoon after lunch; by tomorrow I should be almost back to normal. And definitely in peak form by Sunday."

"Don't forget, we're expecting you and Michael at the

beach Saturday afternoon. My son has organized a volley-ball game and we require your assistance on our team. Now I must go quickly."

I met the gang at the round table for our version of the Maundy Thursday last supper. Or in our case, lunch.

"Hey, Kel, I hear you pulled the Sleeping Beauty bit yesterday," said Jerry.

"The story with the poisoned apple is Snow White, Jerry," said Abby.

"Who cares," said Jerry, "they're always about a broad who falls asleep and gets kissed awake by a prince. Which is the one with the bunch of short guys in it?"

"*Snow White and the Seven Dwarfs*," said Abby.

"That's the one I meant."

"I'm so glad it wasn't Pinocchio," I quipped.

"Watch the nose jokes," said Jerry.

"Bag the short jokes, Jerry," Michael retorted.

"Make nice, boys," said Margo.

I ordered a large bowl of vichyssoise and iced tea for lunch, salivating when Michael bit into a medium-rare swiss cheeseburger with bacon and mushrooms. I never thought I'd tire of ice cream, but knew I'd be glad to be back on solid food when my throat healed.

"Kel, Paul and I are having everyone over for snacks and drinks tomorrow at noon. Can you make it?"

Good Friday is the only day in the year when alcohol cannot be sold anywhere on St. Chris until after four P.M. All the bars, restaurants and businesses islandwide would be shuttered during the day while church services were in progress. Life at WBZE would go on as usual, but with only the deejays on duty.

"Sure, I'll be there when I get through at the station."

"You're invited, too, Michael. Don't forget, Kel, we're on for our usual turtle walk tomorrow night at six."

Chapter
47

THE FRIDAY NIGHT sky was as dark as the dress I'd worn to Mrs. H's bon voyage party. The moon was three nights past full and wouldn't rise until close to ten. It was a perfect night for turtle nesting, the white sand a sharp contrast to the dark sea and sky.

We logged our first turtle at seven-thirty. I was almost at the far east end and ready for a rest break when Margo radioed me.

"Kel, haul ass to the twin palms. I've got a surprise for you."

By the time I got there, Eve had already begun digging her nest and was oblivious to our presence.

"Margo, look. There's something wrong with her right front flipper."

A plastic ring from a six-pack of soda was wedged tight on the flipper like a wedding band grown too small. I grabbed the Swiss Army knife from my fanny pack and carefully cut away the plastic. The flipper looked otherwise uninjured.

"Damn all piggy people," said Margo, making a note on her log sheet. "Don't they know better than to dump their trash where animals will get into it? When I see a plastic bag floating in the water I want to strangle someone. I wonder how many leatherbacks mistake them for jellyfish and suffocate when they try to swallow them."

Eve had chosen a good nesting site, far enough above the high tide line so the one hundred eggs she laid that night would stay dry and warm until they hatched. It seemed fitting that new life would begin in a spot where one had ended.

We watched until the nesting process was complete and Eve was safely out to sea. She would return to the beach to lay one more clutch of eggs before beginning her long journey to African waters. The round-trip back to St. Chris would take her two years.

At nine-thirty I was on the western edge of the beach taking a rest break. I spotted bright Jupiter on the ecliptic path high in the eastern sky near Virgo, Sirius lower toward the west, and directly ahead of me the Southern Cross lay tilted left immediately above the horizon.

It was exactly four weeks from the night I had discovered Zena's body on the beach.

I thought back to that night. I remembered sitting with Angie, eating trail mix while we stargazed. Hearing the party sounds and the reggae band from a home in the hills, and then a car with a bad muffler. I was half asleep at the time. Where had the sound come from? East or west? I stared at the Southern Cross, trying to remember.

The party house was to the east. The car must have come from the west.

I turned to look at the hills behind me. Yes, there was the party house in the east. I recognized the broad terrace where the band played.

There were only three homes visible in the west. They were fairly close together, probably served by a common road, and each overlooked the sea. Anyone watching with binoculars or a telescope had a clear view of Leatherback Bay and the turtle beach.

Every turtle team—with the exception of Jerry's, where more time was spent limin' than walking the beach—followed a similar routine. The partners would meet at the point and split, each going in a different direction. A rest break at the end of the beach, followed by a trek back to the point for another rest stop. A team would break the pattern only when a nesting turtle was spotted. It would be easy for anyone to time using an ordinary wristwatch. The twin palms were an easily spotted landmark only a few yards from the dirt road. How long would it take to pull a body from a car and drag it onto the beach? Less time than it took to walk from the far end of the bay back to the point.

I knew I had to check out those houses.

Margo and I parted company at midnight. We logged two more turtles, marked the nest locations on our beach charts and called it a night. I didn't tell her what I was planning to do.

I let Margo take off ahead of me, saying I needed to make a pit stop before I went to meet Michael at the radio station. I watched the taillights of her car fade to red specks in the distance.

I grabbed a St. Chris road map, a freebie from Island Palms Real Estate, from my glove compartment, and studied it by flashlight. A quarter-mile north, a road cut off to the left from the Leatherback Bay beach road, then snaked back toward the south. It was the only possible access to the three homes in the west.

I found the cutoff road, turned my car around for a fast getaway and parked it in the bush next to a trash Dumpster, then proceeded on foot. Jupiter was now directly overhead. The three-quarter moon had been up for almost three hours, illuminating the path ahead of me like a torch. My darkened flashlight hung on a lanyard around my neck, bobbing against my chest. I made sure my car keys were secure in my fanny pack and my car was locked.

I trudged up the inclined road, pausing every few steps to get my bearings, wishing I'd been smart enough to wear my Reeboks instead of flip-flops. I hoped all the Friday night partygoers were tucked in their wee little beds or sacked out in tents at Columbus Bay and any prowlers were seeking easier pickings.

The first house was gated. I peered through the iron rods but didn't recognize any of the cars parked in the drive. As I approached the second house, dogs began to bark. I quickly squatted in the bush, remaining motionless until the barking ceased.

The third house was set apart from the other two. None of the houses was marked with signs identifying the name of the occupants or the address of the dwelling. We have no rural postal delivery; every country dweller rents a post office box in town, so there were no mailboxes to examine.

I cautiously made my way across the uneven, broken pavement to the third driveway. Undulating vines hung over my head like snakes and the night breeze rustled the seed pods of the Mother Tongue trees in a rattler's warning. My palms began to sweat. I nervously wiped my hands on my jeans, glad I'd worn dark clothing for camouflage.

Very, very slowly, I inched my way forward. My foot struck a pothole. I jammed my fist in my mouth to keep from making any sound and stood absolutely still until the pain in my twisted ankle subsided.

I advanced one baby step at a time until I reached the third house. There were no gates, no dogs, no lights, no visible signs of activity within. But I knew someone was home.

Hidden in the shadows of the third driveway was a car I'd seen before. I crept closer to get a better look.

The license plate number was an exact match with the one I copied from the parking lot at Columbus Bay.

It confirmed what I already knew without a doubt. The person who killed Zena, the one who tried to poison me and the one who lay slumbering within were the same.

A deep cough coming from inside spooked me. I knew I'd overstayed my welcome and got the hell out of there fast.

Chapter
48

IT APPEARED AS if all twenty-eight thousand residents of St. Chris had moved to Columbus Bay for the extended Easter weekend.

The parking lot was jammed to overflowing. Cars were backed up all the way to the north shore road. Michael and I arrived on his Harley, cautiously weaving our way through the traffic, secured the bike to the closest tree, making our way on foot to the beach.

Benjamin and his eight-year-old son Trevor were waiting at our designated meeting place. Trevor had Benjamin's stocky build and his easy, smiling disposition.

"Where are we going to play?" I asked. "There isn't enough room here for even a volleyball, not to mention a playing area."

"In the water," said Trevor. "We always play in the water when we camp, right Dad?"

"It's a good thing we wore our swimsuits," said Michael.

Trevor tugged at Benjamin's hand. "C'mon, Dad, let's go. The game starts in ten minutes."

We picked our way along the sand, waving to people we knew, finally arriving at Benjamin's campsite on the far western end of the beach. Under a canopy sat Miss Maude and Miss Lucinda, sipping cold drinks with Camille.

"We're here to be your cheering section," said Miss Maude. "I'm sorry we didn't see you this morning for our eleven o'clock rum swizzle, but I quite understand."

"I was still waiting in the bank line," I said. "I should have camped at the bank overnight to be the first one inside when the door opened at nine this morning."

"C'mon, Dad. They're going to start without us."

We left our sandals and gear at the campsite. I used a rubber strap to secure my sunglasses, and tightened the adjustable Velcro backstrap on my plastic visor. The sand was blistering hot under my bare feet. I danced sideways like a sand crab toward the water.

"Mama, you're a wimp," said Michael.

"I don't notice you offering to carry me," I retorted.

"If you score even one point, I'll carry you back to the campsite when the game's over."

"And if I don't?"

"Then you're under your own power and you buy the drinks. Deal?"

"Deal." We shook hands and raced to the water's edge, spraying sand on irritated sunbathers in our wake.

After two grueling hours of play, our team finally won three games to two. I was absolutely whipped. I hadn't jumped, stretched or been dunked that many times since my childhood days at summer camp. I knew for sure I'd never pay to go to a gym to exercise. Why buy torture?

Michael carried me back to the campsite.

Benjamin had beer on ice waiting in a cooler at his

campsite. I grabbed a cold Heineken and sat cross-legged on the ground next to Miss Lucinda. We briefly reviewed the parade arrangements for the following Saturday.

"You'll be in the lead car as grand marshal. When you reach Government House, you'll be escorted to a seat on the reviewing stand for the rest of the parade. You and Miss Maude will sit with the governor and his wife. Then you'll announce the awards at the end of the parade."

"Oh, it'll be like opening a fête. I used to do that quite often in England." She clapped her hands together joyfully, then a frown clouded her face. "But I won't have to make a speech, will I? I do so dislike making speeches." Miss Lucinda sounded three sheets to the wind. How much rum had she been drinking?

"Lucy, all you have to do is announce the prizewinners. Don't worry, dear, I'll be right there with you."

"That's quite all right, then," said Miss Lucinda. The smile returned to her face like the sun reappearing after an eclipse. "I believe I'll have one more wee drinkie."

"Lucy, dear, I think it's time we went home," said Miss Maude. "We've had quite enough sun and fresh air for today. Tomorrow is Easter Sunday, after all, and you need to be up quite early for the morning service."

After thanking Camille and Benjamin for a pleasant afternoon, the two elderly ladies majestically made their way arm in arm down the beach. They paused briefly to chat with Mr. Daniel, waved at Reverend Cal and smiled graciously at assorted friends on the way to the parking lot.

"Camille, I'm going to town for more ice," said Benjamin. "Is there anything else you need?"

"Are you sure you won't join us for dinner?" Camille asked us.

"We're having hamburgers and corn on the cob," said Trevor. "I'm going to eat four ears all by myself."

"Another time," said Michael. "I promised Mama I'd

cook for her tonight and I can't break a promise. After all, she did score two points in the game."

"You scored seven; guess that means I have to do the cleanup," I said smiling.

"Why do you call her Mama?" Trevor asked earnestly. "She's not your mother."

"Trevor!" said Camille, with a slight scolding tone in her voice. Michael motioned that it was okay, he'd deal with it.

I waited eagerly to hear how Michael was going to talk his way out of this one. Benjamin and Camille tried to hide the smiles on their faces.

"I call her that because . . ."

"Because why?" asked Trevor, looking at Michael with his head cocked, waiting for a logical answer.

"Well," said Michael, giving the matter serious consideration, "because I like her."

"I think it sounds silly," said Trevor. "If you really like her you should call her 'honey.' That's what Dad calls my mom."

"I don't think Kelly would like that word, Trevor," said Benjamin.

"Why not?" Trevor looked at me. "Are you allergic to bees? A girl at my school is allergic to bees."

"You might say that," I replied.

"That's okay. There aren't any bees at the beach. Come back tomorrow and we'll play volleyball again," said Trevor. Turning to Benjamin, he added, "I want to go back in the water right now."

"Trevor, help your mother get the grill started for dinner. We'll swim again when I return with more ice."

Benjamin walked with us to the parking lot. Michael ran ahead when he spotted a group of kids fiddling with his bike.

"The morning mail was most gratifying," Benjamin said when Michael was out of earshot. "Reports from departments of vital statistics and institutions of high learning in the States confirmed what we already suspected. And the lab report came back positive. We will proceed according to plan in the morning."

Benjamin took off in the direction of his Blazer and I headed toward Michael.

Maubi called out from his van parked near a clump of sea grape trees. "Michael, Morning Lady, come for a cold drink."

We walked the bike over to Maubi's van.

"How come you're not at your usual spot in town?" I asked.

"Gotta be where the action is," Maubi replied.

"And the money," said Michael.

Maubi slapped his thigh and laughed. "What'll it be? I got the Heineken you like chilling on ice."

"We'll each have one," said Michael, handing Maubi a sodden ten-dollar bill, "and take one for yourself."

"Put that wet money away," said Maubi, "this be my Easter treat for you. And for me also."

When Maubi turned to get the beers from the cooler, Michael slipped his ten-dollar bill into Maubi's tip jar.

We toasted Maubi with our bottles. "To your health."

"Morning Lady, you ready for tomorrow? Quincy got that boat all gassed up and ready."

"As ready as I'll ever be," I said.

"You got nothing to fret yourself about," said Maubi. "My boy take real good care of you. Did you know he got a special award from the coast guard? And a thousand dollars for his college expenses. He mighty proud of that award."

Michael gave me a knowing look and squeezed my hand.

"Quincy should be proud, he earned it," I said. "And you're proud of him."

"Ain't that the truth," said Maubi, "ain't that God's honest truth."

Michael and I went back to my house to spend a quiet evening.

I drooled for solid food, but my throat still felt raw and scratchy. Michael grilled a steak for himself and fixed a large bowl of cold cream of chicken soup garnished with snipped chives for me. He cooked the meal, served it on the gallery, and even did the washing up after dinner.

We polished off a pint of ice cream while curling up on the couch watching a Steven Seagal action movie on video.

I felt like a condemned woman on death row being prepped for a dawn execution.

Chapter
49

EASTER SUNDAY DAWNED clear and calm.

I sat on the gallery love seat, where I'd spent most of the night, drinking a breakfast Tab while watching the smooth, flat sea unfurl its peacock colors in the morning light. Overhead the wind chimes hung mute. Minx curled beside me with her warm back against my thigh, vigorously licking her left front paw, then rubbing it in a circular motion over her face.

I'd forgotten what it was like to have someone spend the night in my little house.

When I couldn't sleep I'd crept out of bed, tiptoeing across the floor to the loo. Then I moved to the gallery where I spent the remaining hours sitting in the dark staring at the moon, stars and ocean, trying to boost my courage for the morning ahead.

Had I been alone it would have been a different story.

I would have turned on lights, watched the telly, listened to music, or read books. I wouldn't have thought twice about making noise.

After drinking Tab for most of the night I really needed to flush, but knew the roaring sound of the outside water pump would probably wake Michael.

When the sky turned pink a few minutes before five, I filled the coffeemaker and flipped the switch to On. The coffee had been ready for almost two hours.

Bare arms reached around me from behind. I swear I jumped a foot.

"Is that coffee I smell, Mama?" Michael's lips moved across the back of my neck.

"Fresh brewed and waiting for you," I said, turning toward him.

Michael stretched and yawned while peering through the gallery screens at the unruffled ocean. "We couldn't have picked a better day. Are you okay?"

"I'm nervous as hell, if you really want to know."

"Could've fooled me," he said, heading for the kitchen.

I dashed to the loo to flush before I needed to use a plunger to clear the pipes leading to my septic tank.

Michael stood in the kitchen wolfing down his first cup of coffee. He reminded me of a vampire in need of a fast transfusion.

"Do you want some breakfast?" I asked, hoping he'd say no.

"I've got a better idea than breakfast," he said with a smirk. "Let's play shepherd."

"Michael, what in the hell are you talking about? I'm not in the mood for games."

"Mama, let's get the flock out of here before you totally lose your sense of humor. Quincy said he'd be at the dock at seven-thirty."

Jerry, Abby, Margo and Paul were sitting on wooden benches at Dockside waiting to take the ferry over to Harborview. At their feet rested a large cooler the size of a small coffin. They were all dressed for the beach, with

large towels slung over their shoulders and chests like se-
rapes, drinking mimosas out of paper cups.

Jerry, self-appointed majordomo, made a big production
out of pouring us plastic cups of cheap champagne. I took
a pass on the orange juice mixer. My stomach was knotted
as tight as a fist and I didn't need my allergy kicking in
to add to my discomfort.

"Kel, the last time I was up this early on a Sunday
morning was a New Year's Day in New York when I
hadn't been to bed from the night before," said Margo.

"This is going to be a lot more fun than freezing your
buns off in Times Square watching the ball drop," said
Jerry.

"Bad choice of words, Jer," said Abby, "I'd rephrase
that if I were you."

"Whatever," said Jerry, digging into the cooler. He held
aloft a bottle of Perrier-Jouët, the very expensive fleur bottle embossed with flowers, his prize for logging the first
turtle. "I'm saving the good stuff for later. We're not popping the cork until you get back, Kel. Then we're all going
to my house for breakfast. Heidi's making her famous cin-
namon rolls from scratch."

"Let's give Kel her Easter present," said Margo. "On
the count of three. Ready?"

They all stood up. When Margo called out "three," they
flipped the towels from their shoulders to reveal matching
T-shirts.

Under a cartoon of a motorboat towing a parasailor high
in the sky were the words "Kelly's Ground Crew."

"We had a special one made for you, Kel." Margo
handed me a tissue-wrapped package.

Mine had the same art, but said "Once Is Enough." I
put it on over my swimsuit and cotton shorts.

Michael donned his crew shirt. Margo handed me another T-shirt, saying, "We got an extra crew shirt for
Quincy."

The ferry was waiting to take us over to Harborview.

The gang settled themselves in a semicircle of sand chairs on the Harborview beach. I heard a cork pop as Michael and I walked over to the water sports pavilion where Quincy was waiting at the parasail boat.

"Hi, Morning Lady. Happy Easter."

"Happy Easter to you, Quincy. Thanks for getting up so early."

"No big t'ing. I do it every Sunday morning during season," he replied.

"Here's an Easter present for you," I said, handing him the T-shirt.

He put it on over his navy Harborview polo shirt. "You know what you're going to do?"

"Michael and I went through a dry run the other day," I replied.

"Good. Let's get you ready to fly."

He handed me a foam-lined safety helmet and a life jacket. I stripped off my shorts and put the life jacket on over my T-shirt and one-piece bathing suit. I was wearing my kayaking surf shoes, and my sunglasses were firmly affixed to my head with the rubber strap I'd used for volleyball.

"We'll get you into the harness first, then you can put on the helmet before we take off."

I climbed off the dock into the powerboat, feeling I'd just left the security of the Titanic for a tiny lifeboat.

"Remember, Mama," said Michael, "you're going to sit on the back like a homecoming queen and when we get going the wind will lift you in the air."

Quincy handed me a pair of nubby palmed diving gloves with the fingertips cut off. "You might find it easier to hang on to the harness with these. Michael said your hands get wet when you're nervous. There's nothing to be afraid of. I've taken little kids up in this. Do you know Benjamin's son Trevor? He went up with me a month ago and loved it."

"Don't forget the hand signals we practiced," said Michael.

Their well-intentioned chatter made me want to scream. "Enough, you two. If we don't go now I'm going to lose my nerve. Let's get this show on the road."

Quincy cast off from the dock, and Michael took the seat next to the winch. I sat on the back like a starlet, with my tush firmly centered on the sling seat like it had been attached with rivets.

My ground crew jumped to their feet, waving and hollering. Jerry stuck his fingers in his mouth to emit a piercing whistle.

"Go get 'em, Kel!"

I waved briefly, then gripped the harness so tight I thought my fingers would cramp.

Quincy revved the engines. We were on our way.

We headed north from Papaya Quay through the shoals, following the channel markers toward the open ocean— the same path the Park Service launch had taken the day of Zena's funeral.

One minute I was looking straight into Michael's eyes, the next I was being gently whooshed into the air, watching his face grow smaller and smaller.

He gave me a thumbs-up and let out more cable.

I went higher and higher, the twenty-six foot parachute open above me in a bright nylon canopy.

My mouth was drier than the Sahara. All the liquid in my body felt concentrated in my aching bladder.

Inside the gloves, my hands were dripping wet. My feet squished inside my surf shoes.

I didn't feel like Peter Pan. I felt like shark bait dangling from an orange-and-white bobber.

When we safely negotiated the maze of shoals and were in the deep-water cobalt sea where Columbus first sighted

Papaya Quay and the Isabeya harbor after his swift exit
from the Caribs at Columbus Bay, the same area where
the Ramirez twins caught up with me on their jet skis,
Quincy turned the boat on a course due west.

To my right was the ocean. Lots of ocean. Very cautiously I turned my head a few degrees and saw the familiar shapes of the out islands forty miles north.

Looking sideways made me dizzy. I slowly turned my
head to face straight ahead.

No way was I going to look up. Ever. Down I could
handle. Sort of. But not up. My ankles always feel like
melting wax and I think I need to hang onto something to
keep from falling. Even when I was a kid on a swing set
I always felt queasy when I looked up. I gave up snow
skiing after my first time on a chairlift. I was the one who
once fell off a rope tow on the bunny hill to flop spread-
eagled facedown in the snow. On Santorini in the Greek
islands I climbed hundreds of dung-splotched steps to
reach the village on top of the island rather than take the
cable car or ride a mule.

To my left was the St. Chris shoreline. Isabeya and the
harbor were behind us. In the distance was the entrance to
Columbus Bay. I could see waves breaking on the reef a
quarter-mile out from shore.

The ride was surprisingly smooth. I've been on planes
that were bumpier. Even in first class with unlimited free
drinks to dull the rough edges.

It was like being in a swing with a balloon over my
head. But it still wasn't my idea of a great time. I wished
I had a seatback and footrest. And a porta-potty.

Quincy yelled to Michael. "How's she doing?"

"Hard to tell, but she looks okay."

"How much cable have you got out?"

"Not even fifty feet. She'll barely skim the treetops."

"That's probably high enough for her first ride."

"Quincy, I don't think there will ever be a second one.

Did you get a look at the message printed on Mama's shirt?"

Quincy laughed and maintained course for Columbus Bay.

From my catbird seat I could see the parking lot and Maubi's van, then the tent city on the beach. The volleyball net was still strung across the shallows.

In a clearing on the point past the parking lot, close to the location of the Stamp Day tent, Reverend Cal was beginning his Easter morning service.

He stood at a plywood podium, with his back to the ocean, in front of a crowd of people sitting cross-legged on the sand.

The motorboat passed the point, the sound of the engine drowning Reverend Cal's words.

Quincy steered the boat along the length of the beach just inside the reef. He made a graceful turn to port when he passed Benjamin's campsite. Benjamin waved and continued jogging above the tide line toward the parking area. I could see Trevor and Camille preparing breakfast in front of their tent.

The powerboat came back along the beach heading east.

When he reached the spot where Reverend Cal was standing, Quincy angled north toward the cut where Columbus's fleet once anchored.

The crowd of worshipers jumped to its feet and gasped, pointing at the back of the parasail.

In large white block letters on the orange parasail were the words BEWARE FALSE PROPHETS.

Reverend Cal whipped around to look. He began bellowing like an enraged grizzly about to strike.

He reached under his vestment and pulled out a small gun. He fired high into the air in front of the powerboat.

The sound of the shot sent the crowd of Easter Sunday worshipers screaming into the bush.

"What the hell?" yelled Michael. "Quincy, that son of a bitch is firing at us."

Reverend Cal reloaded, fired again, then started running for the parking lot.

Michael yelled at Quincy, "Mama's in danger. Get her out of here fast."

Quincy increased his speed. I hung on for dear life.

Benjamin sprinted through the sand after Reverend Cal, tackling him in a flying leap and wrestling him to the ground near Maubi's van.

A flare exploded in the air above me.

Michael cranked on the winch as Quincy shot the powerboat through the reef cut to the open ocean and back toward Harborview.

A second flare exploded. I felt like I was flying through a Macy's Fourth of July fireworks flak zone.

Benjamin cuffed Reverend Cal's hands behind his back.

"You are under arrest for the murders of Zena Sheffield, Catherine Sheffield, and the attempted murder of Kelly Ryan. You have the right to remain silent."

Chapter
50

JERRY POPPED THE cork on the Perrier-Jouët bottle as the bell from the Anglican church tolled nine.

"Pour fast, Jerry. I want to know what in the hell was going on out there. I've never seen fireworks on Easter before," said Margo, grabbing a cup of champagne and handing it to me. "Bottoms up, Kel, then dish. How did you know it was Reverend Cal?"

I sat cross-legged on the beach at Harborview with Michael, Quincy and my ground crew, waiting quietly until everyone had a cup of champagne. Hercule Poirot never had a more attentive audience.

"For openers, he's not a real minister," I said, smiling.

"Son of a bitch," said Jerry. "His act was a con? I want my money back. How did you know he was a fake?"

"I was tipped off when Zena called Cal a false prophet during her last parade committee meeting. Then I saw an ad in the back of a magazine for the Church of the Wayward Sheep mail-order ministry. Benjamin checked it out and a fax confirmed we were right."

"Every time he saw the vicar my dad would mutter, 'Jackass don't wear jacket,'" said Quincy, quoting an island proverb. "He'll be pleased to know he was right."

"Wait, it gets even better," I said, handing Jerry my empty cup for a refill. "His name isn't Calvin Stowe, it's really Charles Sheffield."

"Hot damn," yelled Margo, pounding the sand with her fist. "How did you ever figure that out?"

"By rereading Agatha Christie. The killer in *A Murder Is Announced* had a double identity and that started me thinking. Once a fake, always a fake."

"That would make Zena Sheffield his ex-wife," Abby said matter of factly.

"Not exactly," I replied. "Zena was his current wife. They were never divorced. Charles Sheffield was listed as the father on Kit's birth certificate. But when Kit said she never knew her father, that he died before she was born and Zena hadn't remarried, I figured Cal jumped ship while Zena was pregnant. I don't think Zena laid eyes on her husband for almost forty years until she came here."

"How did she find him?" asked Margo.

"Kit remarked that Zena was obsessed by her husband's memory," I said. "I'll bet Zena tracked him like a bloodhound, but didn't make contact until after she lost her job and needed money. She soon found out Cal was also broke, but Zena kept her cool until her last committee meeting when she really lost her temper. Cal knew then he had to get rid of her fast or be exposed."

"Wait a minute," said Jerry. "I don't get it. How did he poison the Island Delights with manchineel?"

"With a juice extractor and a syringe," I replied. "At my first committee meeting Zena offered to share her box of Island Delights, but Cal declined because he was a diabetic. When Benjamin found a black button in a grove of manchineel at Columbus Bay, about an hour after I saw Cal while I was out kayaking last week, he also picked up a used syringe that tested positive for insulin."

"Mama, that's pretty circumstantial," said Michael. "What else gave him away?"

"His hands," I replied, smiling smugly.

"My God," said Margo, shaking her head. "The funeral. We all saw him."

I nodded. "But at Zena's funeral he wore gloves. I didn't get it right away because the pallbearers were also wearing gloves, it's custom. When I saw Cal at the garage the day I picked up my car, he was wearing a long-sleeved shirt and his hands were bandaged. He said it was skin cancer and he'd just come back that morning after getting treatment in Puerto Rico. Jump-Up night the bandages were gone and his hands looked like my sunburned back. He burned them with manchineel while he was poisoning the Island Delights."

"So that's why you asked if he was on my flight back from San Juan," said Abby with a grin.

"And why you had me checking airline passenger lists," added Paul.

"Right on both counts. Cal wasn't in San Juan when Kit was killed by a hit-and-run driver, he was in Boston. It wasn't until yesterday that Avis confirmed Cal rented a car at Logan. Once we knew that, Benjamin and I went ahead with our plan to trap Cal in public this morning during his Easter service."

"Bravo, Kel!" said Abby, giving me a round of applause. "If you ever want a new job, I'll hire you as my investigator in a heartbeat."

"And leave show business?" I said with a smile. Michael laughed and put his arm around me, pulling me close.

"There's still one loose end," I said. "I can't link Cal to the Ramirez twins."

"I think I've got the answer," said Abby. "Yesterday when I was reviewing the twins' court file, I found a letter typed on a machine with a broken *e*. It was signed by Mr.

Daniel. But I can't prove he was behind the dirty tricks against you, because the twins still aren't talking."

I thought about it for a minute. "That makes sense. Mr. Daniel was on a power trip and really wanted to chair the parade committee."

"There's a man who needs to brush up on his people skills if he hopes to get elected to the Senate next fall," said Margo. "Jerry, stop hoarding the champagne. I want to toast Kelly's success as a sleuth."

"We're out of champagne and it's time for breakfast," said Jerry, handing me the empty Perrier-Jouët bottle. "Keep this as a souvenir, Kel, you've earned it. Haul ass, guys—you too, Quincy—the ferry's on its way over here from Dockside."

The ferry arrived at Harborview with one passenger aboard. Benjamin jumped onto the dock to greet me with a beaming smile and a bear hug. "Kelly, you were great. Everything went according to plan, but I wasn't expecting the flares. Are you okay?"

I nodded and turned to Quincy. "The next time I go up, can we do it without fireworks?"

Everyone laughed as we boarded the ferry back to Isabeya.